Lord Whittington buttoned her up, his large hands fumbling against her back.

She huffed as he slowly worked the multitude of tiny beads into the slotted tabs. "If I wasn't so upset about my situation, I'd laugh. You've taken longer than any maid to button me. Haven't you ever helped a woman into her dress?"

He had her half done when he abruptly stopped. She spun around. "Don't tell me I've offended you again. You'd be a rake if you buttoned me up quickly." She threw herself at the man, her arms locked around his back, her face pressed up against his chest. Started to cry. Wanted someone, anyone to hold her. No, she wasn't being truthful. She wanted this man to hold her and tell her he was over his anger.

Strong arms wrapped around her body as she babbled sorry over and over again. Lord Whittington pressed up against her and absentmindedly, he finished fastening her dress.

"I was considered a rake in my salad days, Miss Barrett. As you can see, my skill returned the minute you were in my arms." His voice sounded like finely aged whiskey, blended, deep, and strong.

She glanced up at the man she loved. The return look made her want him as one wanted a delicious delicacy. A shiver of need spread down her spine and into her toes.

Praise for Donna Ann Brown

"The story provides a quick read of suspense and romance with a sci-fi twist."

~Patricia Morgan

~*~

"This dialogue-driven time travel is a fun read. The characters come to life making the story believable. The second book about Elizabeth had me laughing out loud. One could definitely see how a person from the 1800s would believe they had landed in Purgatory when they land in Hollywood."

~Jessica Plumley

~*~

"A debutante turned actress, a wager, and the Regency Era. Highly entertaining."

~Patricia Tomljanovich

~*~

"The original storyline shows the polarity of living in a large family. Cathrine's brothers both love and smother her. No wonder she finds herself in trouble when another man enters the scene."

~Jillian Alexander

To my sparkley
friend Helen
from Donna
☺

Elizabeth Barrett
and
Cupid's Brooch

by

Donna Ann Brown

A Trade in Time

Elizabeth Barrett and Cupid's Brooch

Cover Art by *Debbie Taylor*

The Wild Rose Press, Inc.
PO Box 708
Adams Basin, NY 14410-0708
Visit us at www.thewildrosepress.com

Publishing History
First Fantasy Rose Edition, 2020
Print ISBN 978-1-5092-2960-4
Digital ISBN 978-1-5092-2961-1

A Trade in Time
Published in the United States of America

Dedication

To Leslie Webster, Critic Partner Extraordinaire.
Thank you for pushing me
to send my manuscript to Wild Rose Press.
Without you,
this book would still be an unsent document.

Chapter One

Liz Barrett
California, 2012

"You're fired!" Liz's voice echoed across the stage where she normally rehearsed. The props for her television show, and the fact that the other actors had left for the day, made her voice sound powerful. Her hands shook, and butterflies swirled in her stomach. The eggs she ate for breakfast threatened to empty all over the director's jeans. Acting seemed different than practicing words with her boss for a real-world situation.

Jeff Ledger, boyfriend and soon-to-be terminated agent, played one too many games. While one might optimistically like to believe someone's intentions are unintentional, they can be deliberate. Hence her need to practice.

Vince shook his head. Gave her a thumbs down. "You sound iffy."

"Iffy? I hardened my tone and used crisp pronunciation. "What do you mean iffy?" She wanted to growl at the man who hadn't been helpful. He could fire her agent for her. Most directors did the nasty jobs, yet he refused. Said this would teach her a lesson.

The man made a circular motion with his finger. She hesitated before turning around. They walked in tandem off location toward her dressing room. She came to an abrupt halt a step away from the entrance. Before she could say a word, her mentor spoke. "Your voice lessons paid off. But I know you Liz. You don't sound believable. You have a hitch in your pitch. Jeff will notice. I warned you about him. He won't leave without a fight. And it's not the studio's fight."

"Funny. I didn't need voice lessons for my leading role on the hottest televised show this season but," she paused. Considered what she wanted to convey. "I certainly need them for this unfortunate task. What a colossal mistake I've made." Her hands trembled so she stepped into a pose learned from an acting coach.

"You'll be fine." The big man patted her on her shoulder in a reassuring manner. "You were nervous the day I met you, Red, and you nailed your scene. Stop acting twitchy."

"Twitchy. I've never been twitchy in my life." The idea of how she appeared put steel in her spine.

Note to self. *Never allow a boyfriend to interfere with work.*

The furious producer had already pulled Jeff's Studio pass. He would never be allowed to step foot on the lot again.

"We hired you as the star of *Times Past* because you act prim and proper one moment and can get riled when needed. You've never appeared cowardly before. I mistakenly believed you wanted to let him go."

"I'm not a coward. I can breathe fire and brimstone," she snapped. Remembered how she had battled with the show's investor to stay off the couch. "I can do this." Her voice sounded strong.

"I like the determination you project. Stay feisty

and kick that kiss-ass off our set."

She didn't plan to kick Jeff off the set. Decided to be kind. Would politely explain why he couldn't work with her. Her reasons to let him go could not be disputed. How to break up with him as her boyfriend would come next. "I should write a book called Virgins Beware. Men who seem too good to be true, are too good to be true."

"You have great business sense, but you act naïve. What red blooded man carries Band-Aids in his backpack for your sole benefit? He's a douchebag who crept into your heart because you wear uncomfortable shoes. The book you want to write should be called Once Upon a Blister."

She turned to face her boss. Wondered how he would react if she jabbed him with her stylish heel. He'd need one of those Band-Aids the douchebag carried. She realized her boss, with all his loud, boorish, in-your-face ways, genuinely cared. She sighed with a heaviness she felt all the way to her pinched toes. "I want him gone as much as you do."

The director looked into the dressing room. "The museum guard has an invoice in his hand. The studio won't pay a penny for another prop we will never use."

His flushed face and angry voice worried her. Vince had an angina attack last month. She could do this. "Calm down. I don't want to go over budget any more than you do. I can manage my boyfriend."

The director glared and motioned for her to enter the room. She stepped through the door, walked past the guard, and immediately noticed a wooden box in the middle of her dressing table. The box hadn't been in the room thirty minutes ago. Thanked her lucky stars she didn't have to shoot a scene today. Most of her colleagues had already left for home. She collected her thoughts before she spoke. "I need a moment of your time, Jeff." The request sounded pleasant.

"Oh Liz, you won't believe the legend of Cupid's Brooch." The man barely glanced at her. "I'll tell you the history, so you'll understand why we have to borrow this jewel."

"You're too funny. When I borrow items, I use them for free. This isn't free!" Her cheeks warmed—part of her redheaded curse. The fact he didn't look at her made her nerves twang. He hadn't paid attention in a long time. "We need to talk so please look at me."

Her soon-to-be ex continued to focus intently on whatever lay inside the wooden box.

The object commanding attention had her bend forward. A horrified gasp escaped her lips. "This piece is hideous."

"I've committed you to the project whether you like it or not." Jeff's facial expression all but shouted Nanny-Nanny-Boo-Boo.

She had no intention of sticking her head in dog do. Her body froze icy hot and her voice sounded rough and cold. "You're fired, and the studio plans to return Cupid's thing-a-ma-jig." She didn't mean to blurt but his upturned eyebrow caused an over-reaction.

"I'll have a new scene written for you. A time travel piece." He looked around as if he had never been in the room before. "Where can we stow our jewel? You have a safe in here, don't you?"

"You have a safe in here," she sniped. "You insisted. Part of the astronomical expense I'm forced to pay on your behalf. In the middle of my fight to get the writers a raise, you had that monstrosity delivered. The safe became last season's joke. I've let you undermine me since the series began. Three years, Jeff," she held up three fingers to emphasize her point.

"I'm not a child, Elizabeth. I can count."

"You haven't counted how much you've gone over budget. I'm finished with your extravagance. This," she waved her hand toward the dull pin, "gets returned today. I've talked to the producer and we've come to an agreement." She hoped he didn't notice the strain in her voice.

"I'm your agent, Liz. I know what's best for you." He looked down his perfect nose at her. A nose she had paid for. He would look more real if she popped him in his perfect, plastic nose.

Through gritted teeth she said, "You're not my agent any longer. I told you, you're fired."

He smiled at her and she could not help but notice the beautifully capped teeth. Another expense she paid.

"You can't fire me, Liz. My contract is airtight." He looked so sure of himself she experienced a moment of panic.

"Really? Airtight?" She would never give him the satisfaction of knowing he upset her. "Yes. I can. The director is outside with his assistant who will escort you off the property. Our contract has been reviewed by the company attorney. You don't have my best interests at heart and this," she glared at Cupid's brooch, angry with the pin, as well as Jeff, "this final extravagance is one of the reasons I can let you go. You've signed my name once too often without permission."

She frowned at the item instead of looking at the man. "The brooch doesn't sparkle. What possessed you to pick up a tarnished antique you weren't authorized to procure?"

He didn't answer. Instead, turned his back on her, leaned over the dressing table, refused to respond. After a long few minutes, he glanced up with soulful eyes, smiled congenially and his breath sync'd up with hers. He had done this in the past. Would run his hand in a pattern over her arm and she wondered if he tried to use covert hypnosis on her.

What took me so long to realize he's a con artist? Everyone else realized he used her as a meal ticket which stung her pride. She stood tall in a deliberate way.

He mimicked her exact movement.

"Did you look at the literature I left for you? This is Cupid's Brooch. You know Cupid, don't you? The God of love." He tried to touch her arm as he talked but she backed away before he could. "We have a great opportunity here. I went by your house yesterday evening to discuss this, but no one answered the buzzer. I even called your cell. Did you mistakenly turn off your device again?"

She muttered loudly, "Thank God for electric gates and surveillance systems."

Jeff blinked. Looked confused.

As a top-notch actress, she nailed scenes in one shoot. Encounters with him were never as easy as her scenes.

Her newly fired agent sniffed, turned his perfect nose up in a defiant gesture. "The house phone rang but no one answered. I noticed your car in the drive. You need to fire Maria." He sounded like a general giving orders.

I'm not your troop she mouthed off silently in her head. Stared at him with what she hoped looked like haughty eyes.

"I'll find you a maid who answers when I ring," he continued in a cold, no nonsense tone.

How dare he tell me to fire Maria as I fire him? Jeff's termination would turn into this season's joke if she didn't nip it in the bud. Deliberately she enunciated, "You're. Fired."

He stepped closer, towered over her. "Stop the uppity act," he snarled.

"Uppity?" He might try to threaten her, but she would never back down.

His eyes narrowed. He grunted, turned his back and hunkered down, once again to stare at the unsightly brooch. "Yes, uppity. I'm your agent. I look out for your best interests. Everyone on the set received an earful." He glanced up. "I won't have you ruin your reputation because you're on the rag."

"Stop acting crass. You've been terminated, so I need you to leave now. I won't discuss this with you further." She sounded tired because she was tired. Would they have to drag him off the lot? She hoped not.

"You know the fans would hate to find out you're a drama queen. I will ruin your reputation if you continue to challenge my authority."

The silky soft threat made her snap to attention. She motioned for the museum guard. The man acted as if his shoes were glued to the spot where he stood. "We won't use this brooch. Please return the item."

Jeff snatched the brooch from the box and reverently held the object up, out of her reach.

The guard looked confused.

"Where should I sign?" Jeff asked.

She stood between Jeff and the clipboard. "This trinket gets returned. The company won't pay this invoice."

"Payments been guaranteed." Jeff darted around Liz, snatched the clipboard with the necessary documents from the museum guard using his left hand. He continued to hold the brooch up in the air with his right.

Her patience snapped like a twig. She jumped up and snatched the brooch out of his hand, held the trinket behind her. "You don't have authority to sign. You no longer work here." *Where's the director?*

"I had *you* guarantee the brooch." Jeff dropped the clipboard on the floor as he tried to maneuver around her again. The stunned guard backed out of the room.

Liz raised the piece of jewelry upward before she swiftly lowered her arm. Made sure the item stayed out of Jeff's reach. "Look at me Jeff. I didn't authorize this." Incensed by his temerity, she deliberately waved the piece in front of his face. "The brooch doesn't belong on the set." She waved it again for good measure.

"Don't over react." He shouted as he grabbed for the brooch.

She swiftly shifted sideways. Out of the corner of her eye, she noticed the director stood in the hallway, a frown the size of the Grand Canyon on his face. He couldn't get into the room because the museum guard blocked the way.

Jeff made another grab for the brooch. As her arm came downward, she wondered if she would ever find true love. The dull stone flashed bright.

"Liz, you're overwrought. I'll send the brooch back after the first scene. We'll talk about my employment when you feel like yourself again."

"I am myself." Violently, she waved the brooch to get his attention. The man's eyes no longer looked at her. They were glued to the object.

The guard scooted behind the director. "I can't return to the museum without a signature."

Jeff looked crazed, whined. "What do you want?"

"I want a man who loves me, not my position." She flung the brooch in the air. A glint of red flashed.

"What does love have to do with this situation?" He asked without taking his eyes off the sparkly antique.

"Deluded love got me into this mess." Liz's hand continued to move of its own volition. Her body quivered as outrage vibrated in every cell.

His eyes followed the brooch, as if mesmerized.

She was caught up in a swirl of strong emotions she couldn't accurately identify. A spiral of electricity cascaded from her head to her toes. Her hand lifted, propelled by some otherworldly energy. "I want to be loved for myself, not for my position," she said in a sing-song voice she didn't recognize.

Jeff stayed fixated on the brooch. "Your fans love you."

"No. My fans adore me. They have no clue what makes me smile, or how I like my coffee. They believe my favorite color is pink. My favorite color happens to be red." She waved the brooch under his perfect nose for emphasis. "You released the wrong information to the fan club. When did I say I liked pink?"

She waved the brooch as she waited for an answer. The trinket somehow had a life force of its own.

"Well, you're the only redhead I know who can wear pink, so you must like pink." He didn't sound apologetic.

Tears gathered as her feelings intensified. "I wore pink because you liked the color," she explained. "But I told you I loved the color red." *Had he ever listened?*

"Jeff, I want someone who loves me," her hand waved in a lazy eight motion and she became powerless to stop the movement. Emotional truth poured from her lips, "I crave love. I want to be able to complete someone's sentences. I want to respect the person I wake up with each morning. I want so much more than what you have to offer."

An overwhelming need gripped her. A need to…to be loved. Her hand continued to move. Her voice became calm. "I want to be loved for who I am, not my position."

A light flashed…her body spun. Then spun around again.

She could hear the faint echo of voices…laughter…moans.

Sounds harmonized…became discordant.

Men yacked…women whispered.

Giggles cascaded in waves across her body.

Liz sensed cold air…warm water…a desert breeze.

Energy ran up and down her spine.

Feather like touches caressed her skin.

The air became heavy, like molasses, then fluffy, like a cloud. Her breathing became rapid, then slowed to a faint nothingness.

A beam of golden light surrounded her…turned

pink…white…yellow…teal.

After long moments, a multicolored rainbow enveloped her body.

Gravity lifted her up…forced her down. Pushed her body forward…backward…

Rocked, pulled, and thrust her through a whirling tunnel.

She no longer perceived the direction of the wind, the position of the sun, the latitude of the moon. Rapidly she hit rock bottom.

Hard.

Her body filled with pain and she found she couldn't open her eyes. Stars danced in her vision behind eyelids that fluttered furiously. Blackness descended as she slipped away.

Chapter Two

"I feel her breath upon my ungloved hand, Mama. I do believe she lives." The voice sounded young and panicked. Almost hysterical.

"Don't wave the ladies reviver in her face you silly chit. Put the glass vial under her nose." Those harsh words were followed by a thwacking sound, as if someone had been hit. Liz tried to open her eyes but couldn't.

A nauseous smell overwhelmed her senses. She gagged, instinctively shoved the substance away with her right hand and forcefully blinked herself awake. An unadorned, plain-faced teenager peered at her. Not the normal type actress even though she wore a period piece dress. *Why am I on set?*

The young girl leaned back on her knees, the glass vial nestled in her ungloved hand. A fat double chinned woman in a bright yellow colored dress stood over the girl's shoulder. Bumped the poor child with her knee.

"Pass the fainting concoction again," the overweight, over-dressed woman demanded.

She coughed and pushed the vial away from her when the noxious vapors passed under her nose for the third time.

"I say, what the devil happened?" The male voice held a deep melodious tone and came from behind Big Bird—her name for the oversized woman. "Move aside

Lady Coldwell." His demand seemed peevish, yet his tone sounded delightfully robust. She realized this voice belonged to a manly man. A shiver of delight tickled her spine at the masculine sound.

"Your charge is a missish gel. Prone to hysteria!" The ridiculously dressed matron made it sound like she was a Drama Queen.

The audacity. She took note of the horrid outfit encasing her like a sausage. Realized the woman hadn't budged from her spot. Positioned herself at the forefront of this strange sideshow. *A bulldozer couldn't move her.*

The incessant pounding of hammer-like devices inside her head made her cantankerous. She didn't want to be mean, but she could feel her temper start to take hold, so she closed her eyes. Inhaled. Exhaled. Hoped the Director would clear the set.

"Emily, give her another sniff before she swoons again."

Swoons? Really? The over-large woman had an over-loud opinion.

She gently stopped the girl's hand from placing the nasty vial under her nose. "Thank you but I'll be fine in a moment. Let me lie here and catch my breath." She noticed her body vibrated to the thumps in her head— like energy currents, tapping out a steady, painful rhythm.

Big Bird stomped her foot. Her motion revealed a large pair of old fashioned, garish green shoes. She wanted to touch the grotesque but finely crafted workmanship on the shoes only...her back had been glued to the floor. *Why am I on the floor?*

She looked upward from her position, noticed a

painted fresco on the ceiling. Stretched her arm toward the artwork, whispered, "How lovely."

She realized the coolness of the floor seeped into her bones. Tile? Marble? No—who did a floor in marble these days? Way too expensive! The man's handsome face peered at her. This could be her new leading man. He looked spectacular dressed in stark black evening attire. He seemed tall from her perspective. Of course, even the girl on her knees looked tall from her prone position on the ground.

She realized she lay flat on her back in the middle of some…her head turned left, then right. She had to be in an entry way. One belonging to a grand mansion. "At least Jeff got one detail right," she mumbled as the man squatted next to her. His descent to her side forced Big Bird to back away.

"Give her some air," the man admonished. His voice seemed low and rich. He had sexy lips, a tad larger than usual. Thick black hair crowned his head. She wanted to touch his locks, see if they were as soft as they looked. One errant curl fell onto his forehead as he leaned over her. A love lock. The urge to tug on the strand seemed perfectly normal, yet her arms refused to move. Thick, nicely curved brows rose above slate gray eyes. His long nose had a slight bump—and his chin seemed firm. What a face. Maybe thirty years of age. He flashed a friendly smile and she noted his teeth were the color of ivory piano keys. Obviously, he hadn't been an actor for long. Teeth were the first body part the studio made you fix.

This man had good old-fashioned sex appeal. He even smelled yummy. She blinked at her waywardness. Sniffed. He smelt clean. Fresh. Foreign. She inhaled deeply—shaving soap and…another scent not entirely definable. No Tom Ford for him.

She closed her eyes to linger a little longer in his presence when she noticed the shooting pains in her head. She must have hit hard because she didn't know the who, what, when, where or why creating this awkward situation.

"Can you open those beautiful emerald eyes for me?"

The somber request from the man sent a shiver of pleasure down her back. Butterflies stirred in her stomach. That, or the knock on her head made her nervous. *Beautiful eyes?* Another charmer. Hadn't Jeff made similar remarks?

She opened one eye and noted his look of concern. Tried to sit up but couldn't bend at the waist because her corset restricted her movements. Were they filming? Did she have an accident? Tried to remember. Couldn't because her head swam.

"I have a terrible head ache and…" she paused, took another deep breath. "I need to eat. I'm famished." Her stomach growled as if to confirm the truth of her remark. She loved food. Couldn't tolerate junk and never snacked. Ate three solid meals a day and never gained an ounce. The hollow under her ribs made her stomach feel as if she had missed a few meals. *Hollow under her ribs?* Even my self-talk sounds weird. When had she ever used such vernacular?

"You broke your fast with me this morning," the man stated in a deliberate, no nonsense tone.

Broke her fast? Okay. He too seemed to use last century jargon. Might be the type to take his role a bit too seriously. Probably why the studio hired him. He would be *that* guy. The actor who stayed in character while he ate lunch. She, on the other hand, laughed, talked, and on occasion, dropped a spoon. This man would sit rigid, cut his food into teeny pieces before he put the fork in his mouth. Probably chew the required thirty-six times. Might even act like Jeff. A wave of disappointment surged through her achy body.

"If you get up, I promise you will have some sustenance. But first I want to examine the back of your head."

Her eyes shut automatically as he started to explore her skull with long, sensuous fingers. He gently massaged every square inch of her head. The persistent stoke of his gentle touch lulled her. When his fingers stopped, she opened her eyes and asked, "What happened to me?"

Big Bird peered at her and huffed out. "You had a fit of emotion is what happened."

"Not like any faint I've ever seen," came the solemn voice of the young girl who squatted on her left side. "You stood straight like a Lady should and then…" Her teeth bite into her lip nervously. Her eyes widened. Finally, she continued, "Looked as if someone lifted you off the ground before they purposely dropped you."

Big Bird smacked the girl's shoulder with her yellow fan. "Nonsense child. She had a fit of emotion and fell backwards."

A groan of protest escaped her lips. How she wanted to snap the fan in two. Realized she couldn't stand. Clenched her teeth and ground out, "my head hurts."

"That's what happens when you have a fit of

emotion." Green shoes tapped angrily on the floor. The noise intensified the hammers pounding out a discordant beat inside her noggin.

"Your skull hit the floor when you fell." The man laid his hand on her shoulder and she received a shock. A mega-ton of electrical currents rushed through her body. Her entire being jerked with the sensation.

The man pulled his hand away as if he'd been burned and she witnessed a blue spark move from her shoulder into his palm. Strange because they were not on carpet.

"What just happened?" she asked.

"I am not sure." His eyebrows drew together. His hand trembled slightly, and the kindly gentleman suddenly became unapproachable. "Can you move?" His tone of voice sounded way too polite.

She swung her right leg to the right side, then back to the original position. Did the same with her left leg. Finally managed to raise her right arm up off the floor and gasped in horror. "What happened to my nails?" she moaned. The French Manicure was gone, replaced by stubby, chewed digits.

"You had them for a meal." The woman's tone sounded as colorful as her dress. "Ate your nails. Such a filthy habit. Biting and gnawing like a rat, you were. Not like my dearest daughter, Emily. She would never eat her nails."

Enough was enough. This woman infuriated her. She thrust her arm out in front of her, pointed at Big Bird. "Off the set," she told her in a cold, regal manner. "I have no clue why the director hired you. Pick up your final pay and be gone."

The young girl looked at the woman, terror in her

eyes.

Her tormentor gasped. "Final pay? Off the set? Whatever is wrong with the gel?" The woman's large, oversized chest heaved in indignation. Her ornate fan snapped open and fluttered back and forth. Probably to hide her flushed face.

"You are what's wrong with me. I need to eat. Then I want a detailed explanation as to why I am flat on my back in some strange place." Her tone sounded peevish to her own ears. For some reason, she didn't want to sound peevish in front of this man.

"Please stay calm." His voice soothed her. Gently, he curled the finger she aimed at the terminated woman into her palm. Next, he rubbed the back of her hand. Her arm went slightly limp as tingles shot from her fingertip through her arm down to the pit of her belly and into her hoo-ha. She seemed hungry for more than food. This concerned her more than she cared to admit.

"When did you last eat?"

"I…I don't remember." *Couldn't remember and seriously didn't care. How odd.*

"You broke your fast with me this morning in the breakfast room. Have you eaten since then?"

"I haven't the faintest idea." The delightful man stroked her in such a pleasant way. Sensuous waves of deliciousness enveloped her. Her nipples hardened. *When have I ever been aroused by a simple touch?* Her musings horrified her, yet she couldn't make herself stop his caress.

The gorgeous man turned toward the overweight woman. "When did she last eat?"

The woman frowned. "My Lord, she has not been in leading strings since her childhood. Need I remind you, I am not her Mama! I am here at your bequest to manage her season. Please do not chastise me."

"Mother helped Miss Barrett prepare and Miss Barrett had no time to eat," the girl volunteered.

The situation grew weirder by the minute. This actress was the second person she fired today, and here she stood, rooted to the ground, uncooperative in an extreme way. The same insolence Jeff exhibited. Okay, so she did remember a snippet from the immediate past. *Why did this woman act like she didn't hear me? Doesn't anyone listen?* The voice in her head whispered, "you can learn a lot if you listen."

The situation along with the voice in her head made her panic. "Where's Jeff?" she whispered. The man looked at her, his mouth opened and shut, as if he were surprised. She noticed his perfect lips. Kissable lips. A mouth pleading to be...*what is wrong with me?*

"Come, let me try and help you stand. Slowly. You may have done some damage. You," the man pointed to someone she could not see, "go ask cook to warm food."

"What a muddle this is." The woman grumbled. "Get her up off the floor before the Duke of Silverman arrives."

"Calm yourself, Lady Coldwell. You," he pointed to the girl, "summon the butler. Have him send for a Doctor. You," he pointed to Big Bird, "go into the parlor and wait for the Duke. We must get Miss Barrett up off the floor and settled more comfortably."

"I'll tell him the clumsy gel fell down the stairs." Her voice came out strident, harsh.

"You will not embellish. Tell him she fell down from hunger." His voice sounded sharp.

The man stuck up for me. Utterly charming. *Utterly charming?*

"Never, my Lord, never. He will think you a cheese nip, sir. I shall tell him she has the headache. All gentlemen understand 'The Headache'." Her yellow feather bobbed from the back of her head as she turned on her green shoe and stomped from the area.

Why did the older woman wear a feather? They did away with the silly plumes in the first season of the show. "Did she call you a cracker?" She asked as she struggled to sit up. Her head spun again, and she became woozy, fell back into strong arms that braced her.

The helpful man tried to sit her upright. The corset wouldn't bend at the waist, making the situation impossible. She would have to tell the wardrobe department they had overdone the wire contraption.

The man's hand supported her back and made her feel warm and secure even though her body seemed cold and her mind confused.

"This blasted corset. The strings are way too tight."

"You talk of unmentionables?" The man smiled, his gray eyes dancing with amusement. "What happened to the prim and proper miss?"

The young girl slid to a stop on the polished floor near her legs, almost collided with her body. "I rang for the maid."

The man swooped down, put his hand under her arms for support, his other hand under her upper legs and proceeded to lift her swiftly. He cradled her to his chest.

"Heavens above," the fat women yelped. "What will his Grace think if he witnesses this...this...flap-doodle."

Flap Doodle? Obviously, Big Bird didn't follow anyone's instructions. She had been consigned to the drawing room. But nooooooo. Here she stood, arms waving.

"Yes, what should I think?" growled a cold, hard voice from the doorway.

She couldn't see who talked because her face pressed up against her leading man's jacket. The smell of his aftershave intoxicated her once again. Almost as if his scent drugged her.

The man's hold stiffened. "I see the butler let you in," he replied as he slowly released her legs to the floor, then helped move her into a position so she could stand on her own.

When he stepped away, she swayed. He steadied her by placing two large, comforting arms around her waist. "Can you stand?"

She shook her head yes even though she wanted to say no. Now she understood. The reason she had been on her back was to enact this role. She must have pretended to faint, like all genteel women of past generations, and actually hit her head by mistake. A good explanation for why she had trouble remembering current events. One did not mention corsets in this era. The word would be considered scandalous. The director should have called cut but he allowed them to ad lib on occasion and this must be one of those occasions.

"Good Job," she congratulated the fat lady with a thumbs up signal. "How much film did we put in the can?"

"I would like to know what takes place in this residence." The voice sounded stern, demanding. The newcomer stood ramrod straight, his clothes without a wrinkle. Brown, slicked back hair had been greased with some sticky substance. A quizzing glass was propped in his eye. She immediately noticed his green orb and the displeasure emanating from the magnified glass. He peered at her, his lips thin with displeasure, his mouth grim.

"Wow. You look like a genuine, stick up your ass aristocrat." Suddenly blackness started to descend. Large, gentle hands broke her fall, the world tilted as she faded into the inky fog.

Chapter Three

Chester Langford, Earl of Whittington, looked at the stunned faces gathered in his entryway as he held the other man's fiancée in his arms. A sorry situation. Even so, he wanted to laugh. A first for him since his return to England.

The American hoyden told the richest man in England he had a stick up his backside. He wondered if she realized her betrothal might become strained after this episode. From the look of anger on the Duke's face, he half expected the man to challenge him to a duel. The Duke might even go so far as to rescind his offer of marriage.

"Miss Barrett fainted. She hit her head on the floor and has a lump the size of an egg on the back of her head. We finally had her stand on her own when…" he looked down at the peaceful features of the beauty he held. He would try to remedy the situation. "She fainted a second time. Earlier she used nonsensical words. I believe she's delirious." He sniffed. One of those English gestures used in situations such as this.

Lady Coldwell bobbed her head in agreement, the yellow feather bouncing in all directions. "She wanted to know if I called his Lordship a cracker. Why would I call the man a sea biscuit?"

Lord Whittington stifled the urge to grin. Restrained himself because the farce could turn into a major theatrical production if he weren't careful.

"Would you put my betrothed down this instant," the Duke snarled and stamped his ebony cane on the marble floor. A thwacking sound echoed in the entry way. A groom rushed over, as did the butler. The door stood wide and any passing carriage would be able to see into the house on St. James Street. An older man with a black bag rushed up the front steps, led by a young footman who wore his livery.

"Your man mentioned a nasty fall." The doctor noticed the unconscious woman and walked over to where Whittington held her. He lifted one of Liz's eyelids and pronounced, "Out in slumber land."

The doctor took control of the situation and said, "Let's get her to a place where she will be comfortable, and I can examine her head."

"Lead the way to her room," he told Emily.

The Duke blocked his entry to the stairs. "Your servants can take her to her room. You," he pointed at Lady Coldwell "will go with the doctor and report back on her status. I want an explanation for what I witnessed when I entered this household."

He allowed the strong page, to lift Miss Barrett from his arms. Had a sense of loss once the weight left him. He looked at Emily and said, "Why don't you go with Miss Barrett and the Doctor? Show him her room and get her comfortable. We'll wait for you to give us word in the parlor." He straightened the cuffs of his shirt and brushed off his coat. When he looked up, he noticed the Duke's glare.

"Let's retire to the receiving room, Your Grace and Lady Coldwell." He gestured with his hand for the Duke to precede him. Lady Coldwell gaped like a fish out of water. He understood her dilemma. He also realized those extra stones she carried made the stairs a challenge.

The Duke marched toward the sitting room and he followed. Lady Coldwell's footsteps clumped slowly after him. Relief washed through his body, glad she obeyed his orders instead of the Dukes. This entire evening had played out like a farce. A comical one.

"A glass of port is called for," he said as they entered the room. "Please make yourselves at home and I'll pour." He walked over to a cabinet, decanted the top of a bottle and splashed a tot into two crystal glasses on the silver tray. He had his back turned and hoped neither of them could see his expression.

A stick up the Duke's backside! Who would have guessed his young charge could be so bold. She rarely spoke since her arrival. The quintessential relative of a relative of a relative who got sent to him because no one wanted to be her guardian. He stifled his grin and turned to face his guests.

"Would you like a glass of sherry?" he asked the older woman. She nodded. Her inability to speak made him want to laugh aloud. He detested her whine and only asked her to live here when she applied to him for her daughter. She showed up the same day Miss Barrett's solicitor dumped her on his door step. A fateful intervention. Lady Coldwell could capably plan a season for Miss Barrett and her own daughter, Miss Emily Coldwell. His responsibilities would be taken care of. Only, the arrangement hadn't worked out the way he envisioned.

His duty should have ended when he made Lady Coldwell the chaperon. The only reason why he let her stay. Well, mayhap not the only reason. He did have a conscience. This morning he had been told, not asked, but informed by the old dragon, how he would escort them to a social function this evening. England had disadvantages. Especially when one happened to be a Lord of the Realm.

His mind wandered to the Duke of Silverman. Why had he sent his man of business to negotiate a marital contract before Miss Barrett had engaged in the season's events? Lady Coldwell assured him his charge needed lots of preparation before she would be ready to enter society. Marriage to a Duke would trust her into the midst of the beau monde. Why did this man want to marry Miss Barrett? Then again, he wouldn't mind marriage to someone with spunk.

He never considered the formal arrangement. Remembered how he politely asked her if she wanted to marry a Duke. Deliberately mentioned his wealth since the girl came from Boston. Her own father had been a second son turned merchant which meant she wouldn't be insulted like most young ladies.

He became contrite once he realized he had wanted a quick way to get rid of her. Had even congratulated himself on the ease of the situation. Miss Barrett consented with a discreet nod. Never actually said a word. He recalled the interaction. Recognized their interview had been a one-sided exchange. Bother. Would his role as chaperon to these unfortunate women cause him grief?

The wood crackled and hissed in the fire place. The mantel clock ticked out long seconds. He missed the comfortable silence of his home. He shook his head to clear away the melancholy. Melancholy threatening to

26

engulf him.

He delivered the crystal glass of sherry to Lady Coldwell. Noted she sat on the only piece of sturdy furniture in the room. Glad to see the chair held her weight. Wanted to grin for no good reason. Did not contain the smile when he handed the other glass to his favorite enemy.

Geoffrey Froth, His Grace, The Duke of Silverman sat perched in a high-backed chair, one elegantly clad leg over the other. He remembered how his charge had asked for Jeff. They called the Duke by that name many years ago when he had been an ordinary chap with no title in sight. She must have met him when her father was alive. Mayhap they had a shared history he did not know about. Could be the reason why the man offered for her. He might have known she'd been stranded far from home and needed a protector. As he looked into the cold face of his ex friend, he experienced a twinge of doubt.

"Your Grace," he bowed slightly, his voice polite, before he turned to get his own glass.

"Bring the decanter on your way back," the Duke commanded.

Instead of bringing the decanter to His Grace, he walked to the bell pull and rang. The Duke had already downed his glass. Lady Coldwell gulped instead of sipped. The butler entered the room. "Please take the tray of libations and place them on the table nearest The Duke, stoke the fire, then bring us news about Miss Barrett's condition."

"What goes on in his house?" The aristocrat demanded as soon as the butler left the room. "You failed to return when your father died last year. When you did arrive, you did so in the middle of the night. Within a fortnight you become a guardian to a beautiful young lady who is guided by Lady Coldwell. A woman who hasn't been seen in years. I say, this set up baffles me. Very strange, indeed!

He folded his body into a chair near Lady Coldwell. "Not unusual a'tall. I came home as soon as I received news of father's death. I did have to sail from India." He didn't tell the man he almost died because of a pirate ship. Wondered whether his feet would touch English soil again. The crew eventually listed into port. Thankful to be home, he stepped onto his homeland's soil and walked through the fog filled streets. Savored the journey to his dwelling.

The Duke sniffed in the manner one does to insult another. "You went on business, I presume."

He decided not to respond. "Let's talk about my fosterlings. What can I tell you? Miss Barrett's eager solicitor dropped her on my doorstep. Not so strange because her father did die. The relatives couldn't afford to give her a season after her year of mourning." He deliberately raised both eyebrows in a challenging manner.

The Duke motioned him to continue with his hand. Pretended to sip at his drink. Acted bored. Whittington recognized he wasn't bored. His tell showed. The movement of the cup turning in his hand kept him from squirming in his chair.

He decided to continue. "Lady Coldwell hasn't been in England due to her husband's health. He died a few years ago which is the reason she is not all trussed up in black. I invited her here once I learned she had a young daughter who needed a man's protection." A varnished version of the truth would be safe. He never wanted Lady Coldwell to look desperate. A look she wore the day she turned up on his doorstep, destitute. He liked her much better now she had a little of her spirit back.

He paused to see how Lord Silverman took the news. The man didn't flick an eyelash, so he decided to forge on. "We were ready to attend the Opera and awaited your presence. Miss Barrett and Miss Coldwell were at the bottom of the stairs nattering on to one another as young ladies do. Lady Coldwell had already checked their wardrobes when Miss Barrett toppled backwards. The sound of her head hitting the marble..." An ugly thunkity-thunk. Had Lady Coldwell pushed Miss Barrett? He left the library, where he had been settling accounts, when raised voices captured his attention. He could not let His Grace know he had doubts about what transpired.

"Lady Coldwell instructed her daughter to get out her smelling salts and revive the young woman. Once she came around, I helped her up. She told me," he considered what to say, decided to be melodramatic. Placed his hand under his chin as if he had to think deeply. "Told me the strings were too tight on her corset."

The man's face reddened, became hard. "Don't mock me."

Whittington looked at his old friend and yearned for the way they used to be. Why had they never made peace with one another? "I know we've had our differences in the past, but I do not mock you. Let us leave our animosities behind for this discussion. This may look bad, but I picked her up because, frankly, I could see no other way to get my charge off the floor. She could not bend at the waist. Corsets don't allow flexibility. Why women wear those contraptions has never made any sense." He could feel his agitation. Wondered why he never noticed how hard being a woman could be.

Lady Coldwell opened the stringed reticule wrapped around her arm and pulled the cloth bag open. Produced a vial of smelling salts. She clutched her sherry glass in one hand, the vial in the other hand. "Please do not speak about unmentionables. We have barely recovered from one tragic incident."

"What we have is a situation where my fiancée may be ruined." The Duke stood up.

He remained seated. "Damn it, Jeff. I didn't ruin her. I picked her up off the floor. I know the rules of society, but you were the only witnesses to my…my indiscreet behavior. Surely you don't plan to jilt her?"

"Like I jilted my last fiancée?" He slammed his glass on the table top and grabbed his walking stick.

"You're not a jilt." Whittington told the other man who towered over him while he sat sedately. He deliberately uncrossed his legs. "The last incident between us…well, I did the deed in a way you have not forgiven. But you planned to marry a trollop. Yea Gads, man. Have you not seen her make a fool of the man she wedded? She is no better than a doxy. I saved you when I set her up. I wanted you to find out about her unfaithfulness before you got leg shackled."

The Duke paced around the room. Stopped at the fire place and looked up at the painting of Whittington's father. "Hindsight makes us see a lot of incidents in a different light," he commented before he

30

once again roamed the room. He restlessly picked up objects of art and knickknacks as if to examine them.

Lady Coldwell kept an eye on the two men without uttering a sound. She looked fearful and her hands shook.

"I think Lady Coldwell needs to explain to me how she viewed the incident." The Duke's voice sounded composed. He walked over to her chair and glared down at her.

"I…well…I," she hung onto her glass as she would a last crust of bread, clutched close to her chest. Had already stuffed the vial back in her bag. "The gel is delirious, like Lord Whittington told you. She talked oddities and," her voice became a whisper, "a curse word slipped from her lips. No other words after the cursing incident. I prayed for her. Yes. I became busy. Prayed to God." The fat woman shuddered, her double chin jiggled.

He could not contain his mirth. "Laying it on a bit thick, don't you think Lady Coldwell?"

Emily paused at the double doors and knocked to get their attention before she entered. Curtseyed to the Duke and waited for permission to speak. Whittington wanted to roll his eyes. They resided in his house, but the ranking peer would be deferred to no matter whose home they were in. The rigid rules had been relaxed in India. At this moment, he longed to return.

Once Emily got the nod to speak, she told them, "Miss Barrett woke up and told the Doctor she has a dreadful headache. She started to ask strange questions. Questions that don't make sense. The doctor is concerned and told me to tell you he intends to stay with her for another hour or two. He doesn't want her to go to sleep because she might not wake up. It happens to people who hit their head."

"We shall attend the Opera as planned," the Duke told the group.

Lady Coldwell set her glass down on the table at her elbow, had an eager look upon her face.

Her daughter, Emily, frowned. "I beg you to excuse me, kind sir, but entertainment will do no good when my friend is upstairs in pain."

"How do you intend to help? Do you have a magic potion to take away the pain?" His cane stomped on the carpet.

The young lady's features showed no fear. Her manner remained calm. "I can be nearby. Ready to reassure her. She is alone and frightened. Keeps repeating stuff and nonsense. Might try to leave the house because she is confused. I can't let that happen." She directed her statement to the Duke.

He looked the girl up and down. "And who exactly are you?" He popped his monocle in his eye.

The young woman curtsied. "I am Miss Emily Coldwell, daughter of The Honorable Thomas Coldwell of Thistle Manor."

"Baron Coldwell's daughter. I met your father." He stared at her for a long time. Finally, he uttered, "You have the courage of your convictions and can still be charming, and polite. Go attend your friend." She curtsied before she left the room.

"I am at a loss as to what to do," the Duke told Whittington. Sincerity rang in his tone.

"I say we retire to the library and have a long discussion." He would apologize for their previous misunderstanding. Stood up and started to walk toward the door. The Duke followed him from the room.

Lady Coldwell rang for a maid after the two men left. Food would settle her nerves. "Please bring me some biscuits and tea." When the maid left, she hurried over to the port decanter and poured herself a glass, swallowed rapidly. The liquor burned on the way down, but she needed liquid courage. Her nerves were frayed.

"I wish I had a home of my own," she told the painting on the wall. Then she remembered she had kicked the brooch out of the way when she followed Lord Whittington into this room. What a dustup. Her body was overtired. Her nerves were spent so she could not look for the dreadful pin this night. She picked up the box the brooch came in from the side table and put the bulky item in her reticule. She would ask a maid to find the pin in the morning. Now, she needed sustenance.

Chapter Four

The creak of wood as she stepped down onto the first stair step made Liz wince. Darn, darn, darn. *Would someone hear the noise?* She listened intently. Tip-toed onto the next step. This thread didn't make any noise. *Good.* The stairs were hard to navigate due to the heavy layers of clothing she had been forced to put on. Could have been worse but she refused a few essential undergarments.

How did one have sex with all these clothes? A valid reason why most men had mistresses during the eighteen hundreds. Demi-reps ran around, comfortable in their homes, a few articles of apparel on. But 'respectable ladies' were another story. They had been forced to wear a multitude of items weighing up to seventy pounds. Somehow these crazed fans wanted to re-enact this time frame and had forced her to wear uncomfortable, heavy layers.

Miss Emily Coldwell turned out to be an excellent young actress. So did the doctor who had a conniption fit when he found her in a shift. Acted like she was naked. His anger convinced her she had to escape. Downright scary how his fists clenched. Both Emily and the Doctor had taken on the persona of the characters they played.

What had the girl told her? Said she lived in England in the year eighteen twelve. Her television show was being filmed in America in two thousand and twelve. Why this elaborate farce? Who played this sick game? Had to be Jeff's handiwork.

Liz tried to trick Emily with questions about the King and the Prince Regent. Forced herself to remember every detail she had ever learned. Found the effort hard because she never studied European history. Because of *Times Past*, she understood more than the average American but that hadn't helped.

Everyone tried to convince her she lost her mind. When she asked for her Blackberry, the servant brought her a bowl of berries with clotted cream and unrefined sugar. Surprised herself when she howled like a banshee as the maid handed her the china bowl. The pretend servant threw her apron over her face and fled. Her performance would never win an Emmy.

The doctor had barreled into her room like a runaway horse. Thunderous, ear-piercing rants stopped her own response. The man left her room with loud promises of cold baths and solitude—a cure for delirium. He pulled the skeleton key from the door, slammed the wooden portal, and locked her in. His actions sobered her. Created fear. Who were these people? And why did she keep using old fashioned words like portal instead of door?

Liz cried first, ate the blackberries second, then set her mind to formulating a plan of escape. The iron hair pins she used were large and sturdy. Antiquated. She kissed the pin once the lock clicked open. Timidly swung the door inward. Peered out the portal to her left. A long hall stretched empty. To the right lay freedom. Stairs leading down. One step closer to the front door.

Her mind circled—why had she been kidnapped?

The only story that made sense was a kidnapping. Her last memory had been a fight with Jeff.

As she thought back to the incident, she remembered how she yelled at him and waved the stupid brooch in his face. Next, she woke up on a marble floor in someone's out dated mansion. Her own story didn't make sense. Had someone come up behind and clobbered her over the head? Did Jeff drug her with some mysterious liquid painted on the pin? Why didn't the director step in? He should have stopped this foolishness.

Her foot touched the bottom step at the same time a door opened. *Drat.* Masculine voices drifted from the hall on her left. She ducked into the room on the right, made another immediate right once in the room. Her thigh bumped a table, almost toppled the contents, which she quickly righted. She looked around and noticed the old-fashioned parlor. One overstuffed with too much furniture and no place to hide.

The doctor said, "I believe an asylum is where you need to take Miss Barrett."

She gasped aloud, stuffed her fist into her mouth. Only a few more steps to freedom. The front door called to her. She couldn't make a sound. These fanatics planned to keep her here. She would not allow them to stick her in someone's basement with bars so they could enact a morbid story line. Never comprehended until this moment how dangerous a television star's life could be.

The pretend Earl told the doctor, "I want to give her more time to recover. Miss Coldwell believes Miss Barrett is a good person who has had a hard time coming to terms with her situation. She came here from

America with her father. You have to remember the man dropped dead in a rented carriage while she sat next to him. Her relatives refused to keep her because her dowry is tied up. Instead, they sent her from one kinsman to another. I don't know the whole story, but I believe they relocated her three times within a few fortnights."

"The relatives relocated her because she believes she's from the future. Next, she'll talk about women's brains being as large as a man's."

She bit her cheek to keep from screaming. Wanted to yell, rant, and rave. Were these people so into their own fantasy world they believed the earth flat? Why would Lord Whittington continue to play his part? They had connected when she woke up on the floor. The emotional tug and sizzle should have been enough for him to stop the charade. He played a different role with the doctor. Could this be a plot to . . to . . .what?

The situation puzzled her. When the doctor talked about her father, she could visualize a lovable man. Not her biological dad who didn't have a lovable bone in his body. She realized she relived someone else's memory. Saw pictures in her head belonging to a faint-hearted person called Elizabeth. Decided to look around the room, run her fingers along the wall.

The gentlemen's discussion became heated in the foyer, but she tuned them out. Took her time hunting for electrical plugs. Diligently fingered every inch of two walls. Found no outlets. Drat, drat and double drat.

Maybe she could find cameras. Hidden cameras in some of the knickknacks crowding the room. Lord Whittington might be a bachelor, but this place didn't look like a bachelor's domain with all the clocks, vases, and tassels.

Even her gay friends didn't have curtains with this much fringe. She picked up a china shepherd girl. Turned it over and noticed a Dresden trademark on the bottom. Did this brand even exist in eighteen twelve? Breathing deeply, she viewed the room with a jaundiced eye. The wall held numerous pictures and a magnificent mirror.

The mirror had to be one of those two-way jobs. If they filmed her without permission, she'd sue. Two days in this nightmarish environment made her desperation high. Had they drugged her? Had she been hit, or had she fallen? She had a bump which meant she suffered some form of trauma.

But...she became confused. The father in her head wasn't her real father. Her biological dad was a steely eyed preacher who refused to talk to her. This other man brought tears to her eyes. A jovial fellow. Again, she had the distinct impression she had two personalities with two different sets of memories inside her head. These notions *would* put her in the insane asylum.

The entrance door closed. She froze, listened to the silence. Waited for the sound of footsteps. Instead, a clock chimed. Eleven times followed by stillness. Outside street noises became evident. A carriage rolled by on the cobblestones. She had been unfamiliar with the creaks and rattles until she realized she recognized the sound of carriages and cobblestones from yesterday.

The view from her bed chamber showed an upscale neighborhood reminiscent of England. She wasn't desperate enough to hurl herself out the window and break bones. Instead, she practiced picking the lock with hair pins. Another skill to add to her resume. She counted to a hundred. Surely, Lord Traitor had gone back to his man cave. She walked to the large mirror covering most of the wall. Put her hand between the framed glass and the wall behind, tried to find cords or holes or strange wires. The wall seemed solid. At least as far as she could feel with her hand. Frustration overwhelmed her. She looked up, into the mirror.

The traitor stood like a sentinel. Stared into the mirror in the entry way. She could tell by his uplifted eyebrows the moment he realized she stared at him while he stared at her.

***

The coat rack is a necessary convenience in a bachelor's home, used to hang hats, coats and scarves. Lord Whittington had a fancy rack with a mirror above the brass hooks embedded in the wood. As he discussed Miss Barrett with the doctor, he noticed her derriere. She crouched on the floor, buttocks in the air, cheek on the ground as she looked under the sofa in the blue room. He had a stunning view of her backside reflected from the mirror on the wall in the parlor.

To protect her reputation, he ushered the doctor in front of him so only he could see her rummage around for whatever it was she looked for. He had trouble concentrating on the doctor's words. Wondered if she lost a button or hair pin? Became fascinated the longer he stared. Noticed she bit her full lip when concentrating. Observed her touching every square inch of the wall. A piece of hair came free of the neat twist at the back of her head. She waved her hand, as if hot, and opened the top two buttons of her walking dress. He had seen a million women bare their breasts in evening gowns, but the unfastening of those top two buttons seemed exceeding enticing.

The doctor finally left but he couldn't. He stood silent like a bothersome thirteen-year-old, peeping into a brothel for the first time. This unconventional vixen had him enthralled. He should have sent her to the asylum. But Emily had fought for her to be given more time. Told him, "We cannot focus on the weaknesses of one another and evoke strength. When I first met Miss Barrett, she acted timid, shy. Please allow her a few more days before you make such a drastic decision."

He stayed away on purpose. Had to. Allowed Emily to interact with his confused charge. The evening she hit her head confounded him. She looked the same yet acted different. He remembered the red-headed poppet, not this dark-haired fox. He never would have taken *her* into his home. Wanted to blame the hair treatment. Lady Coldwell had assured him she would never be accepted in society if they didn't darken her hair.

Only hair color didn't explain disposition differences. The look in her eyes had transformed. Before the green gaze seemed pain-filled. Now, they brimmed with mischief.

He recalled her sprawled on the floor. Her eyes communicated without words. Muddled his senses. She had gazed as if he were Hercules. Her emerald orbs were windows to her soul, and he had seen a spark of...of naughtiness. The youngster he had taken in seemed like a demure miss who needed a husband to guide her. The woman on the floor had a bit of the wild. More tiger than kitten. He foolishly blurted her eyes were beautiful—words never spoken to another woman.

A feature he had rarely, if ever, noticed.

Strange, intense heat ran from her hand into his body, causing her to jerk. Her green eyes opened wide, her confused innocence showed. His carnal nature rose. Made him ready and able. A first for him. If he touched her again, would he have the same sensation? He sincerely hoped the answer would be a resounding no.

Didn't like treading on dangerous ground. His role should be one of protector, not debaucher. She would be leg-shackled to Jeff soon. He had a duty to both of them. Tried to erase her from his mind. His powers of reasoning shut down and he couldn't stop thoughts of corset strings. His lips quirked up without permission. Not even mistresses talked about unmentionables.

The English were a fickle society. Behind closed doors they did all manner of deeds. But even if one did the forbidden, one never talked about taboo subjects. This young lady seemed different. Part of her difference could be her American heritage. His mother told him many of the debutantes hid who they were while on the hunt for a husband.

Miss Barrett looked into the mirror and he could tell precisely when she knew he stood like an inappropriate, thimble-witted, gaping ape. Her full mouth formed a perfect O, her arched eyebrows shot upward, her elegant hands stilled. He observed her, wondered what she would do next. She rearranged the long tendril of hair. He rather liked the freed strand dangling from her top knot. She deliberately tucked the curl back into her bun as her eyes narrowed. A simple, enticing gesture. The nonchalant motion created ripples of want in his loins. His charge tugged on her skirt, strutted toward him. He wanted nothing more than to meet her in the middle of the room.

"Good afternoon." She walked quickly, not at all like the young, timid woman who originally required him to become her guardian.

"Did you find what you were looking for?" he asked.

The imp looked at the floor, then to her right. "A hair pin. Yes. I found my hair pin."

He grunt-laughed. "I guess you found the missing item behind the mirror?" Her lively expression entertained. Would she tell a falsehood?

"I looked for a hidden camera. Electrical outlets. Couldn't find either. Emily tells me I live in England in the year eighteen fourteen."

"Miss Coldwell would be wrong. You are in England in the year eighteen twelve. The month is March. The day is the second, which is also a Monday. They say Monday's child is fair of face. You look like Monday's child." He smiled and noticed her mouth open in an O. He better not trifle with her or he would find himself in deep water. "There are no objects hidden behind my mirror. My silver is in a box in my desk drawer. If you are in need, I will be more than happy to give you pin money."

Her features contorted, her beautiful green eyes glittered. "I don't plan to steal from you."

They stood, stared at one another. The air crackled with tension. "What do you need?"

"I need to go outside."

Disappointment of some odd sort settled upon him.

"If I am in the year eighteen twelve," she continued, "I would like to explore the streets. You won't be able to continue your little game when I find electricity and telephone poles. Might even see an airplane overhead. The type of scenery I'm used to viewing on a Monday in April in the year two thousand and twelve."

He tried not to sigh. *How could such a beautiful young lady be so moonstruck?* Another, stranger reflection flitted through his mind. *I could live with her affliction.* The whispered consideration stopped him cold. High time he found himself a mistress.

Emily galloped down the stairs, a look of relief on her face when she spied them together by the front door. "I'm so glad you feel well today Miss Barrett. Mayhap we can go to the park? Would you like to spend time out-of-doors?"

Miss Barrett nodded agreement, placed her fingernail in her mouth. Her brows knit together after a few ticks from the clock and she yanked her fingers away, glared at her nails. Placed her hands behind her back. Odd reaction to get so poked up about one's own habit.

He cleared his throat. "I have to go down to the ship yard today. I'll have the horse and carriage brought around." He rang for the butler. "Send for the open carriage. Today's a beautiful day and Miss Barrett and Miss Coldwell want to see the sights of London."

Maybe fresh air would help her remember. "Emily, do you think your mother would like to join us?"

She shook her head no, but Miss Barrett interrupted. "I believe we need an escort."

"Lord Whittington can escort us since he's our legal guardian." Emily responded.

"I'll feel safe with your mother along for the ride. I've only seen her while I lay flat on my back. I recognize I've put her though an ordeal. Noticed she's taken to her room and hasn't come out. High time I met my chaperon up close."

Emily looked fearful.

Whittington motioned to the footman who sat in his chair at the rear of the long hall. "Send the housekeeper up to Lady Coldwell's room. Tell her we need her services as a chaperon, and I won't take no for an answer. You two run along and get your hats and gloves and whatnots."

Miss Barrett asked Emily, "Please get my hat and gloves. I've completely forgotten where I put them and what color matches this dress. I'll wait here with Lord Whittington."

They stood in awkward silence as Miss Barrett eyed the front door. A few heart-felt sighs escaped her lush lips. They might have a long wait since women had all sorts of gewgaws they gathered before stepping out. "Would you like to have a seat in the drawing room?"

Her eyebrow shot up, her eyes darted back and forth, and she stepped closer to the exit.

"I believe Lady Coldwell needs a few minutes before she can present herself. We would be more comfortable in the other room."

"Thank you for asking but no way, Jose. I think I shall stand and wait for Emily to bring me my gloves."

He nodded even though he didn't comprehend some of her words.

"I'll bet Lady Coldwell's eating again and has to change her dress. The maid brings one tray after another to her room." The tone of her voice could not conceal her complaint.

A full, involuntary belly laugh escaped from his lips.

Emily charged down the stairs, beetle-browed and fretful. Did she believe him a threat to her friend? Botheration. A chamber maid trailed after her with three heavy cloaks. Lady Coldwell followed slowly.

Miss Barrett's eyes narrowed, and she poked him in the ribs with her elbow and whispered. "Crumbs. She has them all over her massive bosom."

He could not contain his mirth.

Miss Barrett huffed, did not understand.

He whispered, "Women do not talk body parts and very few ever say what they mean."

Emily must have overheard because she bent her head, gazed at the floor. Lady Coldwell opened and closed her mouth as she sputtered for air.

"What a pleasure to have you three reside in my abode," he said to the strange trio. All three women scrutinized him. He wondered if the Coldwell ladies questioned his sanity as much as he questioned Ms. Barrett's.

Chapter Five

Liz inspected the open carriage. "This is an exquisite piece of workmanship," she told Emily and Lord Whittington as she bent down to look at the wooden spokes. The hand-crafted vehicle had perfectly fitted wheels. She bent lower to see the undercarriage and caught the traitor admiring her backside, straightened. "Absolutely exquisite," she told him.

"I'll say," he retorted.

Did he mean me or the carriage?

His coachman opened the side door and pulled the steps down. Lady Coldwell entered first. The conveyance tipped low when the overlarge woman teetered on the running board, making the rig bounce on the springs. The servant held her bulk and the carriage swayed as she plopped onto the seat.

She tried not to show her astonishment as Lady Coldwell arranged her skirts. Acted as if the rocking held no importance. She glanced at her so-called guardian and noticed his face remained stoic. The twinkle in his eye told a different story.

He motioned for her to get in next, held his hand out so she could use him as a counter balance.

"Most women want to know how plush the seats are, not what the undercarriage looks like," he said as he held her gloved hand a moment longer than necessary.

She flashed him her award-winning smile, then sat across from Lady Coldwell and inspected the leather seats, the brass fittings, and the man who steered the horses. What was the correct term? They hadn't used carriages when filming her show, so she didn't know what to call the horse handler. Was he a driver or a coachman?

Lord Whittington held out his hand for Emily. "Miss Coldwell, allow me."

Emily sat primly on the seat next to her. Looked serene. The young lady had perfected the art of concealed emotions. It took Liz two days to unearth her warmth. His Lordship seated himself across from them.

Everyone in the carriage eyed her. Intense and unnatural. She planned to throw caution to the wind. Anticipation built like steam in a kettle. Could she crawl over them and jump from the vehicle when the right moment approached?

"I believe fresh air does everyone good." Lord Whittington adjusted his hat as he spoke.

"I don't think Miss Barrett is ready for Hyde Park, my Lord. She has the fidgets. Do sit still, gel, please do. A lady never gawks as you do." Lady Coldwell wrung her hands as the carriage pulled away from the front step and into the cobblestone lane.

"We will leave Hyde Park for another day," his Lordship told them.

"The charade will be up soon," she said. Hated how she couldn't keep her mouth shut. Now they would be extra vigilant.

The older woman sniffed in disapproval. Addressed her next comment to his Lordship. "She still believes the cock and bull story she made up about living in the future? What shall we do with her?" She twisted her gloved hands. "Oh, what shall we do?"

She glanced at her chaperon, huddled next to Lord Whittington. Noticed a hint of fear on her face. "Stop the act. You won't be able to hold me against my will much longer."

Decided to stand on the floor of the carriage and balance herself as they traveled over the cobbles. Lord Whittington and Lady Coldwell exchange startled glances. Good. She had them worried. Tried to figure out how to jump with the dress she wore. She could stand on the seat, realized desperation made her thoughts unreasonable.

Lady Coldwell screeched, "Sit down, gel. Sit down. What you do is dangerous." The woman glared at his Lordship. "Bats in her belfry, I tell you. What if someone sees her actions? My daughter shall be tarred with the same brush as Miss Barrett."

She turned away from the hysterical woman and knelt on the seat, held on to the brass bar running across the front of the carriage. Embraced the cool, crisp air on her cheeks. The sky looked slightly overcast, the temperature chilly—like the older lady's demeanor. She untied her cape, didn't want to get the material caught in the spokes when she fled. Hated to leave the warm comfortable garment behind if and when she jumped. The ride would have been fun except for the smell. "Are we close to the sewers?" she asked.

No one responded.

The horses meandered slowly down the street allowing her to hear traders call out their wares. "Where did you find these actors?"

Emily pulled her down in the seat next to her.

"Please stay seated and I will answer all your questions. Let me point out the mouse-trap man—see his cages?"

She looked for the mice. Would they be dead or alive? How did the man catch them? Then she noticed a girl whose back had to hurt with all the weight she carried. "Why does the child transport water jugs on a pole? What does she yell?"

"She's a water-carrier and she cries out, so residents know to come out and fill their water buckets."

Her mother sniffed. "Hard to understand the diction of the uneducated."

Her daughter ignored the comment, continued, "You can get whatever you wish for in London. See the knife grinder?" Her slender finger pointed to a man who had set up shop on the street corner. A group of women stood close by. They looked as if they gossiped with each other while the man worked a knife across a whet stone.

"Over here is an ink seller." She nodded at the man who carried pens and his ink-bottle slung on a stick. His song sounded cheerful. *"Come buy good ink as black as jet, a varnish like gloss on a writing 'twill set."* He carried a small barrel, with a pint-measure and funnel.

Emily continued to talk. "The jolly fellow near the bakery is the muffin man and those are egg girls. I see an earthenware seller to my right. The street vendors are necessary in this town."

She witnessed the boisterous city life with awe. The clamoring, wandering people dressed in rags and silly costumes with rips, tears, and patches. The workers carried their shops on their heads or in baskets and carts. Smoke rose from various buildings. Smells assaulted her nostrils.

The vegetable man and his donkey, or 'little moke' which is what Emily called the set-up, had its back laden with panniers, and seemed to be a common sight. No fixed cries came from the vegetable sellers, as their shouts varied with their stock, which included asparagus, potatoes, carrots, peas, and turnips. A man on their right called out, *"Cabbages, O! Turnips! Two bunches a penny, turnips, ho!"*

At some point she realized she could not be on a set. They had traveled too far for the scene unfolding to be anything other than what it appeared. Soot hung in the air and the smells of London stuck to her skin and clothes. The fine day became misty as fog rolled in. She could not help but notice lamps, not lights; cobbles instead of pavement; running filth in the streets instead of sewers.

Her guardian switched places with Emily. Took up where the young lady left off. "Regent Street has fashionable shops." He pointed. "Swan and Edgar, the world-famous drapers and mercers. Mechi is the genius of razors and Nicolls, the great inventor of paletots."

"What's a paletot?" she asked.

He nodded toward a lady who walked out of a shop, a maid trailing behind. She had on a short heavy coat over her ankle length dress. She assumed the short coat was called a paletot.

The man continued in a soothing voice. His presence kept her calm. "We approach Houbigant, purveyor of dainty gloves and rare perfumes. I believe you will like shopping in these establishments. And," he nodded toward a store front, "Lewis and Allonby are celebrated for their silks and shawls. We won't stroll today but one morning you and Miss Coldwell can spend your pin money while your chaperon advises you on the latest styles."

"I do not believe I shall take her advice," she whispered to the charmer who sat close to her without touching. "First, she wore a too-tight, gaudy, yellow dress. Now she has a hat with real apples on the rim."

He leaned toward her, their shoulders touching momentarily and said in a hushed tone, "I believe Lady Coldwell needs food near her at all times. Mayhap you can give her direction in choosing her wardrobe. A bit less ostentatious." He looked her in the eye, and it seemed as if they were alone. The carriage stopped abruptly, ending the special moment. *Why did this man affect her the way he did?*

"Regent Street exhibits a spectacle of wealth, splendor, and bravery no other city in the world can equal. This street becomes exceedingly busy during the season." He continued his running monologue, talking loud enough to include Lady and Miss Coldwell.

"Observe, on your right, the Archbishop's Chapel; and on the left, near Oxford Street, Hanover Chapel, designed by Mr. Cockerell, the architect."

Liz noticed the lower, working classes darted among the slow-moving pace of the upper, better dressed population.

"Why does the man wear...?" She waved her hand toward a fellow strutting out of a shop. His hat taller than a top hat, his waistcoat canary yellow. He had six watch fobs hanging from six different pockets. His pants were red, his platform shoes encased large feet. He could belong to the circus only the other fellows who trailed after him dressed in the same silly manner.

"We call them dandies, m'dear. Gentlemen of fashion." Lord Whittington's tone held a note of derision.

Her guardian wore elegant buff pants, shiny black boots, a starched shirt. The overall picture elegant but simple. "And you? Are you not a man of fashion?" she asked.

His full lip curled, frost appeared in his eye. "I am not."

A genuine laugh burst from her lips. "I would be embarrassed to be seen with you if you looked like..." she waved her hand in the direction of the dandy, unable to come up with a proper adjective to describe him.

He defrosted before her eyes and she wondered why he had been so insulted. A moment of silence ensued before he continued to advise the group about the city. "Crossing Oxford Street, we pass, on our right, the National Institute of Fine Arts. Over here," he nodded to their left, "is the German Bazaar. Yonder church, with the peculiar tower and spire, is All Souls'. The builders name is John Nash who is the Prince Regent's favorite architect. Our Regent wants an eye-catching monument where the newly laid-out Regent Street links with Piccadilly—his idea of progress. The church is built with Bath stone and the unique spire, when finished, will be made of seventeen concave sides encircled by a *peripteros* of Corinthian columns. Who knows when the building will be completed and what the final cost will be?"

Had she been sucked into a time warp? This had to be London in eighteen twelve. A time when women were chattels. She had seen All Souls Church on her tour of England in two thousand and nine—one of the last surviving churches designed by John Nash. Bile rose in her throat. Her body shook and her head started to ache. She might never return home. "Please take me back. I think I've seen enough for one day." Her voice sounded wimpy. Unsure.

"What's the matter, Miss Barrett? Too much air?" Lord Whittington asked in a concerned tone.

"I believe I need to rest. My head aches."

A young girl called out, *"Fine Seville oranges, fine, fine, fine; round, sound, and tender, inside thee rine."* The too young child did not hide the fact she might deliver a baby soon. Her cloak tented out around her stomach. Liz' heart went out to the youngster who couldn't be more than thirteen. "I'd like an orange, if you please."

Emily gasped and held her hand to her mouth. Lady Coldwell thwacked her daughter with her fan and told her, "Stop acting like a gutter snipe."

"Did I say something wrong?" she asked her so-called guardian.

He shook his head no and called to the driver. The carriage came to a halt and a young boy playing nearby was sent to purchase four oranges. He had rags wrapped around his feet instead of shoes.

Emily lowered her voice and whispered. "Oranges are extremely rare this time of year."

When the boy returned, Lord Whittington handed each lady an orange and told the child, "I am not sure I want one. Take this from me, if you please." The boy looked at the man as if he were crazy, snatched the orange from his outstretched hand and started to run in the opposite direction.

"Lord Whittington," Emily cried. "You have gotten the boy's hopes up. This may be the only time the lad ever eats an orange."

Even in her confusion to discover oranges were rare, she had to smile at the generosity of the man seated next to her. Most of the Lords and Ladies of this time period didn't care for the plight of those beneath their station. He seemed different. Or at least, she hoped he had a charitable heart and it wasn't because he hated oranges.

Why had she been transported to another era? If she didn't pop back into the future soon, she would have to become independent. Find a way to make money of her own. Remembered the conversation between her guardian and the doctor. Some relative had dumped her on the Earl's doorstep. The poor, poor man. First her and then the horrid Lady Coldwell.

What a pickle barrel they were in. Pondered for a moment at the old-fashioned thought. Pickle barrel? Gathered her wits and reminded herself the quack of a doctor wanted her locked up. A shudder ran down her spine. No one would believe her a time traveler. An asylum would definitely be worse than the place she now resided.

Without thinking, she set the orange in her lap, pulled off one glove, bit her nail. Realized the body she invaded looked like her but wasn't her. She fully intended to break the habit. Deliberately placed her hand in her lap, held the orange tight. A precious item. One she might never taste again. Oranges grew throughout California. But this precious fruit had been gifted to her. The only item in the world she possessed. Tears pooled in her eyes and she desperately tried to sniff them away.

The man beside her pulled a handkerchief from his inside pocket, handed her the linen square without a glance. Went back to pointing out landmarks as he ordered the coachman to head home. She listened, took in the sights. Decided to learn this city and her housemates.

"Lady Coldwell? How does one eat an orange?" she asked. Both Emily and her mother reverently handled the fruit as if they were exotic.

"One doesn't eat an orange in public," her chaperon responded with a sniff and a lift of her nose.

"I would like instructions once we are at Lord Whittington's home. I also need you to instruct me in manners."

The older woman's jowls jiggled as her mouth dropped open.

"I do believe Miss Barrett is over her unfortunate head bump," Lord Whittington said. Liz looked him in the eye and, once again, felt a strange pull. Both of them quickly looked away.

Did this man realize she would never be a 'milk and water' miss? Wondered how he would react to her vocation. After all, actresses were considered prostitutes in this date and time.

Chapter Six

Liz stepped from the tin tub. Black scum swam in the water, along with rose petals and plant stems she could not identify. How she missed shower heads and steam. Most of the black extract dousing her red hair disappeared. The smell of roses made the task pleasant. She stood naked in front of the mirror and stared at her reflection.

Her body appeared similar, right down to the mole over her left breast. She turned and noticed the beauty mark on her backside. Okay—her figure, skin and hair seemed to be original. The same as she had before the capped teeth, false nails, and strategically placed golden highlights.

Her personality had been altered. She used to give orders and command people. This timid mousey personality seemed to be afraid at her own shadow. Became shy when forced to start a conversation. Bit her nails without notice. Didn't have an opinion. God, what a milquetoast.

Once again, she used odd, old-fashioned terminology. She should have said pussy. She said the word out loud. "You," she pointed to herself in the looking glass, "are a pussy." Speaking forcefully made her feel better. Realized she should have said mirror.

A memory surfaced. In her mind's eye she noticed a man…her father…a portly, fun fellow who had loved her. Sadness and grief crept through her system, tendrils of loss and heartache. She detected tears on her cheeks. Brushed them away with her hand in an angry manner. She needed to concentrate on her past—not her past from the future, but the one this body had led. Then she would make important decisions on how to proceed.

She exited her bedroom two hours later—a woman on a mission with a plan. She knocked on Emily's door and her friend immediately answered. "The sound of your shoes alerted me to your approach."

"Why are you dressed like an ostentatious Christmas package?" The girl had ribbons and bows from head to toe. "Did your mother insist?"

The young lady ducked her head and she realized she embarrassed her when she spoke without thinking. Rushed to let her know they could resolve the situation. "I have a plan that will have us both bang up to snuff." She pushed Emily into her bedroom and followed, closed the door behind.

An hour later they walked down the hall arm in arm to Lady Coldwell's withdrawing room.

"Mama will be eating. Again!"

"Her overeating will be my bargaining chip. Let me do the talking." Bile rose in her throat. She realized Elizabeth's personality intruded. Well, she planned to do this no matter how challenging. She pushed the timid, meek part of herself she called Elizabeth away. Put her hands on her hips in the wonder woman stance and her confidence returned. Knocked on the door.

Lady Coldwell called out, "enter." Sure enough, the woman sat in a chair, a tray table at her side. Cheese, bread, and other half-eaten foodstuff littered the area. She walked over to the buffet and motioned

Emily to stand across from her. They lifted the tray table away from her reach. Lady Coldwell protested loudly.

Liz picked up the infamous fan and smacked the tyrant on her arm. The fat woman yelped. "I won't hit you with the fan if you promise not to hit your daughter with this…this weapon."

The woman sniffed back a tear. "You hurt me."

"Do you think others like to be hit with your fan?" When the woman didn't reply, she waved the gadget in a menacing fashion. Lady Coldwell shrieked and put her hands to her face. With a sense of satisfaction, she realized all bullies back down when confronted.

"Emily, dear. Don't let her hit me again," the woman pleaded. "I never realized I caused you pain. Lady Jensen uses her fan and…"

Liz recognized she had become the bully. Drat. Maybe the insecure woman needed someone to assume responsibility. She reminded herself she could be a take-charge person. Set the fan down gently in Lady Coldwell's lap. Pushed the settee next to her chair and motioned Emily to have a seat opposite.

"I plan to take over the way we dress. I know you don't believe this Lady Coldwell, but I am from the future. In the future I know how to act and dress. All these hideous frills and flounces will be ripped out and redone. But I need your help. You must show me how to act like a lady. You help me, and I'll help you lose weight and," she paused to let her final offer sink in, "I will find your daughter a husband."

Lady Coldwell's expressive face glowed when she mentioned a husband. Then she deflated. "Emily doesn't have a dowry."

"I have one, don't I?"

"I'm not sure. I've never been privy to accounts and such. I had a shock when Barron Coldwell died. He left us...lacking." The woman started to cry, and Liz could smell her fear. In this era, women without relatives were thrown out on the street like yesterday's garbage.

"Three of us working together can come up with a strategy to navigate society." There was no doubt in her mind she could rise to the top. Had done so in Hollywood and would do so in London.

Two hours later they returned to their rooms to dress for the theater, leaving Lady Coldwell to change clothes. Emily entered her room while she continued down the hall, then down the stairs. She looked into the room on the right, then the one on the left. Lord Whittington remained out of sight. She walked the hall to the right of the stairs and found a set of double doors. They were closed. She knocked and his sexy, masculine voice called, "Enter." She opened the doors and peeped in.

The Earl sat behind a massive desk. He had a quill in one hand, paperwork in front of him. Stacks of papers littered the work space. She became intimidated, then realized her body had become intimidated. Clear your mind of self-doubt, she demanded of herself. *This body will not betray me.* Deliberately, she marched across the room to his desk. The man looked at her with amusement upon his face and she softened, smiled in return.

"I say. Your hair is back to normal. No more ridiculous beauty treatments for you."

"What possessed me to dye my hair?"

"You mayhap followed Lady Coldwell's direction. I'm not sure she's the best chaperon for you."

She agreed but the two women had made a pact, so she didn't want another chaperon. Walking around the side of his desk, she pushed a stack of papers out of the way and hopped up. Made herself comfortable, crossed her legs and started to swing them.

A peculiar looked crossed the man's face. As if he had poker'd up for a high stakes game.

"I guess a lady doesn't perch on a gentleman's desk?" she quizzed.

"No. A lady doesn't perch on a gentleman's desk." He agreed.

"Well sir. In your house I won't be a lady. Outside of your house, I promise, cross my heart," she crossed her heart with her hand, "I will act appropriately. Do you know someone who can help me master manners?"

When he smiled, her fear melted. "Yes. I have a sister. She left town before you arrived but should be back by now. I'll send a note for her to attend us in the morning."

"Can you get us a formal dance instructor?" She allowed her legs to swing free, a nervous habit she had in both bodies. Funny that.

"I think Regina knows a dance master. What else can I do for you?"

She jumped off the desk, stood up, and looked over his shoulder. She loved to stand close to him. Became whole. Complete. Immediately wanted to gag. *Complete? Really?* Scanning the account book that lay open before him, she pointed to a column of numbers. "Your numbers are off by one here and here and here," she told him.

He nodded his agreement. "If only my secretary was as good with numbers as you seem to be.

Because he grinned, she continued. "I'm placing Lady Coldwell on a diet."

"What?" The man looked befuddled.

She wondered what words to use in this century. Diet obviously hadn't entered anyone's vocabulary. Overweight people were considered well-heeled and envied. She inhaled and caught a whiff of Bay Rum. The man smelled absolutely delicious, so she needed to end this conversation before she acted inappropriate.

"We are going to restrict what Lady Coldwell eats. The extra weight she carries will kill her. Can I instruct your Chef in the food to be served?"

He nodded but didn't speak. She adjusted the cloth around his neck, so it laid perfect. Her tiny hands worked rapidly. She had done this a million times on set. Patted his chest when she accomplished the task and experienced those tingling sensations. His eyes widened a second before he became ramrod straight. It pleased her to know he noticed the chemistry he tried so hard not to show.

The thrill of his touch reassured her. He had been the first one to stroke her hand after her unusual arrival. Even picked her up with strong arms. Held her tight. It seemed like…lust. Took her a while to figure out the emotion because this body smacked of innocence. She would ruminate later because she needed to figure out finances.

"I have a delicate subject I need to discuss with you." She examined his face and noticed his cheeks reddened. Decided they needed space and walked to the other side of the desk. She risked much with her next question. Realized he might not be honest with her. Lady Coldwell warned her finances were a man's domain and women were not allowed to intrude.

"Do I have any assets?"

Lord Whittington's mouth dropped open. "Assets?" She noticed he looked at her shoes and the wall but never at her chest. *He thinks about me sexually but doesn't want me to know. How refreshing.*

"I mean…who pays for my dresses and…all the items we three ladies need?"

"You do not need to worry about those matters."

"But I do. Worry. Lady Coldwell has dressed us in flounces and all sorts of ghastly lace. We need to redo our wardrobes. If I have money, I would like to pay for Emily and myself."

One lone eyebrow rose. Liz had the urge to reach across the desk and soothe it back into place. Wanted to grab his cravat and pull him out of the chair. Maybe kiss him silly.

Instead, she forced her hands behind her back and asked a sensible question. "I know money is a vulgar topic, but I need to know if I have any."

He pushed his chair back and rose. They were squared off across the work table, held together by energetic cords of want yet buffered by common sense. He stood a few inches taller. She would fit nicely up against his body. Her face reddened. *Naughty, naughty.*

The man took another step backwards. They had an entire desk and extra space between them. But it was as if they were both afraid to get too close. Might start a fire. Or, burst into flames.

He looked away. Pulled his sleeves down with a jerk. Glanced back at her without an ounce of expression on his now stoic face. An expression he apparently perfected. Probably used with cheating tradesmen. Or errant charges who confounded his sense of morality.

"I have enough blunt to take care of you and Miss Coldwell. I will settle a nice amount on both of you before you marry. Lady Coldwell can live with her daughter if need be. Please get the flounces fixed," he walked to the side of the desk. Stood closer yet his attitude seemed far away. "Whatsoever you need can be done. I will make sure you are taken care of."

"Why?"

"Why?" He gulped, looked confused again. A long silence ensued as she held his gaze. Finally, he spoke in a crisp tone. "I take my duty seriously."

She wanted to cry. Literally scream out her frustration. Pulled herself together before she told him duty be damned. Stared at the carpet beneath her feet. "You're a good man. I'll go talk with the Chef."

"The Chef is a Cook and she's temperamental. Please treat her with kid gloves Miss Barrett."

She flashed him her fake smile. Quickly walked toward the door. "I will tell her what excellent food she prepares and request a few favorites. I plan to forbid delivery of trays to Lady Coldwell's room. She will eat all meals with us from this time forward."

She waggled her hand and walked away, cursed herself for the silly gesture. One didn't wave one's hands at a benefactor who had basically given her what she requested. Where were her manners?

***

Lord Whittington watched her leave. Ruminated on that jaunty little hand motion. So innocent yet entirely too seductive. The English rosebud had turned into a wild Irish flower right before his eyes. Their moment started when she perched herself on his desk. Questioned whether a lady acted like she acted. He assured her ladies didn't. They smiled at one another, as if they had discovered a secret. He liked her perched on the desk, legs swinging. A comfortable, devil may care act.

The familiarity between them didn't bode well for an Englishman. Especially when she emphatically stated she would not act like a lady in his house. He didn't want her to act a lady which made his temperature rise along with his over excitable imagination. When she crossed her heart, he experienced a compulsion to take a peek at her chest. Not really a peek. More like a hard stare which he might have done if etiquette hadn't been drilled into him. Actually, wanted to rip off her bodice. He had never wanted to rip off anyone's bodice before.

This young lady had become dangerous. Made him long for her in an improper way. One should never want to sully a woman under one's protection. He walked to the other side of his desk, plopped into his comfortable chair, tried to forget their tête-à-tête. The chair no longer seemed warm and friendly. Miss Barrett had…she had disrupted his peace. What in tarnation had she done to him?

His mind circled back. Her jump from the desk to the ground, the closeness of her body as she stood over his shoulder. Oh, how he liked her casualness. He had expected her to lean down and kiss him. And why would he expect a kiss? Because he yearned for her in a way he never yearned for another. Maybe a shake of his head would put these silly notions in perspective.

Yes. She came to talk to him about Lady Coldwell's eating habits. He had agreed to…what?

His mind circled again. Like a mad dog stalks a lone street vendor until the animal can snatch a piece of mutton pie. Miss Barrett had straightened his cravat. An intimate act. One, his sister, Regina, had done a hundred times before. This slip of a Miss had started to fold the cloth and he had become…well, one could not think about what had happened in his nether regions. Too unseemly.

Only…he could not stop his speculations. Had become like the mad dog. Wanted to follow her. Had to pull his cravat loose because it seemed noose-like.

Spiraled back to when she had laid her hand on his chest. He believed she planned to pull him close, kiss him. Ludicrous. Only light skirts acted boldly. And, she wasn't a light skirt. Miss Barrett came to him an innocent and she would leave his household in the same manner. She might wreak havoc with his glandular system, but he didn't have to act on base impulses.

He remembered how she'd asked about her assets. Almost jumped out of his skin. He understood she asked an innocent question yet…could not resist the involuntary pull toward her. Tried to reassure her when he had been the one needing reassurance. Completely forgot to tell her she had funds of her own.

Miss Barrett had an indulgent father. She had an acceptable dowry, along with a bigger, substantial sum, which would always be hers to control. One of the reasons why no one wanted to take her in. The relatives didn't have access to those funds. A newfangled notion in England. Did all the colonials act in this manner? He had no idea.

His next reflection stopped him cold. Would the Duke appreciate how unique Miss Barrett acted? He seriously doubted the man would. Told his mind to stop worrying about a situation he could not control. When had he become so involved? These ruminations about her had engulfed him. No more. Cease and desist. He picked up the next piece of correspondence in the pile.

And what did his brainbox do? Circle back to the atmosphere between the two. Remembered how she changed when he talked about duty. The air had somehow gone flat between them. Women generally liked men who were conscientious of their responsibilities. Well, he did have a duty to her and yearning after her didn't meet the mark. When she left the room to talk to Cook, he experienced loneliness for the first time. Preposterous. Utter rubbish.

He shook his head, forced himself to speculate on when it would next rain. Decided to write a note to Regina. Needed reinforcement from his ever-practical sister. She would find a dance master and another Cook if Miss Barrett ran this one off.

He looked at the numbers on the sheet of paper before him. Realized his warehouse man had been cheating him for years. A penny here, a penny there. Miss Barrett had caught the mistake as she glanced at the paperwork. She might be better at arithmetic than he. Noooooo. Women couldn't keep numbers in their pretty little heads. Or could they? Regina learned alongside him when they were children. He walked to the opened door and looked right, then left. He could still smell Miss Barrett's hair even though he couldn't locate her. Suddenly, her vibrant laugh from the downstairs kitchen had him smiling. He envisioned the tigress and the temperamental Cook, who chuckled at her verbiage. The woman did unconventional in an appealing way. Used strange, fascinating language. Captivated him.

He marched to the front entrance and picked up his hat, caped coat, and cane. Needed to walk off excess tension. His sister only lived a few streets over. He would go see her in person instead of sending a note.

The lingering smell of roses stayed with him the entire way.

Chapter Seven

Lord Whittington perceived the moment Miss Barrett walked into the breakfast area. Noticed her even before she uttered a cheerful "Good morning." He stayed hidden behind his paper. Mayhap she would ignore him, even if his libido couldn't ignore her.

The temptress brushed past his chair, headed for the sideboard. The clatter of the silver lid being lifted from each chafing dish made him grin. Would she poke her cute nose into every container?

Curiosity made him look over the top of his newspaper to see what she chose. The plate held scrambled eggs, two slices of bacon, and tomato slices heaped with sautéed onions. Odd choices to break one's fast. Where were her kippers? The toast and jam?

Loud, plodding steps thumped down the hall, alerting him to the presence of Lady Coldwell. The woman never ate with him, which had been a relief since she tended to talk about inane matters. Instead, she had trays of food brought to her room. Her daughter trailed close behind. He would have been surprised if she hadn't. The older women clung to her child like a lifeline.

"Good morning, Lady Coldwell. Your plate is filled with goodies. Please be seated." Miss Barrett pulled out the woman's chair to indicate where she wanted her to sit.

He sat in shocked silence. The tigress bossed the old lady around? Could not help himself, lowered his barrier to glimpse the chaperone's facial expression. She stared in his direction.

"Good morning to you, sir." Her face looked serious, her voice polite, yet her hands trembled.

He caught the butler glaring into the room.

"We have help, Miss Barrett. You can serve yourself breakfast from the side table, but the help pours the tea and seats everyone." He pointed to the boy in the corner of the room. Obviously, she wasn't aware of her guffaw.

"I'll be happy to instruct the butler on how I like my tea." She waved the man over. The normally stoic servant gawked, then remembered his manners and walked sedately to where she stood.

The mother daughter duo took their seats. Lady Coldwell glared at her plate. A pout formed on her lips. He propped his newspaper back into place so none of the women could see his grin.

The sweet, soft whisper of words coming from Miss Barrett's direction piqued his curiosity. A glance around his flimsy fortress showed the butler smiling. He watched as the man nodded his head in understanding. Sat her like one would seat The Queen. *My Queen. What a queer notion.*

Coffee was poured for the Colonial Queen and the rest of them received a bracing cup of tea.

"You have a great view from this room," Miss Barrett said. He lowered his paper again. Noticed her steadfast gaze. Those glittering green eyes held a hint of humor. Did she know he tried to ignore her?

"Yes. I must say the flowers have started to show

themselves. Another month and you will see a riot of colors."

She smiled warmly, turned her head. "I haven't said Good Morning yet, Emily. You look like you slept well."

Lady Coldwell coughed. "Good morning, Miss Coldwell. You look like you slept well."

"Isn't that what I said?"

"No, m'dear. You used her first name." The voice belonged to his sister who entered through the door. "One does not call other women by their first name in mixed company. I do say, you did use a nice way to correct her without actually correcting her." The petite, full figured, beauty nodded toward Lady Coldwell.

All three ladies studied his sister, Lady Moreland, as she sauntered into the room. He beamed at Regina, glad to see someone who could take charge of his three responsibilities. She seemed happy. Had rosy cheeks and, he noticed, flattering curves. His skinny, little sister had grown up. Her dark shiny hair had been piled high on her head and she wore the latest fashion.

Lady Coldwell put her fork down and preened at his sister's compliment.

Miss Barrett rolled her eyes.

Miss Coldwell looked as if she tried to suppress laughter.

He decided introductions were in order. "Ladies, you remember my sister, Lady Moreland."

Lady Coldwell and Miss Coldwell stood. Miss Barrett followed a second behind the other two, mimicked their actions, including the polite nods. Well, well, well. Why did she suddenly try to fit in?

He motioned to his sister, "I will not bow to you,

m'dear. Too early for such nonsense."

"You are the same rank as my husband, but manners dictate you stand."

He grumped but stood and kissed his sister's rounded cheek.

"Would you care to join us?" Miss Barrett asked.

Everyone turned to stare at her except him. He turned away. Didn't want to encourage her rash generosity even though he enjoyed her candidness.

"Whatever did I do wrong this time?" She asked in a shaky voice. Her fingers became buried in her mouth. Once again, she pulled her hand away, glared at her fingertips, and put her offending digits behind her back.

"You cannot invite someone of a higher rank to Lord Whittington's table. Only he can ask Lady Moreland to dine," the chaperone explained.

"We don't stand on ceremony in this house," he interjected. "Regina, have a seat and my man will get you some tea."

After she had been served, Regina broke into a one-sided, running dialogue of her plans for the group. He started to read his paper in earnest. Noticed he liked the sound of friendly chatter in the background. He had grown up with the sound of his mother and sister nattering like magpies.

His father always pretended he couldn't bother to listen but every once in a while, he would interject a comment. His mother reigned supreme over the table. She had been a plain, plump woman with a smiling countenance. He still missed her warmth. Recognized his sister had become like their mother. What a splendid notion.

The butler opened the door and announced, "Lord

Silverman awaits in the green room."

"I guess I'm not allowed to ask him to join us either," Miss Barrett asked as she pulled his newspaper down. Her emerald eyes locked onto his face. She lowered her voice. "He took us to the theater last night. Don't you think we should invite him? Cook has berries and cream for dessert."

His forthright charge quickly turned away, patted Lady Coldwell's arm. "I arranged this treat for you." The older woman beamed. Obviously, the two of them had called a truce.

"Show Lord Silverman in," Regina told the butler. "I haven't seen him in an age. Dessert, you say? I didn't know one had dessert with the first meal of the day. Don't tell my three-year-old or he'll demand sweets at every meal."

The ladies were laughing at an anecdote his sister told when Lord Silverman appeared. Everyone stood.

"Good morning, Lord Silverman." Miss Barrett's smile seemed welcoming.

He wanted to tell the interloper he wasn't welcome. Didn't because manners dictated, he be polite.

"Please sit next to Miss Coldwell. She is alone on that side of the table." His charge sounded like a teacher instructing a dimwitted pupil.

His sister's eyes twinkled at the social error. "Now the table has an even number. If this were a dinner party, you," she pointed to the Duke, "would be considered a blessing."

Whittington groaned. Noticed he hadn't been annoyed until his nemesis arrived. "Yes. Please do be seated. We have berries and cream. A special treat." His voice sounded sarcastic to his own ears. A sharp kick to his shin made him drop his paper. "Why did you kick me?"

Miss Barrett looked away. "Lord Whittington is such a grump in the mornings. Manners are not his strong suit."

He muttered under his breath.

"What are your plans this fair day?" his sister asked the Duke.

"I came to see if the ladies would like to take in the sights this afternoon."

"The dance master will be here soon. Please stay?" Regina sounded like a colonel ordering a soldier.

Lord Silverman's eyebrows lifted, and the monocle went up toward his eye. He wanted to laugh. That eyepiece wouldn't deter Regina who cleared her throat. "We learn country dances today and need enough people to form lines."

The Duke shrank in his chair. "I would be delighted to stay."

Why did he feel sorry for the man? His sister cocked her head toward him like an eagle does his prey and he understood he, too, would be required to dance.

The women smiled indulgently at him, so he slapped his paper on top of the table.

"I feel the need for another cup of tea." He motioned for his servant.

"Tea solves every problem in England," Lady Coldwell said, then looked at Miss Barrett. "Has the time come for our berries?"

Miss Barrett motioned with her hand to the table boy, who disappeared. A moment later, a young girl came in with a tray holding small bowls of cream and berries. She gave everyone a dish. "Thank you, Molly.

These look scrumptious. Tell Cook I loved her eggs. Scrambled easy—exactly how I like them." Molly giggled and left the room.

Miss Barrett didn't seem to notice all heads turned toward her again. Instead, she focused on Lady Coldwell. "You have approximately two tablespoons of berries and a smaller amount of cream. Enough to sweeten up the end of our meal. I say, love foods that love you back. We eat, then we dance. The exercise will do us good."

The berries were devoured in record time. Soon thereafter, the butler announced, "The dancing master has arrived. He awaits you in the ball room."

"Thank you, Henry. I don't have a clue where the ballroom is, so we'll let Lord Whittington lead the way." Miss Barrett stood.

Did she call the butler by his name?

Regina frowned at him. The Duke told Lady Moreland, "you have much to instruct. Mayhap you can deal with a colonial who doesn't know her place."

He wanted to tell the Duke to stuff his opinion but understood his charge would marry the rigid man. Suddenly wanted to help. Like he had upon her arrival.

He hadn't exchanged more than a few words with the grieving girl the day she showed up on his doorstep. Her solicitor informed him they were distant relatives. Thoroughly explained he was her last hope. Talked about her father's sudden death. Miss Barrett had tears of embarrassment on her cheeks. Her gloved hands shook as she clutched the strings on her reticule. His mother would have a conniption in heaven if he neglected his duty.

Once the solicitor left, he made a few polite

remarks before he had his housekeeper show her around and take her to her room. He hadn't seen her until the evening meal.

They had dined in the way he did at his club with some of the stuffier, older members. He carried the weight of the entire conversation. After her fall, she had suddenly become the center of every conversation. Stood with her head up and her back straight. Engaged on a first named basis with his staff. He left those details to the housekeeper and butler. This is how his mother ran their household at the Grange. The warm place where he grew up. His house had started to feel like a home.

He didn't notice he had a grin from ear to ear. But his staff, his sister, and Lord Silverman did.

Chapter Eight

Liz sauntered into the ballroom. The instant the bottom of her worn slipper hit the wood floor, she slid. Carefully traversed the big room and didn't stop until she had walked the entire space. The tall ceiling brought the imp out in her. Would it echo? "Hello Room."

Her voice bounced around and faded. She looked toward the group, did a jaunty bow instead of a curtsy, then ran toward her friends who stood gaping in the door way. At the last minute she set both feet sideways to stop. Instead, she crashed into Lord Silverman. He quickly righted her, a frown upon his rigid face.

Lord Whittington laughed. "Remember how we used to slide when we were boys?" he asked his friend.

Lady Moreland replied, "You two played cowboys and Indians in this room. Used the piano as your fort and ruined Mama's best comforter when you tried to design a teepee."

The Duke's face looked like thunder until he sniffed, sighed, said, "I remember a time or two you joined us."

"Yes. Well, I guess we're all grown up now and have to mind our Ps and Qs." Lady Moreland giggled at her own words.

"Adulthood has nothing to do with age." The room became silent, so Liz walked toward the dance master sitting on the piano bench and introduced herself.

"I believe everyone has grown up with the exception of Miss Barrett." The mighty Duke glared at her. Turned to her guardian, "What happened to the brown-haired mouse and who is this unruly, red head?"

Anger rose from the pit of her stomach. Who was this pompous ass? He might be a Lord, but he would never be her master. "Expressing ones greatness means showing up as yourself without any apology."

Emily slid to a stop beside her, grabbed her hand and led her around the piano. She allowed herself the luxury of being pulled along. Didn't want to be mean spirited. Lady Coldwell had told her time and time again, her biggest fault was her impetuous nature. Her impetuous nature had been her biggest asset when she had a career. How did one turn a liability into an asset in this day and age?

She decided to cool her heels near the piano bench as Lady Moreland and Lady Coldwell talked about what needed to be learned. Like a magnet, she found herself standing too close to Lord Whittington. Lord Stick-Up-His-Butt stood directly across from her and Emily had been arranged by his side, directly in front of them. The dance master started to explain their moves. Showed them how they would bow and prance and change places on the downbeat.

"Who will play the music?" she asked.

Lady Moreland told them she would be honored. Insisted Lady Coldwell and the instructor dance along, so they formed lines. She learned the steps quickly and found herself in good spirits. Enjoyed the movement of her body and the intricate steps.

"Let's begin again," the master clapped. They

stood in formation. Lord Silverman bowed, she curtsied. Made a pass using four steps and stood across from each other. Miss Coldwell and Lord Whittington did the same, then took four steps to the side. This left them partnered with the opposite person.

"You're a much better sport than Lord Stick-Up-His-Backside," she whispered to Lord Whittington when she made her pass. He missed a step. The next pass had her mischievous side up. She winked. Enjoyed seeing him ruffled. He could be so alive with humor one moment and so…so priggishly British the next.

They rehearsed a few times and once again she found herself partnered with her guardian. In a hushed voice he told her, "Lady Coldwell melts like a large chunk of ice. Do you intend to intervene or shall I?"

She looked at her chaperon and realized how red her face appeared. Her brow shined with sweat. On their next pass, she replied, "I think she needs at least five more minutes. Twenty minutes of rapid heartbeat is a great cardiovascular exercise." He looked as if he didn't understand a word, she said but he took his pocket watch from his vest and glanced at the time. Five minutes later, he called a halt. Asked Lady Coldwell to play for a while. "Regina needs to participate. Dance does a body good."

She nodded in agreement. What a great guy. Noticed Emily stared at the Duke with awe. The man ignored her friend because he was too busy glaring in her direction. "What?" she demanded.

He blinked rapidly.

Could he do anything but glare, stare and make her feel like the smallest bug needing to be squashed? Didn't he realize Emily considered him the greatest invention since sliced bread? Too bad they hadn't invented sliced bread.

"Children let's not squabble," Lord Whittington told his friend as he slapped him on the back, rolled up his shirt sleeves.

His Grace straightened his jacket and cuffs. Again. Next, he adjusted his cravat. Really? The hot and stuffy room made one want to take clothes off and this high and mighty gent buttoned up rather than roll up his sleeves. Did he want to be presentable or comfortable?

"We shall move on to the Waltz," the dance master told his students, oblivious to the tension in the room. "The dance has been introduced to England and I want you to be one of the first to know the steps."

"I think Emily and Lord Silverman should go first," she told the group. Lord Whittington agreed, and Lady Coldwell started to play. The dance master called the steps, "One, two, three, one two, three, one to three, turn, turn, no don't stop, turn as you move."

"They look uncomfortable," Lord Whittington told her and his sister.

Lady Moreland grinned. "I'll say. They haven't looked each other in the eye since the dance began." The unlucky couple did a few more turns around the ballroom. Looked worse instead of better.

The dance master turned to her, "Your turn."

"Let's show them the right way to do this." She placed her hand in Lord Whittington's. Tingled at his touch. The music started, and they skimmed across the floor, his hand guiding her. Their movements were synchronized, as if they were one. He exerted pressure on her waist which signaled when to turn and when to move backward. A perfect dance partner. She enjoyed gliding elegantly around the room.

The bubble burst when Regina called loudly, "You can stop now. The music ended."

"We showed them how to dance, didn't we?" Pride sounded in her voice. She felt invisible heat building between them. Giggled.

Her partner grabbed her hand and they raced across the room, slid to a stop in front of the group who gathered around the piano. They continued to hold hands. Lord Whittington gallantly extended his hand, holding hers, then turned her over to his friend. "The lady is the perfect partner. Even you can't mess this up."

His Grace put his hand around her waist and started to move with the beat of the piano. They bumped heads.

She laughed. He didn't.

The dance never got better. When they stopped, she wanted to pull off her slippers and tend her bruised toes.

Lady Moreland took the Duke's hand and told him, "This is the latest rage. You must learn the Waltz. I will count slowly, and you follow." They took a spin around the room and the dance instructor followed. He appeared much more graceful than when he had danced with her and Emily.

"Emily, if you can play, do. Allow Lady Coldwell a turn with Lord Whittington. He waltzes gracefully. He will sail your mother around the room."

Lady Coldwell looked stunned. "I am too old to dance a waltz."

"Au contraire, m'dear. You must take a twirl around the room. And," he pointed at her. "Men are not graceful. We are poised."

"Yes, Lord Loftiness," she replied.

His sister poked her brother in the ribs, and everyone laughed.

The dance master clapped his hands again. "Lord Whittington and Lady Coldwell will start here." He placed them on an invisible spot on the floor. "And," he pointed to her, "Miss Barrett and Lord Silverman will start here. You will circle the dance floor without bumping into one another."

She was breathless when they finished. Not because she had fun and laughed as she spun. It took effort to keep the Duke on course. A lot of effort. Her toes and legs cramped. She noticed Lady Coldwell beamed at Lord Whittington and her spirits lifted. The man had glided the big woman around the room. Made their twirl seem effortless, given the older woman a much-needed boost in confidence.

Lady Moreland called a halt to the lessons and sent the dance instructor on his way. "I won't see you in the park this afternoon because I promised to take Mathew to the menagerie at the palace."

"Can we come?" she asked.

"Didn't you plan to take the air with Lord Silverman?"

"We can breathe air at the menagerie," she responded.

Lord Silverman looked at Lord Whittington.

Lord Whittington looked at Lady Coldwell.

Lady Coldwell looked at her daughter. Her daughter, Emily, told Lady Moreland, "We'd love to see the menagerie, but we've already promised Lord Silverman we would accept his invitation."

Lord Silverman interrupted. "As Miss Barrett

pointed out, air is at the menagerie. I would be honored to escort you ladies."

"Count me out," Lord Whittington told the group.

She stomped on his toe.

He scowled at her before he turned to his sister with a straight face. "I would be delighted to attend the menagerie. Let's hope the lion doesn't get loose again."

"You're joking, right?"

Lady Moreland gave her a strange look. "My husband will be with us."

As if that explains everything.

"He plans to bring his gun!" Without another comment, she made her goodbyes.

Lady Coldwell decided to take a nap.

The two men went off together while Emily and Liz helped the housemaids take rows of flounces off their dresses. Soon enough, they put on their unadorned outfits and were ready to leave.

Eagerness washed over her. To see the palace would be a delight. She didn't know about the menagerie, so she asked questions non-stop on their ride over. Her comfort level dimmed when Lord Moreland exited his carriage, a rifle slung over his shoulder. Lord Whittington opened the boot of the closed carriage they had ridden in and pulled out a similar gun. A reminder she no longer lived in America. This might not be safe. She resided in London. In an era where bears got loose, and people were mauled.

"Where's your gun?" she asked Lord Silverman.

The man pulled at his cuffs. Pointedly ignored her. What little respect she felt withered away.

Emily stared at him like one stares at a forbidden dessert. She recognized an attraction when she witnessed one. Wonder how such an ice chip, who had no intention of protecting the women could attract anyone. Classified the man as a bored neighbor who had naught else to do but tag along with them for the ride. She could barely tolerate him. Considered being rude...only, Emily liked the man.

She continued to look at Emily who blatantly stared at The Duke. Whispered, 'he's a great catch.' Emily gave her a pained look. She hoped the girl would catch him because she had no intention of hooking that fish.

Chapter Nine

"It's been two months since I've been under your roof acting like the perfect Lady. I've been dragged to thirty-five balls, forty parties, twenty-one dinners and eleven breakfasts. To shop and spread gossip seems to be the two favored activities during the season. Now, I want you to take me somewhere so I can see the other side of life in this magnificent city." Liz uncrossed her arms. Demands rarely worked with His Lordship.

Lord Whittington's black brows shot upwards. "Dragged? Yea, gads. I hope the dancing hasn't ruined another pair of slippers. Then you might be forced to shop. Again! I do remember I asked for one night in and you told me 'the season is too short to stay home.'" He mimicked her voice and tone perfectly.

She wanted to stay mad but couldn't. "You know I like to dance. This," she sighed loudly and motioned with her hand in the air. "The novelty has finally worn off. You've been through a number of seasons, so you should have predicted I would eventually get bored."

"Bored! I cannot believe you dare to utter the word. You've basically turned my life upside down and now you're bored." He threw his hands up.

"How have I turned your life upside down?" She stood still, stunned by the accusation.

"You've allowed the housekeeper and her maids to sell the bouquets of flowers delivered by your admirers.

The flower girls love the resales. My maids receive extra shillings. Not a word of gossip spreads about this highly unusual practice. Servants know what goes on in every household. I dread the day one of those young pups who sniff after you finds out from his valet, you have sold his heart-filled offering."

He sounded serious but the twinkle in his eyes gave him away. "You can tell anyone who asks it's a Bunbury Tale."

Lord Whittington placed his hands on his hips. "You ask me to lie?"

"No. Button your full lip and look down your elegant nose. Makes you look top drawer and aristocratic." He scowled at her and she decided to find out what other grievances he had. "How else have I turned your life upside down?"

"Cook no longer lets me eat in the kitchen. I am master here and I cannot enter my own kitchen. Then, who did I find sitting in my seat last night after the ball? You." He jabbed his finger at her. "You ate the last of the shortbread."

"Tasted divine." She purposely licked her lips.

"I haven't had a piece of shortbread since the season began. Lady Coldwell has one less chin, which is good for Lady Coldwell, but I, too, need another wardrobe."

"You are bang up to the snuff with your new purchases." She didn't like the fact her pronouncement made him frown. "I used the correct terminology, didn't I?"

"Miss Barrett. You asked me, and I told you how you've turned my life around."

She waved her hand in an encouraging manner.

"By all means. Continue with all the petty annoyances you have against me."

"I found my coach man reading about horses. Who taught him to read?"

"In the future, the masses will be educated," she responded. He didn't look mollified by her remark. In fact, he started to fidget with his cuffs—a sure sign of agitation.

She decided to say what she wanted before he blew a gasket. "A little birdie told me all about the Elgin marbles. Said your ship yard houses the last marbles sent to England. They are part of history two hundred years from now and I want to see them."

"Who told you about my ships? And, how do you know about Lord Elgin? The man is notorious."

"A great debate is in progress amongst the rattlers. I've listened to their speeches."

"Rattlers are the coaches. You mean to say a great debate is going on between the young puppies. Don't you realize they don't have an ounce of logic in their brain boxes? The youngsters can only repeat what their elders say."

"Snakes, dogs, who cares what the terminology is and don't," she poked her finger in his chest, "don't get all holy roller with me."

He took her slender fingers in his and sparks ignited between them. He needed to tell her about her betrothal contract, so he quickly dropped her hand. Lord Silverman signed the document early in the season, but they had not broached the subject again. He wanted to know his friends' mind before he told this firebrand she would be married. And, before Miss Emily Coldwell got hurt.

"You need to get the vernacular correct. I should not get all hoity-toity." He stuck his nose in the air for emphasis.

"I agree. Stop getting hoity-toity and let me go to the ship yard with you. I want to see what the place looks like."

"Ladies don't belong in the yard."

"Where do we belong? Locked up in a house? Attending parties? Those ladies pull their garters down the way light-skirts do when they street walk. I concluded the heir and the spare notion too far-fetched to be true when I lived in the future. Found out I've been wrong. These ladies get married to the first person who offers for them, immediately produce two children and start a torrid affair with whoever will play along. It's perfectly acceptable only..." she took a deep breath and realized anger filled her. "Only, I don't find the behavior acceptable. Do you know what happened in the garden at Lady Sinclair's house?"

He wanted to know but he didn't want to encourage this enticing woman who stormed back and forth in front of him. How had she learned about light skirts? No telling what she'd seen the few times he left her with Lady Coldwell as the sole chaperon. He would have to have a word with the woman. "Why did you go into the garden? Have I not warned you of the dangers?"

"I took air with Lady Coldwell. She likes to sit outside and cool down after a few dances. Who would believe she turned out to be all the rage? We listened to the moans and groans of more than one couple. Emily would never understand so we left her inside. You should hear the corkers these Corinthian's tell the ladies." His eyebrows lifted higher. "Did I get the vernacular correct this time?" she asked sweetly.

"What do the young pups say?"

"You know. The standard chatter hasn't changed much in two hundred years. The boys want to get in the girls' drawers in this century and panties in my century."

He could not control his laughter. "I can never stay angry with you. You know I can't." He smiled sadly.

His tone and the look on his face puzzled her. He was good and kind and gentle. The absolute, perfect gentleman—danced with the wall flowers, took time to talk to the matrons, listened to old codgers' stories without cutting them off mid-sentence. He didn't overindulge in drink or gamble away his inheritance—which seemed to be common. No one understood yet about addictions, but she recognized an addictive personality. The young gents lacked restraint and over indulged.

She wished Whittington had a bit of bad boy in him. Then again, he lived with the notion of honor and she understood he would never make a move on her. Probably didn't even like her but pretended he did. Maybe he even pitied her. She deliberately pushed the maudlin idea away. "I want to go to the ship yard with you. Miss Browne told me she went with her father and helped him from time to time."

"Miss Browne isn't a Lady."

"Neither am I. You and I both know it. Emily's been bred to be a Lady even though her father carried the lesser title of Baron. I've concluded she has a soft spot for Lord Silverman."

"A soft spot? What do you mean?" He sounded

puzzled.

"You know. She has a fondness of the heart or whatever you call puppy love in this day and age. I found a page of silly poems. They were about his eyes. The man has brown eyes, the same color as horse pucks. She said they were cinnamon or some such nonsense. Don't look at me like I've made this up. I never said a word to her about those horrific poems. Wouldn't want to humiliate my dearest friend."

He shook his head, a smile on his lips. "Get your hat, gloves, and Lady Coldwell. We shall go for a jaunt. Emily's a real lady so she has to stay behind and sew or whatever real ladies do to occupy their time."

"Do you realize how many times we have to change clothes?" She muttered. "I'm so sick of dressing and undressing. I would run around in my birthday suit if I could."

He gaped at her, "Your birthday suit?" The quip seemed thick with emotion. Lady Coldwell's footsteps echoed in the hall and both of them jumped.

How had she gotten so close to him? They acted like magnets, pulled toward one another. She sensed his presence in the ballrooms, and, during the long, tedious dinners she attended. When he walked into a room, she perceived his presence. Couldn't sleep until he came home at night, or, early in the morning. Most of the time he stayed with them, but lately, he left Lady Coldwell in charge.

She became moony eyed over the big idiot and he hadn't responded. Wondered if she should seduce him, then instantly rejected the idea. This man had honor. Her odd notions would sully him. She had learned to listen, and, in this era, listening is what women did best.

She forced herself to pay attention to how people mulled ideas over. Even the educated seem slightly ignorant. Everyone but Lord Whittington!

The butler appeared at the same time Lady Coldwell stepped onto the marble floor from the stair thread. "I'll send the maid for your reticule, Lady Coldwell. I believe you're going to the ship yard."

The woman didn't blink an eye, stood and patiently waited for the butler to send a maid after her gloves and other personal items.

"Don't you think Lady Coldwell's hat is stylish?" she asked, as they settled in the closed carriage.

Lord Whittington tapped his cane on the roof of the vehicle, and they swayed as the coach rolled onto the cobblestone lane. "I do believe your hat becomes you, Lady Coldwell."

"I had to throw away the gewgaws. Miss Barrett didn't approve." Lady Coldwell's voice tinged with respect.

Lord Whittington decided to quiz her further. "Should I expect a call from Viscount Erleigh?"

The woman simpered. "I'm a widow, M' Lord. Much too old to have suitors."

He teased the ladies until they arrived at the wharf. Yelled out to the coachman to pull the carriage into the warehouse and they waited impatiently for the steps to be put down. Excitement course through her veins. "I shall finally see the Elgin Marbles."

"Liberate yourself from conventional expectations," he said. Became a good sport and showed them the entire warehouse. The wharf butted up to where the ships docked. Workers unloaded the collection of classic Greek Marble sculptures that had originally been part of the Parthenon in Athens.

"Thomas Bruce, Seventh Earl of Elgin, and the British Ambassador should be here soon," Lord Whittington told her.

"I don't know how to tell you this or how business works in this day and age," she paused. Wondered what would happen if she changed history. Decided she didn't care. "Make the man pay you up front for the storage of his merchandise." Her guardian didn't bat an eye at her pronouncement. She wondered if he believed her or if he pretended because he had gotten used to her 'oddities'.

"Might I inquire why?"

"You already know this acquisition is supported by some. The other critics compare Lord Elgin's actions to vandalism or looting. The British Museum will eventually pick up the cost but not until…around eighteen sixteen. A public debate about the marble placards will be held in Parliament."

A tall, thin man with a wig came strolling toward them from the other side of the docks. Lord Whittington bowed and then introduced them. "Miss Barrett wanted to see the marbles as they were uncrated. We shall discuss how you plan to transport them to your home or the Museum in my office." The men wandered off.

She walked over to the marbles. Inspected them intimately. Then looked at the other goods in Whittington's warehouse. After she had inspected every aisle, she accompanied a bored Lady Coldwell into the office.

Clerks sat at desks where they listed goods and tallied numbers. She couldn't help herself. Looked over a young man's shoulder and noticed a mathematical error. Calculated the sum in her head and pointed out his mistake. The over-large, dull man-child ignored her.

She waved the man in charge over. He limped toward them, stooped backed even though he could not be more than thirty years of age.

"I want to challenge this man to a tallying contest. Give each of us numbers needing to be added and I'll finish faster. I'll also be more accurate." The noise in the room died at her loud pronouncement which had been her intention. "I'm not good with a quill but I'm great with numbers," she boasted. Every man in the room looked insulted.

Lady Coldwell told the young manger, "I wouldn't put her to the test. She is better than good at numbers."

"Will you bet for her, M' Lady?" A clerk in the back demanded.

Lady Coldwell opened the string on her reticule and took out a pound. "How much should we wager?"

"Lady Coldwell, how very crass of you," she said, as if she were shocked.

"Don't let me down, gel, don't let me down," came the whispered reply.

Bets were placed on the man with the exception of Lady Coldwell. She bet on her.

"I see my chaperone is the only one smart enough to pick a winner," she told the room.

"Her Ladyship has too much money to burn." came a boisterous reply. Everyone laughed.

She sat at a desk directly across from the young arrogant gent who she classified as a dullard. Two accounting ledgers were chosen, then placed in front of each of them. The manager told them loud enough for everyone to hear. "When I say go, I want you to tally as many columns in the book as you can. I'll tell you when to stop."

She had done four times the number of columns as the man across from her when the man called halt. Two of the clerks checked their work. Two additional workers verified the findings. Liz had no errors. The red-faced braggart had errors in every column.

"I want to congratulate the winner," the hunch back told the clerks after he viewed the final results.

She stood and curtsied.

"Where did you learn to add so quickly?" asked one of the young men.

"What's your name?"

"I'm pleased to introduce myself. John Leslie." He bowed politely.

She grinned. This young man would publish the Philosophy of Arithmetic in eighteen twenty. "Mr. Leslie, I'll show you a system of learning, but…" she paused for emphasis. "I expect you to share the system with everyone you meet. They are called multiplication tables."

She made the paper chart she had memorized in fourth grade. Took the numbers up to twenty-five times twenty-five When she finished, she glance around the room. Lord Whittington stood tall in the back of the crowd. How much had he witnessed?

Lady Coldwell quickly collected their winnings and the men disbursed.

John Leslie bowed to her over and over again. She admired his excitement. "I must be off," she told the young man, "but remember" she paused, "share this secret of counting with the world. You might want to print this formula for future generations." The man nodded.

Lord Whittington remained quiet until they got in the carriage. "I don't know if you're a witch or a fairy, but I do believe you when you say you know what the future holds."

She smiled at the bewildered look on his face. "What brought this on?" she quizzed.

"Lord Elgin told me the British Museum would not take possession of the marbles. I asked for payment up front, which is not done. He assumed I had facts he didn't and paid me to keep them for the next five years. Told me he planned to get money from his wife's lover and said he would expect a full refund if the matter resolved quicker than the fifth year."

"I wondered why he agreed. He can't know the process will take five years."

"I told him he could pay me for however long he decided he needed my services. Warned him I would take possession of the marbles if he went past the contract date. Said they would end up in the British museum as the Whittington Marbles instead of the Elgin Marbles."

She clapped her hands, delighted at the turn of events. "Bravo, Lord Whittington. Bravo!"

"What did you do while I haggled like a common tradesman with Lord Elgin?"

"I earned money in an honest way."

"Betting isn't honest when you know the outcome," Lady Coldwell admonished her. Then she turned to look at Lord Whittington. "And you, sir, need to remember Miss Barrett is from the future but she most certainly should not hear about a wife's...petticoat hold over another man."

She wondered at the expression—petticoat hold. Terminology confused her—sounded similar yet different. She held out her gloved hand which now had ink blotches.

Lady Coldwell counted out a stack of pound notes, then commented, "You need new gloves again."

Everyone laughed because she ruined more gloves than most young ladies. She couldn't resist. "I've made history by sharing a mathematical table with the man who will be credited for inventing this idea."

What else would she be able to create if she continued to live in this century? What a grand life she lived. Far more entertaining than her life as an actress. When one thing changes, everything shifts. Her life have become adventurous.

A doubt assailed her. How would it all end?

Chapter Ten

Lord Whittington summoned Liz to the library. The place would have been considered a home office in her time, but in this century, they called it a library. Books lined the walls. Shelves were crammed with every conceivable subject bound in fine leather.

She'd had a few delightful afternoons with her new-found family right here. Lord Whittington, Lady Coldwell, and Emily allowed her to read aloud and then listened as she explained the fallacy of the information she read. John Heywood had written a proverb about the moon. Said it was made of green cheese. Many ignorant people believed him.

Today, Lord Whittington did not sit at his desk. Instead, he had settled into one of the two leather couches near the fireplace. Lord Silverman sat directly across from him and Lady Coldwell perched on a Queen Anne chair. The seat managed her bulk nicely. The rest of the furniture in the room held Chippendale style pieces with cabriole legs and ball-and-claw feet. The room normally radiated warmth. Not today.

"Where's Emily?" She asked, as she entered.

"We have a serious matter to discuss, Miss Barrett, so Miss Emily Coldwell has been sent to my sister's for tea."

She did not like the formal tone set by Lord Whittington's words. "I see. Am I allowed to take a seat, or should I send for a blind fold and firing squad?"

Lady Coldwell chuckled. She would not have laughed a few months earlier. Her chest glowed with pride as she realized the woman had definitely blossomed under her tutelage. She, too, had benefited from the relationship. Lady Coldwell no longer acted up-tight and bossy. Actions she had learned from an overly harsh mother-in-law and a cold husband. She turned out to be a pleasant companion once she learned being scared doesn't mean you can't make a difference. Both of them had benefited from their relationship.

"Oh, gel, do be seated. You make me jittery when you stand over me. Lord Whittington's tone suggests this is serious. And it is. Serious, I mean…but, a happy serious."

She gazed at her chaperon, then arranged her skits to sit on the couch next to him. "Well proceed so I can be happy, too."

Lord Whittington cleared his throat. "When you first arrived, you needed my protection. Needed someone to talk to the swains who flocked around you. Always laughed when I informed you of the latest quiz who seemed enamored. I've never allowed anyone to ask for your hand because…" He stopped. Pulled at his cravat. Looked away.

She talked into the thunderous silence. "Because I would say no. I don't want to be married."

"You did say yes to one proposal." Lord Whittington looked at the Duke instead of her.

"I did?" A trickle of fear crept up her spine. Surely, she would remember a proposal of marriage.

Oh, no! Had the original occupant, Elizabeth, said yes to an offer? She might have because of her shelf life. An aged mouse didn't do well on the market. Those who were sixteen and unmarried were stigmatized. Seventeen-and-eighteen-year old's were considered on the brink of extinction. She happened to be twenty-one. Definitely in the old maids' corner. Only her vivacious personality saved her from the back wall.

"You did." He nodded, as if his agreement made it an accomplished fact.

Lady Coldwell cut in, "It happened the day you hit your head. Each of us has changed and somehow the subject never came up."

"How could you do this to me?" she demanded of Lord Whittington.

"Do this to you?" His eyebrow rose upward, and he glared with steely eyes.

"Yes. How come you never mentioned this until today? I hit my head three months ago. If I had a stick of hot wax, I'd apply the mixture to your upturned eyebrow and rip the hair right off your face. This is an impossible situation. I don't remember agreeing to marriage!"

She turned toward Lady Coldwell. Her voice sounded like a plea to her own ears. "If I don't remember, can I get out of the contract?"

Lord Silverman's voice cut her off. "Do you object to all marriages or marriage to me?"

She gaped at the man. Her mouth opened and closed yet no words were spoken. "You?" This had to be a bad joke. No one spoke. "You! Why, you're a Duke and I'm a common miss with an Irish mother. Why would you want to marry me?"

The Duke sputtered.

"Are you hesitant because this is scary or because you're not sure you want this?"

The clock on the mantel ticked steadily and she counted ten tocks. Finally, she broke the uncomfortable silence. "Cat got your tongue?"

The Duke refused to look at her.

She turned her body on the sofa, so she leaned toward Lord Whittington, but she pointed her index finger at the Duke. "This man doesn't even like me. We can't dance without stepping on each other's toes. He constantly chastises me for my actions. And, he smells like cheese. The worst part of this abomination is he can't name one reason," she held up one finger, "why he would marry me. I say, that makes the contract null and void."

The Duke turned red. "I asked for your hand in matrimony. Lord Whittington assured me you agreed. He actually asked your permission, which is more than most guardians would do for an ungrateful, unruly wench like you. You said yes. I see no way out of this debacle." He stood.

She jumped up, rushed to him. Stood toe to toe. "This 'debacle' will get worse if we get married. I foresee a lot of broken china. If I'm so unruly—why continue down this path? We can pretend we never signed the contract and both of us can find someone more suitable." The plan sounded reasonable.

"I will not be a jilt again. Damn you, Whittington. Have you purposely set me up for a second time?"

"Why in blue blazes would you think I set you up on purpose? You have and always will be my best friend. You've seen the difference in Miss Barrett since she hit her head. She used to be a shy, timid young lady. You told me so yourself. Now, she walks in a room and commands attention. We need to talk about this contract. Please, everyone—have a seat."

Everyone was standing except Lady Coldwell who remained seated. Her face looked pasty white, eyes were downcast, and her big body trembled. "We should have mentioned this sooner. Yes. Sooner," she muttered.

The Duke used his cane to repeatedly stamp on the carpet. Then he took a deep breath, regained his composure. His cold British veneer became apparent, his words clipped when he said, "I will not be called a jilt again."

She nodded her understanding. "If no one knows you signed the contract, you can't be called a jilt." Perfectly logical.

The Dukes stony face turned red as he shouted, "My man of business knows."

"Well pay him off," she spat back. "Everyone has a price. I suggest you find his price because I. Will. Not. Marry. You."

"Then you, Miss Barrett, are the jilt. This will not be pleasant. I lived the situation down when Whittington made a fool of my last affianced. The gossip and jibes were not easy for me to deal with and I am a man. A woman won't have the same luxury. You have no credentials AND you shall be tagged, labeled, and tossed over." He pointed at her with an unsteady hand. "No one will come within ten feet of you."

He turned toward Lord Whittington. "I cannot believe I am caught up in a nightmare with you for a second time. I'm sorry you're tied to this eccentric who talks nonsense and uses words no one understands. I did try to do right by her, but I have been rejected."

She clasped her hands together so she wouldn't slap the fool. "Your Grace. Please stop the hysterics and let's talk sensibly. I don't want to be married to you any more than you want to marry me. Marry Emily. She's perfect for you. And, I might add, the only person who can dance with you and make you look stellar on the floor."

He stomped his cane. "A genteel woman would never tell a gentleman he cannot dance."

"You can dance. But only with Emily who, by the by, thinks you're brilliant. Personally, I can see your flaws. And yes, I know my behavior is unbecoming. Women are supposed to bow and scrape."

She had her hand pointed at his chest and decided to thump him. His indignation made her want to grin. She didn't. She had to remedy the situation. No one gave Lord Stick- Up-His-Butt what for. Ever.

"Emily believes you have a sense of humor. She is the perfect person to stand beside you. She might be able to take some of the starch out of your stiff ways. We can redo the contract and put her name in my place. Tell your man of business someone gave you the wrong name. How could you be expected to know a person you witnessed from afar? State someone gave you incorrect information, this doesn't have to be a..."

She heard an object in the hall shatter and froze. Looked toward the door, realized someone backed into the hall table and toppled the vase. She prayed a maid had become clumsy.

"I did not sign a contract with Emily. I mean with Miss Coldwell. I signed a contract with you," Lord Silverman bellowed.

They heard footsteps running down the hall, so she rushed to the door. "Emily," she called, but the girl had already started to run up the stairs.

She decided to go after her, but Lord Whittington blocked her way with his body. Over her shoulder he said, "Lady Coldwell, please see to your daughter."

The Duke shook his head as Lady Coldwell rushed from the room. "We've said all we need to say. I shall always blame you for allowing Miss Coldwell to overhear my remarks. She is a sweet girl. As for you," he pushed pass her guardian. "I cannot believe we are in the stew pot again. Miss Barrett is a jilt. Upon my honor, I will not tell anyone, but should there be chatter, know you are the one responsible."

"What would you say if I said yes to your contract?" What if she called his bluff? Would he back down if she actually agreed?

"Miss Barrett, you had time to make amends before you said my breath smelt like cheese. I would hate to be so cruel as to breathe on you again."

"You're jilting me?" She acted surprised.

"You said no. As a man of honor, I will accept your answer." The Duke straightened his cuffs, looked at his watch fob, quickly glanced at Whittington and then glanced away. "I am sorry we can no longer be friends." He started toward the cane he dropped earlier.

She snatched the walking stick before he could. "I don't intend to marry you. So don't take your anger out on Lord Whittington. You have stuck by our side for months. Dined with us. Played cards. Shared your box at the theater. I never once imagined you eyed me as a potential candidate for matrimony. You don't even like me."

She stomped the cane on the carpet and liked how the dull thud made the men pay attention. Walked around them, stood on the other side of the couch. Held the cane across her chest with both hands. Twirled the stick once and noticed she had both men's undivided attention. She could rectify this situation.

"I happened to be in the dark about this marriage proposal. The bump on my head severely affected me and I've forgotten more than I remember. You," she pointed the cane toward the Duke, "should have mentioned our pledge. Given me some hint or clue. You never claimed me for more than one dance. If you wanted everyone to know your intentions, you would have danced with me three times. That's the signal. You," she twirled the cane again, "didn't send me any signals."

"Emily is another story. You sent her plenty of signals. You danced with her more than you danced with me."

The Duke interrupted her, "As you stated previously, she is easy to dance with, where you are not. You gallop around the room with your long legs. Whittington here is the only one who can waltz with you and make you look graceful."

Gallop? Did this ass deliberately insult me? "Lord Silverman, you secured punch for Emily and tidbits from the refreshment table at every function we attended. I dare say, Lady Coldwell and I seemed to be an afterthought. Let's talk cloak room. You stuff me into my cloak, but you drape Emily in hers. I've even seen you tie her cape strings. An intimate act for someone who is betrothed to another."

Lord Silverman looked as if he wanted to choke

her as he clenched his hands into fists. "What do you imply, Miss Barrett?"

"Your feelings are obvious? You are smitten with Emily. We can change the names on the contract and be done with this mess."

Lord Whittington walked over to her, pried the walking stick from her hands. "I dare say, I don't want you launching this at my friend. Each of us needs to simmer down before we decide what to do."

She turned at the sound of a strangled growl and witnessed Lord Silverman storm from the room.

She wanted to go after him. Turned to the man she trusted. "I've messed this up for Emily, haven't I?"

Lord Whittington agreed with a head shake, unable to mask his disappointment. "I've lost my childhood friend again, Miss Barrett." The look he gave her made her heart sink to her toes. With one last shake of his head, he silently turned on his heels and left.

She plopped down on the nearest chair and tears flowed down her cheeks. She never cried! Then a realization hit her with such force she sucked in her breath. She wanted Lord Silverman for Emily and Lord Whittington for herself. Waterworks streamed down her face as she listened to herself sob. A loud, ugly sound.

A strange sensation made her want to laugh while she cried. Her body didn't belong to her. The vessel her soul lived in belonged to Elizabeth and she realized Elizabeth had been more in touch with emotions than she. Once the torrential tears started, she did not know how to stem them. Embarrassed someone would see her only made the sobs worse.

She cried for a good fifteen minutes before she realized Lord Whittington didn't know how much she liked him. How could he. She hadn't known how much she cared.

How had she allowed herself to fall in love with the man whose only role was guardian? Her fist went to her mouth to stop the wail that launched from cracked lips.

Her heart ached as she realized in the last week Whittington had avoided her. She flew up the stairs and into her room. Threw herself on the bed, pounded her fist into the stuffed mattress, tried to muffle her sobs on the silken bed cover.

The man had done the honorable when he escorted them to functions. Yes, he danced with her. He also danced with every wallflower. Did so because he happened to be a good man. An honor bound man. Dutiful. Had she become another duty?

Never one to languish for long, she decided to stop her commiseration. She only had one true friend. Emily. Had emotionally grown up during this jaunt to the past. Allowed both Emily and her mother into her heart. She hadn't paid attention to her body. This treacherous body discerned emotions in shades other than black and white. She used her handkerchief one last time, stood and walked to her desk. Sat down. Moving from the bed made her feel like her old self and she seemed ready to tackle her newest problem.

How had Emily fallen in love with such an obtuse stick-in-the-mud? The ignoramus had some affection for her because actions speak louder than his words. Only, the old-fashioned topper blundered about in a proper English way. Emily had the same English demeanor. Stiff upper lips ruled the head, not the heart.

Emily might be deeply hurt, but she would stuff

down her emotions and pretend to be right as rain. No one understood the word transparent in this era because everyone acted a hypocrite. Emily would never give voice to her feelings about the Duke. Blast, hell and damnation!

Honor made grown men act childish. Last week one of the members of Parliament fought a duel. How had her life become such a tangle? And why, oh why had she started to act like some love-sick, antiquated woman.

Chapter Eleven

"Lady Moreland's ball is tonight, Emily. We must attend." Liz called to her friend through the closed door. Everyone had gone to their room after the 'incident' yesterday. Lord Whittington left the premise in a snit and did not return until daybreak. Early this morning he told the butler to let callers know they were not at home to visitors. Then he left again.

The atmosphere in the house became solemn. She wondered when someone would hang black crepe from the windows.

The women of the house ate lunch and dinner alone in their respective rooms. The staff tip toed around and talked in hush tones. Downstairs maids whispered.

She cried on and off which left her face red and blotchy. A facial mask would be nice but in this century the tinctures, salves and creams were made of noxious substances. The afternoon dragged into early evening. She dried her tears. They had to attend the ball. After all, Lord Whittington's sister arranged the event in their honor.

The door down the hall opened. His Lordship appeared without a jacket, hair wet from his bath. When did he sneak in? Had he stopped to visit a lady love? She wanted to kick herself. Had to stop speculating about where he'd been the night before.

She noticed bloodshot eyes. The lines on his face

showed lack of sleep. His chin demonstrated displeasure. The twinkle no longer apparent in his eyes. Had she ruined the friendship between them?

He knocked on the door and said, "Miss Coldwell."

Emily's door opened instantaneously.

"I hope you will be ready within the half hour. My sister expects us early. I do believe she requires you and Miss Barrett in her receiving line."

She nodded her head. Had already dressed for the Ball. "I would never embarrass you, M' Lord." She refused to look in her direction.

"I'm sorry Emily. I didn't mean to embarrass you."

"You never mean to embarrass me, Miss Barrett, but this time you went too far. My private feelings and emotions were mine, not yours to divulge."

The sweet girl always called her Liz when they were at home. Now she called her Miss Barrett? Her heart hurt. Really hurt! "I'm so sorry. I don't know what else to say."

Lady Coldwell's door opened. Her feather from the simple head band could be seen before her face appeared. She gave the three of them a sad smile, walked toward them at a fast clip down the long hall. Her features no longer showed emotion. Liz remembered the exact day she learned how to maintain the dispassionate expression.

They had been in Lady Tutwell's receiving room and one of the *tons* worst snipers made a snide remark about her. Had done one of those pretend whispers everyone hears. She told Lady Coldwell to suck it up. The woman didn't understand her terminology but took a deep breath, sucked in air, and gathered her wits about her.

To encourage the older woman, she whispered, "Take your best shot and make sure you land a verbal blow. Isn't her husband the one who pawned all her jewels?"

Lady Coldwell's shoulders went back, her spine straightened, and she faced her tormentor. Peered down at the small, elegantly clad woman with the nasty demeanor.

"I noticed those jewels in the hands of your husband. Had them redone. Such a pity." She looked the matron up and down to make sure everyone understood she wore paste.

The ballroom became silent while the peerage cocked an ear toward the two who squared off. Then the titters started, and her empowered chaperon walked away without a curtsey or a by your leave. As the evening wore on, she received numerous dance invitations from married men whose wives insisted. The older widowers became interested in a woman who could hold her own.

Lady Coldwell had become a big, beautiful woman who carried herself with a jaunty swish of her skirts. "I am ready M'Lord, and my two charges will do as expected." Gave a nod to her daughter, turned to her and asked, "what do you intend to wear this night?"

Liz threw herself at the woman's bosom, started to wail. The big woman hugged her close for a few minutes, then said, "We can't have you two looking like watering pots, can we? I have asked for tea before we leave. A good bracing cup is medicinal. Get dressed quickly and we'll talk downstairs."

She trudged back to her room while Emily and Lady Coldwell went downstairs for tea. Her hair had been done earlier so she unbuttoned her dress and took off her undergarments. Put on her newest cotton short stay which acted like a sports bra.

Next, she pulled on her silk bodice petticoat and tied the strings in the front with impatient fingers. Glad she had given the maids her corsets. Garters and silk stockings were laid out on the bed. She remembered weeks of borrowing hosiery from Emily before she learned how to put them on without poking a hole in the silk. Hated the fact she had to put on two petticoats so the sheer, white muslin gown would flare out at the hem when worn. Finally slipped the high waist ball gown over her head. Dressing was easier with two people and the reason women required chamber maids.

The looking glass showed her face had color. Funny how she no longer thought mirror. The jargon had rubbed off on her, slipping into her consciousness. She decided to hurry. Had a tad bit of hope. Lady Coldwell hadn't appeared to be mad at her.

The green dress she wore had been shot through with gold thread and embroidered with tiny rose buds. The short-puffed sleeves and hem line held the same flowered pattern with a beautiful dark green vine entwined. The workmanship exquisite but she couldn't make herself care. Had to make amends with her dearest friend before the situation became irreconcilable.

Fastening the top button in the back of her dress created a dilemma. She would be unable to do herself up. A million buttons ran down the back. How would she reach them without help? Walked to the bell pull and tugged. No one came immediately, which meant the servants were not within hearing distance.

Usually, Emily helped her, and she helped Emily. As she headed down the hall toward the servants' stairs, she hoped to run into a maid who could fasten her.

Lord Whittington opened his door as she walked past. "Oh, thank God you're still here." She said. "Do me up in the back." She turned her back toward him so he could button the tiny beads. Didn't feel his hands.

Looked over her shoulder and noticed he stared at her back, his mouth slack jawed. "What's wrong?" She pleaded, wanting to wail and gnash her teeth. Recognized another horrid mistake.

He looked at her and choked out, "Where's the maid?"

She bristled.

Whittington's slate gray eyes became storm clouds.

"I don't know where the maid is, but you're here so fasten me into my dress," she said. Waited a second, pleaded, "Please."

He smiled. "Need I remind you Miss Barrett, you're naked."

"Oh, for the love of Pete," she hissed. "You've seen a lady's back before. I have a bodice and petticoats and all kinds of under garments on. Please, please, please button me up so I can go have a talk with Emily. I love that girl." Her shoulders hunched. Her best friend might hate her.

Lord Whittington buttoned her up, his large hands fumbling against her back.

She huffed as he slowly worked the multitude of tiny beads into the slotted tabs. "If I wasn't so upset about my situation, I'd laugh. You've taken longer than any maid to button me. Haven't you ever helped a woman into her dress?"

111

He had her half done when he abruptly stopped. She spun around. "Don't tell me I've offended you again. You'd be a rake if you buttoned me up quickly." She threw herself at the man, her arms locked around his back, her face pressed up against his chest. Started to cry. Wanted someone, anyone to hold her. No, she wasn't being truthful. She wanted this man to hold her and tell her he was over his anger.

Strong arms wrapped around her body as she babbled sorry over and over again. Lord Whittington pressed up against her and absentmindedly, he finished fastening her dress.

"I was considered a rake in my salad days, Miss Barrett. As you can see, my skill returned the minute you were in my arms." His voice sounded like finely aged whiskey, blended, deep, and strong.

She glanced up at the man she loved. The return look made her want him as one wanted a delicious delicacy. A shiver of need spread down her spine and into her toes.

Molly cleared her throat. Lord Whittington removed his arms and stepped away. With bent head, the servant asked, "Someone rang?"

She smiled at the maid. "Lord Whittington has been good enough to do my buttons for me. I'm sorry you had to climb all the stairs, Molly." She turned to Lord Whittington. "I'm ready to face the Lioness in her Den."

He put out his arm and she linked hers through his. They walked the hall and stairs, arm in arm, no words necessary. His nearness comforted her. The feel of his linen jacket and the muscled arm underneath melted her fears. At the bottom of the stairs, he stopped and called to the butler. She continued into the green room.

Lady Coldwell patted the couch as a signal for her to sit. Tea had been arranged on a side table out of reach. "We need to have a comfortable coze the three of us. Emily, dear, stop the sulks. Your face looks as if you have rag manners. Now cry peace, the both of you."

Emily jumped up from her chair and ran toward her as tears flowed. She walked over, pulled her friend onto the couch, sitting between the women. She proceeded to coo soothingly into the girl's ear, patted her back. The torrent of tears lessened, until she became calm enough to dab her eyes with a handkerchief.

Lady Coldwell opened her fan, snapped it shut to command their attention. "We've been in a pickle before and I've always found a way out."

"When were we ever in a pickle?"

"Your father, bless his dull as ditch-water soul, left us without a feather to fly. He could be a kindly man but one without a lot of learning and no common sense. He bought into one scheme after another until we had no resources left. Lord Whittington is in the family tree, but many generations removed."

Emily looked at her mother like she had sprouted horns.

Lady Coldwell didn't care. Continued to talk. "I didn't want to starve. Fear makes a person bold. Bold, I say. I applied to the man for your sake. He has been good enough to give you a season and me a reprieve from becoming a companion to a dullard. The only way I could see to survive. We have a few months of up-coming country house parties. When the weather changes, we will have to figure out how to proceed."

Emily looked at her mother opened mouthed. Lady Coldwell gently reached across her lap and pushed on her daughter's chin so her mouth shut. "You," she pointed to Liz, "need to help me sort this situation. You have what it takes up here," she pointed to her head. "Find a way to get my Emily and Lord Silverman together."

Lord Whittington entered the room. "What did you say?"

Lady Coldwell didn't shrink, as she had in the past. "Do have the servant bring the tea tray closer and let us discuss the situation."

"No one is desperate in this room." His lordship sat in one of the chairs directly facing them. "You may all stay as long as you need. You won't become homeless. I do believe Miss Barrett might need at least one more season. She'll definitely take longer to settle than the rest of you."

The twinkle in his eye gave her a sense of relief even if he had insulted her. She smiled back and he abruptly turned toward the tea tray next to his elbow. The clank of the silver tea pot filled the silence. No wonder men weren't allowed to serve. Her chaperone, who always commented about etiquette blunders had a funny look on her face, quietly stated, "I have a confession to make."

"Yea, Gads, Lady Coldwell. I've had enough heartfelt confessions to last me a month of Sunday's." He added a tot of port to the tea pot before he turned to face them.

"You will listen, M'Lord, so you know the whole sordid tale. Then we can make decisions. My father happened to be a Duke."

Emily's gasp made Liz realize the young lady hadn't been informed of her own lineage.

"Yes, m'dear. You are a blue blood. I should have married a Duke but Lady Thenwhestle got in my way. They called her Miss Clementina Drake in my day. As Miss Barrett would say—a nobody. Her father…well, he collected golds. Not a banker but," she leaned in, whispered, "moneylender."

Liz couldn't help herself, interrupted. "You mean the nasty woman in the market who had squinty eyes and a vicious mouth?"

Lady Coldwell laughed. "I do love your descriptions. Yes, she's the Lady, and I use the word loosely. Very loosely. Do you remember when you raised an eyebrow? Demanded to know, 'Were you born with a silver spoon in your mouth?' Oh, what a rare form of insult."

"You called her a mushroom under your breath and her snooty attitude toward you made me furious."

"You're astute, gel, astute I say. You flashed your fan, gave her the cut direct. You hadn't learned fan signals, so you never realized you indicated yourself as the superior one. She hasn't been seen in London since the season began. No doubt, because of embarrassment. You stirred the gossips to remember her sordid tale. The gel had beauty once upon a time."

She gasped in horror. "The old biddy used to be a beauty? Pray tell us the sordid tale."

"In her younger years, she had a flawless complexion, golden hair, rosy cheeks. A bit plump. Plump signaled well fed. And, she always dressed up to the nines. No one could touch her beauty. No one, I say. The man I loved took a stroll in the gardens and the next day everyone chattered. Somehow her brother bumped into them. In the gardens. My suitor did right by her because he did not want anyone to call him a rake."

"I do not get this honor everyone takes so seriously. One person always gets dishonored. I'm puzzled by the incongruity." She'd seen young girls sullied for no other reason than they were alone with a man.

Lady Coldwell threw up her hands. "All trickery. She might have been a diamond of the first water in front of a looking glass, but her demeanor happened to be vile. They were married and Lord Thenwhestle now lives in the bed he made. You were introduced to him. At the Dowager Duchess's dinner. He's thin and bald and..."

"Is he dull as ditch water?" Emily inquired.

"Don't be fresh, gel. You and Miss Barrett are patterns of the same kind with your mouths."

The flutter of her fan signaled she accepted the back handed compliment. "Lady Coldwell, please stop flattering us and get on with your story."

"I'm at the end of the story. I married the first man who asked, a man who..." she paused, "a simple man. He wanted to get back at Miss Drake who had tormented him about his clothing and hair and all sorts of nonsense. He suggested we run away together to Greta Green."

"Mother, do not tell me you were a run-away bride?"

"Oh, dear girl, that happened a long time ago. Yes, I ran away, and my father cut me off. Without a pence in our pockets, we were. Baron Coldwell took his place in the country and we lived an unadorned life. Then we met Miss Barrett. I must say, you have changed my short-sightedness. I used to eat myself into a stupor until you came along. Starved me, gel. You starved me." She smiled as she said this, and they could tell her words were a compliment.

"You did look as if you were going to cry the few times the bread basket passed in front of your nose," Lord Whittington remarked.

"Yes, my dear Miss Barrett had a purpose when she came to my room." The older woman took both of Liz's hands in hers before she went on. "What you said sounded true—we could learn from each other. At first, I believed you were heartless. You walked me up and down streets and alleys. Looked and poked around where you didn't belong. Inappropriate questions flew from your mouth!" She shook her head. "Didn't take long for me to look forward to our days in the park. Our shopping ventures. I saw the world from a different perspective. You even taught me how to dress." The woman fingered her elegant gown. A gown that covered her excess weight and complimented her full figure.

"I dare say, my mother would have shown me if I hadn't been so impetuous and run off. You, Liz dear, are too impetuous. Behavior has consequences. What you said to Lord Silverman insulted him." She paused to let the words sink in. "I do believe we can put our minds together and find a way to rectify the situation."

The maid bustled into the room, set the tea tray next to Lady Coldwell, asked if they needed more hot water. The conversation stopped as her chaperon acknowledged Nancy and poured everyone a cuppa.

Such a British formality. A large gulp made her gag. The amount of liquor in the brew burned her virgin throat. She recognized alcohol when she tasted it, and this had to be a full-bodied version of some expensive variety.

Lady Coldwell took a tiny sip, frowned at the drink, set the teacup daintily in the saucer. Picked up her story. "Do you remember how you made me sit on the grain scale in the marketplace? First bet I ever made."

Lord Whittington took a sip from his cup, frowned. Rang for the maid before she could get back to the kitchen, asked for a fresh pot for the ladies and had her bring the tray back to his side. Liz deliberately took a gulp of the laced brew, traded her empty cup with Emily's full one.

Lord Whittington noticed. "You two bet on oddities. I'll be happy to provide more pin money should you find yourself in need."

Liz smiled because he didn't chastise her. What game did they play?

"No, sir. You are generous enough," said Lady Coldwell who didn't notice their interplay. "I huffed and puffed around the market as I tried to keep up with my charges. Miss Barrett told me to have a seat on this metal contraption to catch my breath. I sat and suddenly, some young lad cried out, 'see the fat lady, come look, come see,' as if I belonged to the circus."

Lady Coldwell pointed at her. "You put your firm hand under my chin, looked me directly in the eye and said, 'if you can't win them over, join 'em.' Before I understood what you were nattering on about, you started to yell over the lad's voice. A crowd gathered, and I was too tired to stand and leave."

The matron looked at Lord Whittington and jabbed her finger in his direction. "Your charge asked the crowd if they cared to wager on how much weight a lady could lose."

Liz shrugged sheepishly, took another gulp of the spiked tea. "I wanted to see how much you weighed. When that awful boy started making fun at your expense, I decided to turn your embarrassment into a contest. We have a diet plan in my time called Weight Watchers. I realized you could lose at least five to seven pounds in the first week, so I bet you would lose seven."

"You were ruthless, gel, ruthless. My stomach grumbled for weeks."

"Yeah right! I commiserated with you but the money we made had you monitor your own food intake. Especially when coins were delivered into your gloved hands."

Their guardian stared at both women in horror. "I cannot believe you two. Not a' tall ladylike."

Liz crossed her arms. "You bet on raindrops at Brooks or The Beefstake Lounge or whatever you call those men's clubs, then chide us? Please! Gambling is an occupation a woman can participate in as long as we are in the proper environment."

"Yes, but a man holds the money. Who held the money?" He slurped a mouthful of tea.

"I had the man with the scale take the money. Do you know how much trouble I go through to keep my gloves white?"

Lady Coldwell laughed. "Women don't handle money because their gloves become dirty."

"Seriously?"

Lord Whittington looked at them. "I do believe she may be right. Some hoity-toity Lady called money vulgar and women would forever after be sullied by the handling of coins. You do have an eye for our idiosyncrasies, Miss Barrett."

The front door knocker banged three times. She sat up expectantly. Lord Silverman had a habit of joining them before they left for the evening's event. Did he reconsider? Emily bit her lip nervously. The butler came in with a note on a silver slaver. Lord Whittington took the note, tore it opened and scowled.

"Lord Silverman wants his betrothal gift back."

"What betrothal gift?" she asked.

"You mean the ugly brooch?" Lady Coldwell gasped indignantly.

Excitement started to thrum through her veins. "Is it about this big," she motioned with her fingers, "dull gold filigree with a dullish stone?"

"Yes, dear. Such an ugly piece. I remember you waved the brooch with your hand as you fell."

"I've found my way back to the future," she shouted, jumped to her feet and jammed her fist in the air several times. "I waved the brooch around the day I ended up here. The pin transported me from the future. Where is it now?"

She could not contain her excitement. Skipped around the sofa. Could leave and go home. As she celebrated, a still, small voice inside asked *Is this what you want?*

Lord Whittington and Lady Coldwell looked at each other before the woman spoke. "I accidentally kicked the item with my foot the evening you arrived.

So much happened I never looked for it on the floor. I did keep the empty box."

She jumped up and ran into the foyer, scanned the floor. Lady Coldwell and Emily followed. Lord Whittington stood near the coat rack, spying. She encouraged the others to help her. Bent down and thrust her hand behind every table, pillar. Even went so far as to take the fresh flowers out of the vase in the hall.

"Why is your face such a brown study, M' Lord? Brown study, I say. Look behind the coat tree and find the brooch." Lady Coldwell instructed.

Lord Whittington grimaced. *Miss Barrett cannot leave. I do believe I'm in love with her.* Whittington noticed a flash of light from behind the wooden tree. Bent low, slid his hand down the back of the furniture and picked up the ugliest brooch he had ever seen. Had the stone glinted?

He'd had too much to drink the night before. Today too. Needed to…well he didn't know what he needed after he touched Miss Barrett, so he sloshed port into the teapot. He glanced toward the ladies, noticed none of them noticed him. Hastily shoved the pin into the inside pocket of his caped coat hanging on the rack. Didn't stop to consider why he hid the brooch.

The ladies scurried up and down the hall. The woman he loved called to him, "Join our treasure hunt."

Well, he wished he were a pirate. He would steal her away, camp on a deserted island…he stopped himself before he created another erotic dream. *When had she crept under his skin?* "Ladies," he called to the giggling women who he realized were slightly tippled from the liquor. "Time to leave. I'll request the staff look for the piece while we're gone. Mayhap one of them already found the brooch."

The ladies stopped their search and called to the maids to help with their gloves and what-nots. This process took longer than usual as the high-spirited trio laughed and carried on. He waited so he could be the last one out the door. Turned to the butler. "Have my coat taken upstairs and put in my room. The weather has been nice, and I have no further need of it."

The butler immediately handed the coat to the foot man who started up the steps. He raised his voice so the ladies at the curb could take notice. "Have the maids clean the front area and down the hall on both sides of the stairs. Tell them to look for a brooch. I will give a reward of five pounds to whoever finds the antique jewel."

The carriage ride seemed festive with talk about transporting everyone to the future and back again. He did not join in the chatter. Had already deduced Miss Barrett came from another time and space. Mayhap the future. She said her body looked exactly the same down to the mole he dreamed about but had never seen.

Did each person have a double somewhere? Would they be able to find one another if they traveled in time? He realized he did not want to find out.

Chapter Twelve

Liz stood in the receiving line and smiled like a Cheshire Cat. She didn't know if the three cups of tea made her feel tipsy or if going home made her carefree and heedless. Tonight, she didn't care how others might judge her behavior. Ruminated about the convenience of tampons, steamy hot showers, and massage therapists. Tried to remember how her favorite chocolate bar tasted.

How nice to travel back and forth from one era to the other, bringing items with her as she traveled. She had a few books Lord Whittington would want to read, mentally made a list.

Maybe she could transport Emily or allow her friend to transport herself. This could happen once she figured out how to make the brooch work. Then again, the first item on her list was to find the brooch.

Lady Moreland introduced them to everyone who entered the premise. She had met a goodly number of patrons at other parties and teas. About half of the introductions were people she had seen but had not been formally introduced. Only the top echelon of society were invited to the Duke and Duchess' home. They dressed better, spoke as if they were the crème de la crème because they were. Many of the older folks wore wigs. She noticed she no longer had a need to fit in.

The ball room had a Grecian theme, with harp music strummed from every corner. One could dance on the second floor which hosted a card room, powder room, and another area where men played billiards. The entire third floor had been set up with food and drinks. Tables were laden with all sorts of delicacies from a stuffed peacock to lemon tarts.

"What has you fidgeting so? Normally, you can stand with your back straight and no outward signs of nervousness." Lord Whittington uttered under his breath between arrivals.

She stood as close to him as deemed appropriate. Breathed in his scent. Wanted to brush the errant lock from his forehead. Instead she stopped squirming. "I'm about to go home. Can't wait to get back." Her sigh came out chock full of emotion. She wanted to be here in the past and in the present at the same time.

"Can't wait to leave us poor backward sods, can you?" The tick in his jaw became pronounced.

An Earl and his wife were presented. As they ascended the stairs to the next floor, she took the opportunity to disabuse him of the notion. "I've never regarded you as a backward sod. I'm excited at the notion I can flash back and forth through time."

"How do you know the brooch will return you?"

"I had the brooch in my hand in the future when I left. I also had the item in my hand when I arrived at your entry way. I'm positive the trinket will take me back. It seems an eternity already and we haven't cleared the receiving line. Then we must dance, and chat and I so want to go home." The smile on her face charmed him.

Her smile would be gone the moment she got her

hands on the brooch. Liz would disappear. Elizabeth would return.

Sedate, even tempered, Elizabeth. The dull one.

"What about Emily? Do you intend to leave your best friend behind?" His voice made him sound like an unruly child.

"Not until Lord Silverman proposes to her."

"He isn't going to propose." *Mayhap that will keep you here longer.*

She sensed the man's sadness. Understood she had to rectify the situation. Determination rose within. She would get her friend back in contact with the Duke. She could right this wrong. An idea started to form.

The rest of the evening had full dance cards and whispered plans between the three ladies. Lord Whittington disappeared to puff a cloud with other cronies in the Library. The slang fit the description. When the servant opened the door to let people into the room, a literal cloud of smoke could be seen from the cigars and cheroots.

Anxiety built like steam in a kettle. She wanted to get home. Home as in Lord Whittington's mansion. When had she become so entrenched in his establishment?

He sat silently while his friends conversed. Couldn't wait to hide the brooch. Forever. Concluded his strongbox at the shipyard the safest place for the troublesome jewel.

He had noticed Emily waiting anxiously as each patron was introduced. About half way through the ball she looked as if she would cry. Did she finally realize Lord Silverman had no intention of putting in an appearance? Lady Coldwell stuck to Liz like a glue-pot.

Probably trying to figure out how to get her to stay because she needed her. They all needed her.

A million hours later, or so it seemed, Lady Coldwell announced they could leave. The carriage dropped them in front of the mansion. The four walked silently up the stairs.

His Lordship ended the silence by asking the butler. "Has anyone found the brooch?"

The man gave him an odd look and replied, "No one on this floor found the item you wanted us to locate."

Everyone went to their room.

She decided to open her bedroom window for air and to gaze into the sky. England wasn't like California. How did one ever find a star through all the fog? The alcohol had worn off and she became headachy. Wasn't exactly disappointed the staff had not found the pin. Distinctly remembered she had the brooch clutched in her hand when she woke up on the floor. Tried to piece events of the night together in her mind but the entire incident became a jumble.

Didn't mind if she had to stay in this time and place. She had friends who acted like family. Seemed more like flesh and blood relatives than her actual relations.

Wheels, harnesses, and squeaks told her a carriage approached. She examined Lord Silverman as he departed his equipage. The man walked sedately up his front steps, the coachman drove away. Tendrils of fog made him disappear, then reappear. He had dressed for an evening out. Stopped on the last step of the landing and looked across to their mansion.

She ducked her head into the window so he would

not see her. With a flash of inspiration, she decided to go have a word with him before Molly finished undressing Emily.

The sound of footsteps running down the stairs had Lord Whittington on his own feet. He entered the hall from the library in time to see the bottom of Miss Barrett's gown swish through the front door. He had taken off his cuffs and cravat, his shirt sleeves were rolled up, his vest hung from the back of his chair. Where the deuce did Miss Barrett go? Alone. At this time of night? He traversed the hallway quickly and witnessed her sprint across the green toward the Duke's front door.

A deep groan escaped his lips before he called for his butler. "Follow me." The butler motioned for an under servant to stand guard at the front entrance and trotted after his master who ran to catch up with Miss Barrett.

She paused before she walked up the steps of the Duke's residence. Lifted the ostentatious lions head, knocked loudly. The wooden portal swung open and a staid butler gawked at her, alone on the doorstep, at such an unseemly hour. He had his Lordship's coat in his hand and was about to tell the young lady to leave when she pushed past him and let herself in.

Lord Silverman stood on the third step of the stairs. Had stopped his ascent at the sound of the knocker. "Why are you here?" His face looked incredulous, his tone startled.

"We have to talk about Emily. Did you know her grandfather held the title of Duke?"

The man glared at her before he marched down the three steps. He stopped and, once again, they were nose to nose.

Lord Whittington barged through the door breathing heavily. He found them close together, glaring at one another. Wondered if they would start pulling out each other's hair. What a perfect end to an awful day.

"Everyone in my household knows Lady Coldwell's daughter has a Duke for a grandfather, thanks to you. What else would you like to announce to me and my staff at this inappropriate hour?"

She crossed her arms, instinctively tapped her foot on the floor. "Please point the way to a room where we can have a private conversation."

"There is a time and place for private conversations. This is not the time, nor the place."

"It is exactly the right time and place."

When the Duke turned his back on her and started to ascend the stairs once again, she cried out in desperation. "You jilt."

The enraged man turned, fists clenched, the vein in his forehead evident and she experienced a pang of fear. Lord Whittington placed his body between the two of them. A struggle ensued. Started as a shoving match, a few missed punches, and both of them ended up rolling on the floor. The two butlers finally separated the angry lords.

All four men set about straightening their cloths when the scuffle subsided.

Lord Whittington turned to Liz and shouted, "What do you mean to do? Make him accept Emily?" His body vibrated fury.

She became alarmed and aroused instantaneously. Wanted to move away and, in the same instance, embrace him. Stood rooted to the spot unable to comprehend why she couldn't respond.

Lord Silverman sneered at her. His rebuff propelled her to back toward the front door.

The Duke's butler slammed the portal closed before she could escape.

"In the library. Now!" The man she adored snapped out his words like a command.

The sober trio marched into the room without another word. They stood and glared at one another. The click of the door shutting sounded loud.

Lord Whittington broke the tension by saying. "Miss Barrett, do you know what you have done? You entered a man's house without an escort."

She couldn't help herself, rolled her eyes. "You were right behind me so don't you dare say I've been compromised."

"You then proceeded to call his Grace a jilt. Those hurtful words happen to be untrue. This incident will be all over town by morning. I know you decided the brooch will take you into the future, but do you realize the real Miss Barrett will be shamed? No longer received in polite company? What have you accomplished by your actions?"

She twisted her hands together, realized the nervous gesture didn't belong to her. "I want to make the situation right for Lord Silverman and Emily. I hoped I could call him a jilt and he would man up and marry my friend. This didn't exactly work out as I planned. Will my actions be misconstrued in another way?"

"Yes. The chinwags will say you wanted marriage so badly, you couldn't contain yourself."

"Oh please." She threw her hands in the air. "No one would believe I want to marry him. I can barely tolerate the man."

Lord Silverman stepped menacingly toward her, and Lord Whittington had to step between the two of them for a second time.

"By Jove. I shall not stand in my own house and be insulted by this up-start. She is moonstruck. Ready for Bedlam! Emily told me how she believes she is from the future. We can have the Doctor commit her tonight. Let me have my man go roust him from his bed and be done with this debacle." He started toward the door and her guardian, once again, stood in front of him and blocked his way.

Lord Silverman looked Lord Whittington in the eye, shook his head. "Please tell me I read you wrong. Do you love her?" He sounded horrified. His eyes grew big, his expression glum. "I cannot believe this. No. It is too hard to believe." The Duke backed away from the door, sat down hard on the first chair he encountered. Put his shaking head in his hands.

Silent noise filled the room. The clock on the mantel ticked and the wind rattled the panes on the windows.

She gazed at Lord Whittington in wonder. He looked like every other upper crust gent who didn't show emotions except for the nerve jumping in his jaw. Could this be true? Could he love her? That's what she wanted, right? Suddenly the urge to be seated hit her with such force she stumbled over to a chair. Plopped down. "I don't feel well."

"No one in this room is feeling quite up to snuff," came the sober reply of Lord Whittington.

The Duke stood. "I shall marry Miss Emily Coldwell. You were right about the marriage contracts. I didn't know your name and left space, to be filled in with the correct information. I came home and checked. My secretary never received the documents because I locked them in my strong box. I can fill in any name I want as long as Lord Whittington has the legal right to sign as guardian."

"I believe Lady Coldwell has assigned me that right." Lord Whittington's voice sounded strained.

She looked at both men suspiciously. "I don't want you to marry Emily unless you want to."

The staid Duke actually rolled his eyes. "She has manners, grace and breeding. You, on the other hand, are a ninny hammer with more bluster than you can maintain." The man straightened his cuffs and his demeanor. He pulled his pocket watch from his vest, his face once again devoid of all emotion. "It's late. Do you wish to ask another question?"

She opened, then closed her mouth. Finally, she asked the question she needed to know. "Do you love her?"

"What has love got to do with this situation?" The Duke looked as if he would yell and tear out his hair.

"Your friendship for Lord Whittington makes you marry Lady Emily Coldwell. Do you not have strong emotions for her?"

The man didn't respond. His expression shuttered so he appeared unconcerned. He glanced at his watch again to demonstrate he didn't plan to engage further.

"Can you not feel a pleasantness when you are in her presence? Do you know what love is?" How did one puncture an English man's façade?

"Aristocrats do not marry for love. I do like the young lady. In fact, I found I missed her at the Devlin's ball this evening. I will prepare the papers."

She realized this would be the only admission she would get. "No." Her moan sounded desperate. "I don't want you to marry my friend if you don't have feelings for her. You accuse Lord Whittington of love, but you are not allowed to have any?"

"I will not write sappy poems or sing sonnets from the street. I did those acts as a lad. A big mistake. What I feel for the young lady is warmth and contentment. I believe we have the start of a good relationship. You will stop meddling since I have made up my mind."

Lord Whittington stood, walked over to her chair, placed his arm on her elbow and forced her to stand. He started steering her toward the door. "We shall tell everyone you and Emily had a misunderstanding about which ball to attend tonight. Miss Barrett and I came to talk to you about the situation with my butler. My servants will repeat this story. For some reason, they have an unholy affinity for my errant charge. If both of us agree, along with the servants, no one will be ruined."

The Duke walked them toward the doorway. "You, my friend, are the one who has to deal with her. I will tell the lie because I believe you have feelings for this harridan. This is the last act of friendship you shall receive from me."

They exited the safety of the room.

She noticed none of the servants had his or her ear to the door, as they did from time to time at Lord Whittington's. In fact, the two butlers stood at the entrance like sentinels, the under servants nowhere in sight. She walked past the stoic men as serenely as she could.

The Duke trailed after them onto the landing and whispered, "May God have pity on your soul, man." The remark carried in the fog.

She cringed when she noticed Lord Whittington stiffen.

The butler walked three paces behind them.

The trio strolled to the front door without speaking a single word. Lord Whittington released the pressure on her arm and walked down the hall toward his study. Asked the butler and the under footman to attend him.

She noticed he wanted to be as far away from her as he could get. What a fiasco. She had disgraced him in front of his friend.

Sadness enveloped her as she dragged herself up the stairs. How would she break the news to Emily?

Chapter Thirteen

Sun peeked through the drapes as the door knocker sounded. Liz opened the window and tried to see who visited. A tall footman stood on the step holding a silver platter. Definitely a special invitation from Lord Silverman since she recognized the insignia on his black jacket. The man had well-turned legs encased in white stockings worn below black knee breeches. She couldn't see what happened after the Butler invited him inside. Long moments later the servant headed back across the park toward his employer with a reply held up-right on his small tray.

Maids bustled in the hall, but no one knocked at her door as she dressed. She heard Lady Coldwell and her daughter being summoned to Lord Whittington's den. Waited, paced, and wondered. Decided to grab a bite to eat in the morning room and found her toast tasted like sawdust.

Lady Coldwell waltzed into the room with a grin on her face. Sat down and put jam on her bread. Was she stress eating or celebrating? The woman took a bite and said, "I know something happened last night, but I'm not about to question Emily's good fortune. She's in love with the Duke and who am I to deny her happiness? Let us rejoice." She raised her toast in the air. "His Grace came to his senses. Asked for Emily's hand in marriage." She stood. "You made this happen.

Thank you, dearling. So stop the pout and come join us for a walk."

She realized the woman had no clue what transpired. Didn't plan to tell her. "No. I want to wallow in my misery. Even if I find the brooch, I have to give the piece back to the Duke."

The woman patted her arm. "Don't worry dear. I have no intention of leaving you alone with Lord Whittington. I will stick by your side until you marry."

"What if I don't want to marry?"

"Not marry? I know you think me old fashioned, but you will eventually feel the need to tie the knot with someone. The need to marry runs in our blood." Lady Coldwell looked so certain.

Now would not be the time to talk about women's lib. She didn't have the heart to talk about anything. Emily would be furious when she found out what happened. "Will you go with me to the solicitor's office? I need to find out if we can live independently. I'm not sure what I want to do with my life. We will be all right if I have money. I can access some of Elizabeth's memories. She had a wonderful father. I'm sure he would never leave her without a pound."

The woman agreed to go with her the next day and left the room humming.

Lord Whittington entered, bowed. He held the ugly pendant in his hand. "I found the brooch yesterday." His face flushed red.

She eyeballed the horrid piece of jewelry. Watched as he set the brooch down on the table in front of her and backed away. The dull stone glinted for an instant.

She reverently picked up the ornament, unsure if she saw a flicker of light. "Ugly as I remembered."

"The stone is lackluster, and the metal looks tarnished. Can't be made of gold." He stared at the brooch, not her. Had he seen a glint or was he having a pipe dream? He had smoked opium once while traveling. This fanciful feeling seemed similar to smoking the water pipe.

She stood, closed her eyes, held the stone in front of her and clicked her heels three times. Said, "There is no place like home. There is no place like home. There is no place like home."

When Liz opened her eyes, she saw her guardian gawking. "Dorothy did that in the Wizard of Oz. The clicking of heels worked for her! Didn't work for me. I wonder why?"

"I'm not sure." The man beamed at her. Looked positively radiant.

She perceived a jolt of electricity, like one gets when one sticks a needle in a light socket. There were no light sockets in this day and age. Suddenly inspired, she said, "You don't want me to leave, do you?" She glimpsed a flash of light.

The previously happy man glowered at her. "I want you to be happy. If you can't be happy here, go back to the future where you will be. Who is Dorothy? A relative?"

"Dorothy is a girl in a movie. She clicked her glass or was it ruby slippers three times and they took her home. I do believe I have my fairy tales mixed up."

"We have crystal glasses. Glass slippers would break and make you bleed. Why did this Dorothy want to go home?"

"She became homesick."

"What about her new friends? What happened to

them when she left?"

His tone sounded like an accusation. She looked at him and wanted to cry. "They went with her. But that won't happen if I leave. You won't be able to go into the future, will you?" The terrible weight of truth caused pain in her chest and she found herself clutching the brooch to her heart.

She realized she had deep feelings for this man. He could make her laugh at herself. Had a brilliant mind. Deliberate, kind and caring. Made her feel comfortable. Hadn't wanted to commit her. Tried to understand why she believe she came from the future. Recognized she told the truth. And now, he told her to go home so she could be happy. The man considered her feelings instead of his own.

Had Lord Silverman been right when he accused Whittington of loving her last night? How would she know? Love confused her. The brooch glinted.

"I won't try to use this anymore. I'm here and I like my life. Sure, I miss planes and cars, hot showers and saunas but, I can watch the future unfold before me. I know about steam engines and I will make Lady Coldwell enough money so she becomes fearless." She looked up to watch the man she loved and saw him close up like a shutter. Damn the English façade.

"You won't get sick of me and Lady Coldwell, will you?" Her voice cracked as she asked the question.

He cleared his throat, straightened his cuffs, smiled. "I will not catch a fever because of you."

"I didn't mean you would get an illness. I mean will you stop wanting us around. I seem to cause you a lot of trouble and I have not and never will learn to keep my mouth shut."

He smiled. "You bring sunshine into my life."

Emily rushed through the door. "You are never going to believe this. Lord Silverman told us the pendant is called Cupid's Brooch and the jewel has a legend attached."

Lady Coldwell walked sedately into the room several steps behind her daughter. "The brooch has magical powers. Magical powers, I say. We shall have to wait for Lord Silverman to tell us what he knows because he became tight lipped about those powers when we were in the park." She looked at her daughter with upraised brows.

The simple scold worked, and Emily blushed. "How unbecoming of me to rush into the room without announcing my presence."

Lady Coldwell noticed the piece in her hand. "You found it?" Her voice sounded shocked. Her face carried surprise and the line in her forehead increased as it did when she worried.

"Yes. I already tried to go home. My plan didn't work." She shrugged, tried to look sober.

Became decisive. Like her old self. Wanted to stay in this time, in this place near Lord Whittington. She sensed he wanted her too. *Follow your heart instead of your fears.*

Would their relationship turn into a romantic fling or a brother sister exchange? The brooch vibrated. She scoffed at her over active imagination.

The butler interrupted, "His Grace is in the parlor."

"We will join him," said Lord Whittington as he took her elbow and steered her toward the blue room.

Her stomach knotted, and she clutched the piece in her hand as she entered the room. Felt lonely when his

Lordship let go of her elbow, so she could be seated. She didn't want to turn the jewel over to the Duke even though the item belonged to him. If he took possession, she would never get back to the twenty-first century. People died of the common cold in the here and now. She shook the negative notion from her head. She had intense feelings for Lord Whittington. To stand next to him made her whole. How could she be so wishy-washy? One moment she wanted to return and the next she wanted to stay. What she really wanted was the best of both worlds.

The weight of uncertainty engulfed her. She would miss him dreadfully when she disappeared. They would never have sex. Never kiss. Never hug except for the time she needed her dress buttoned. She had cried like Niagara Falls because of Emily and Whittington had held her tenderly. What she would give to be back in his arms.

She realized if she transported to the twenty first century, she would dislike Jeff even more. Women were wired differently than men in some aspects. In others, they were exactly the same. She had been naïve. Decided to experience sex and convinced herself she loved Jeff to make her decision more palatable.

Jeff never made her tingle. Lord Whittington sent shivers down her back with a look. Or a scold. Or a smile.

Her heart beat rapidly, her chest had a warm expanding glow. Hope intervened. Did he want her in the way she wanted him? Disbelief intruded. Maybe he considered her entertaining but didn't care to kiss or touch her in an intimate way.

"Ah, Cupid's Brooch." Lord Silverman's voice cut

into her ruminations. "The dull, unappealing item cost me a pretty penny." He snatched the piece from her limp hand and held it up for all to see. "There is a legend associated with this jewel. I bought it from the curator at the British Museum as a young lad. It sat on a display rack in the back room. I was browsing when my eye caught a glint. When I went to see what caused the flash of light, I found this dull trinket." He held it up. "I see the item still lacks luster. As a lad, I acted fanciful. I doubt the brooch actually glinted."

Everyone started to talk at once. Finally, the maid came and asked if they needed anything. They said no and everyone took a seat. The lack of chatter seemed louder than a volcano and held the same amount of tension.

The Duke sat across from her chaperon, turned the piece over in his hand. "I came into the title when I found this brooch. The museum needed money and I became enthralled with the idea of magic. Planned to use the piece as an enticement to marry at the right time. Only, the time never seemed right."

He looked at Liz with a horrified expression. "I did vow to present it to the person I planned to marry." The last part of his sentence came out as a squeak.

She rolled her eyes. She deserved to be insulted but the man acted like a dimwit. Became embarrassed because he stated the truth. Thank God she didn't have to marry him. *Poor, poor Emily.*

The Duke held both hands up. Looked toward his friend in a symbolic gesture. He should have shouted for help because he obviously needed someone to take his foot out of his mouth.

She became curious. Decided not to let him dangle

a minute longer. "What about the original Lady you sniffed after. Did you not try to give the brooch to her?"

The man did not laugh. Didn't even crack a smile. "Sniff? I have never lusted after a woman in my life." His demeanor became cold. Hard. Glacial.

"I didn't mean to insult you. I mistakenly used incorrect vernacular." She hated to apologize but she also hated to be at odds with the man who would marry her best friend.

Emily interrupted. "Please, your Grace, tell us more about Cupid's Brooch."

He nodded toward Emily and continued his story. "I handed the case to the Lady I planned to marry one evening at a house party. I didn't have to say a word, but she said plenty."

To everyone's astonishment, his voice took on a high false tone, "Are you in your cups? Did you find this in the dust bin and judged I might need a gift for my maid?" His eyes got a faraway look as he palmed the piece.

"Even the brooch perceived her as a lying cheat, or else the jewel would have glinted and glowed when she touched the object." Liz instantly understood how the time-travel piece worked. What would happen if two people in love touched the brooch at the same time?

Lord Silverman cleared his throat. "I guess everyone believed her a lying cheat but me." He peered across the room at his friend. "Could you not have made me understand? Instead, you exposed her treachery and I became a jilt?"

"Please excuse a young man's foolishness." His tone sounded heartfelt.

She wanted to punch both of them in the shoulder.

Men. "You have Emily and she can love enough for two people." She swished her skirts around her legs, loved the sound. When she looked up, all eyes in the room stared at her.

Lord Whittington broke the silence. "Tell us more."

The Duke got comfortable in his seat. Everyone relaxed once he relaxed. "The curator told me the person who previously owned the brooch declared this a miraculous tool. Said he summoned the woman he loved by waving this in the air three times. It's all balderdash."

"How do you know? Did you try?" Emily sounded excited, her smile large, her eyes sparkled with life.

"I was ready to let bygones be bygones when Whittington returned from India but did not know how to approach him. The brooch turned up in an old overcoat pocket and I pointed the piece at this house. Had the brilliant idea to make a marriage contract with his ward. I didn't wave the silly pin around. I had a feeling. One that indicated I needed to meet someone in his household."

Her heart jolted in her chest. "He needed to meet you, Emily." Both Emily and the Duke blushed.

Lady Coldwell held out her hand. "Let me have a go. I do love fairy tales. I, like every other woman, want everlasting love."

His Grace looked dubious but handed her the brooch. Lady Coldwell waved the pin in the air and asked, "Did I move? I didn't experience any tingles like you talked about earlier."

"I believe you need to say an incantation. Try I want to find true love." She said with authority. Hoped this would help Lady Coldwell get an offer. She wasn't too old to remarry, and her first husband had been dull as ditchwater. She needed to believe as much as the rest of them.

The older lady started to laugh. Waved the brooch and said, "I want to find true love." The stone glinted but the woman was caught up in the fun of flinging her arms in the air. Both hands were on the brooch and they started moving in a figure eight motion. The jewel winked again as she said, "I want to find true love."

Lady Coldwell looked as if she had been electrocuted when she said her statement for the third time. Her hair stood on end, her eyes bugged out, her teeth chattered, and waves of energy pulsed around the room. As soon as the words were out of her mouth, she started to slide off her chair toward the floor, her eyes closed.

Lord Whittington tried to stop her from sliding to the floor as the butler announced, "Viscount Erleigh here to see Lady Coldwell."

Lady Coldwell's face went slack. When she finally opened her eyes, she found the Viscount leaning over her. "You need to feed her. I hear you've starved the good lady."

They situated Lady Coldwell in her chair as the Viscount demanded smelling salts and strong, hot tea and a dozen other remedies. Servants scurried to do his bidding. When she was comfortably seated with a tea tray at her elbow and a lemon biscuit in her hand, Viscount Erleigh asked to speak with Lord Whittington in his library for a "much needed discussion."

"I do believe you shall receive an offer of marriage," Emily whispered as the two men left the room.

Lady Coldwell simpered. As quickly as she turned happy, she turned white faced. "I cannot leave you, Miss Barrett. You have no one to look after you."

Emily picked up the brooch from the floor. Carried it over to where she sat. "You're going to swish this brooch in the air and say the words three times. Then you and Lord Whittington will finally know what mother and I have been saying for weeks. You two are the perfect match."

Her friend's pronouncement shocked her. "You think I should marry Lord Whittington?"

The Duke put a damper on the women when he said. "I hate to be the bearer of bad news but how did you have the brooch in the future, and, at the same time, the item is here in the past? And, we don't know Viscount Erleigh plans to ask for Lady Coldwell's hand in marriage."

She jumped out of her seat. "Only one way to find out." Picked up a crystal glass from the sideboard and placed it on the wall between the parlor and the library. A moment later she leaped into the air. "You, my dear Lady Coldwell, shall gain a husband if you so choose."

The woman blushed a delightful shade of pink.

"I refuse to be the one who causes you to lose out on true love. I can always find another chaperone. I remember," she laughed aloud. "The day I arrived, I wished for true love. Then I got zapped from the future. This piece is magical, Lord Silverman. I'm from the future, whether you want to believe me or not. Can we agree to disagree?"

"Agree to disagree?" The staid man frowned. "I say, that is quite the phrase."

They were laughing when Lord Whittington and the Viscount walked back into the parlor. After much ado, the older lady left for a ride in the park with her gentleman caller. Both of them looked pleased.

She impatiently waited until they were out the front door, then picked up the brooch set on the side table. "I want to be with my true love." She said the words and meant them. Believed Lord Whittington would be her man. "I want to be with my true love." Her hand involuntarily moved in a figure eight motion. Listened as an echo of herself said, "I want to be with my true love."

The air became thick, then thin.

She moved up, up, up, then down.

Colors swirled, bells tinkled, the sweet scent of roses filled her nostrils.

A gentle breeze caressed her body as she settled onto Lord Whittington's lap.

"Whaaaat happened?"

"My dear girl. You were across the room, then you were dumped in my lap." His wide smile showed teeth.

"You don't mind, do you?"

"Mind? I have never minded your presence since the day you arrived. I didn't want to let you go back to the future you continuously describe but…" he waved his hand. "I couldn't stand in your way of happiness. I realized a few weeks ago we needed to stop spending time together since you were betrothed to my friend."

"Well, I'm not betrothed to him now."

"No. Do you think it silly if we get married by special license? I'm not sure I want to wait for months to tie the knot."

She understood exactly what he meant as she

snuggled closer. "How does one acquire a special license?"

The Duke picked up the brooch with his handkerchief where it fell to the floor. Held the item away from his body. "We must take this trinket back to the museum. Immediately. I don't know what I witnessed but I would deem it unholy. Miss Barrett flew across the room at an astonishing speed."

Everyone noticed the disquiet in his voice, watched his eyebrows draw together, his face pale. "How she flew without using her feet mystifies me." He shook his head, became instantly British when he noticed everyone stared at him. Cleared his throat. "I don't want to be responsible for anyone getting hurt."

"I respectfully disagree." Emily responded. "We need to find some poor bloke down on his luck or some homely girl and give them the brooch with the promise of magic."

"And where do you propose to find a poor bloke or a homely girl?"

She interrupted them from her comfortable seat atop Lord Whittington. "Our mission is to find people who need love and lend them the brooch."

"What a great idea." Her smiling friend agreed.

"But not before you use the brooch," she said from her secured position.

Lord Silverman moved the handkerchief encased brooch behind his back. She got up from the warm lap of her true love and snatched the brooch from his hand. Decided to toss the brooch at Emily who stood near the Duke. Both Emily and Lord Silverman reached for the brooch at the same time.

A crash, a loud bang, and a sonorant boom echoed

throughout the house. As if thunder had hit the walls and ricocheted into the attic.

Colors flashed around them.

The smell of jasmine filled their nostrils.

Her body swirled and twirled as the air thickened and thinned.

When the flash became a flicker, Liz found herself back on Lord Whittington's lap.

Emily lay on the floor. Her dearly beloved's body covered her, as if he had the need to guard her.

"What the devil happened?" Lord Silverman demanded. Once he realized he was splayed across his intended, he rolled away, sat up, glanced frantically around the room. Scooted across the floor back to Emily. "You are not hurt, my dear. Are you?"

Emily giggled. Put her hand out so he could pull her into a sitting position. She kissed the astonished man on his lips.

Liz also shared a kiss with her man. He must have planned to do the same because their foreheads collided.

Cupid's brooch had done the trick.

Chapter Fourteen

The violin music engulfed the ballroom. Couples danced, others chatted, a few lone individuals strolled from one side of the room to the other. Lady Whittington noticed the debutante peeping at the man from behind her fan. She so wanted to find a woman who searched for true love.

Her husband, who stood behind her, whispered in her ear. "Man's a bird-witted gambler. Never interfere with a gudgeon."

Her eyebrow rose. "Isn't a gudgeon the fish we served at our last dinner party?"

"Yes. Those fish swallow bait with ease and swim eagerly into traps. Moneylenders adore young men who act like gudgeon's. He won't have a pence to his name by the end of this season."

She realized her husband wanted to find someone who needed the use of the mystical brooch as badly as she.

"A better choice for the young lady would be the timid youngster in the corner."

"Never," she scoffed. "He is full of negativity."

Her husband's dark brow rose, his head tilted slightly. She had learned to read the nuances and understood he wanted an explanation.

How did one explain negativity? "You know…a discontented person!"

"You mean a grumbletonian."

"Yes. Different terminology, same connotation. Life is complicated. Love doesn't have to be. I'm in love and I want everyone to experience this delicious emotion."

"This era does not subscribe to true love." His eyes twinkled. "A topic used by poets and on stage. Arranged marriages work."

She poked him with her gloved elbow. "We didn't have an arranged marriage."

"You traveled through time to find me, dearling. You are special. Only a few will ever have what we do." His smile made her insides turn to goo. They had been married for over a year and she never tired of him. Imagine that! She wanted some other lucky lady to experience the magic.

One problem. Her dear friend, Emily, and her stick-up-the-butt husband guarded the brooch like a sentry guard's palace gold. She tried to find the perfect lady. They all tried to find the perfect person, only…the four of them could never agree. What a silly pact they made when they jointly decided everyone had to say yes. No one would receive the brooch because they couldn't come to an understanding.

Her hand covered her stomach as she recognized a small flutter. How she had changed. Pregnancy would have sent her to the nearest abortion clinic in Hollywood. Here, she loved her condition. Interesting how the masses called it increasing. In a weird way, the word made total sense. Mayhap her babe should be the one to use the brooch later in life.

Emily and her husband left the dance floor and walked toward them, smiles the size of platters. She wondered when her friend would find herself in the family way. Shook off her fantasy. Mayhap they beamed because they found someone worthy of the brooch.

"Spill the beans," she demanded as the couple approached the alcove by the potted fern. A place where many a couple got pinned. A quaint term.

"Beans?" Lord Silverman lifted his monocle in his eye. She understood he only acted superior when he became doubtful.

"Don't be mutton-headed. What do you two have to tell us?" Her voice came out like a demand.

"I'm with babe and I'll have a boy," Emily said in a hushed tone. Her face literally glowed.

"I don't see any ultrasounds in this century. How could you possibly know you're having a boy?"

"Whatever is an ultrasound?"

"A machine used by doctors. They put the instrument on your stomach and take a picture of the baby inside you."

All three listeners gawked at her pronouncement.

Emily bent closer. "Mother used a needle and thread. You hold the thread over your stomach and ask if you are going to have a boy or a girl. The needle moves in a circle or a straight line. It circled numerous times so I'm having a boy." Her face filled with excitement, which made her beautiful.

"How come you didn't include me?"

"You always accuse us of being superstitious. I do not subscribe to witch craft," she sniffed. "The midwives used to do this in my mother's time, but we are more advanced now. Midwives have gotten away from making claims because the medical profession laughs at them. Mother subscribes to midwifery."

She gazed at her friend. "When can Lady Coldwell, I mean, when can The Right Honorable Viscountess Erleigh swing her needle and thread over my belly?"

"She'll be at the house before tea time tomorrow. Viscount Erleigh is off to one of his astronomy meetings so she sent a note around to say she planned to call. If you don't poke fun at us, we will see if you are having a boy or a girl."

Her husband stood at her back, close but not touching. They did have to show some decorum. "Can I attend?"

Lord Silverman grunted. "Yes. We can discuss Cupid's Brooch. Need to safeguard the jewel until our children are old enough to have a go."

"I say. We can lend it to the British Museum until they come of age." Her husband exclaimed.

She turned and poked him in the ribs.

"Or we can put the piece in a strong box. Our backyard can become a burial ground." His laughter rang out and those close to the couples turned to stare. You could have fun, but never too much fun at these formal events.

Emily and her husband looked at each other and nodded. "Come over tomorrow morning, we will break our fast, bury the box in the back yard under a shrub or a rose bush, and mother can see whether you will have a boy or a girl."

She and her husband nodded in unison. They had come up with the ideal plan. Cupid's Brooch would remain hidden until their children came of age.

Chapter One

Elizabeth Barrett
London, England 1812

Elizabeth walked past the library and heard her guardian, Lord Whittington, clear his throat—a sure sign of agitation. "She *appears* intelligent," he said.

Lady Coldwell snorted loudly so she stopped in her tracks. Had become acquainted with the grunt-like noise. Meant she disagreed. And when she disagreed, her opinion aggrandized.

She realized she *should* move out of earshot. Instead, her slipper shod feet stepped closer to the door and stopped. Her back pressed against the wall so the occupants of the room could not see her. *Please, please don't let this be about me!*

"She listens. Yes. She listens. Miss Barrett's only virtue is listening." She could not mistake the complaints were about her. Again. She cringed, pressed closer to the entrance. Lady Coldwell's fan made a tap-a-rap-rap on some piece of furniture. Her stomach did a flip and a flop.

"The gel listens when I give her instruction. She is a boon companion when I'm able to force her from her bed chamber. I do believe she has the potential to become a shut in. Mayhap due to her mother's blood. You know that woman originated in Ireland."

She became indignant. Boon companion? Lady Coldwell wanted an audience, and no one dared to naysay her. The reason she made her bed chamber a place of retreat. One where she could read and sew and write letters without censorship or the sound of her chaperon's deadly fan. The fan hurt when she struck. And her mother, bless her deceased soul, had never stepped foot in Ireland. Her grandsire had been one of the original American colonists. If she were a man, she would call for pistols at dawn.

"I have yet to hear an intelligent comment from her. Intelligent? No. I call her conversation insipid. Yes. Insipid is the right word."

Insipid? How could Lady Coldwell know if she talked intelligently when she never allowed her to squeeze in a word?

"I find her dialogue delightful when she has the opportunity to respond." Lord Whittington replied. Elizabeth recognized *that* tone. Soon he would rise from his chair and Lady Coldwell would be escorted from the room. She had seen him do this maneuver on numerous occasions. When he did expel her, the woman would shoot to her side, like an arrow from a bow, and complain about boorish manners from young men with too much income.

"The dance instructor said Miss Barrett has two left feet. Refused to learn the waltz! Refused. One does not refuse the dance instructor."

Two left feet. Her father would be proud. She could not trust an unscrupulous individual who stood too close when Lady Coldwell had her back turned. The dance master used excuses to find ways to touch her hands and arms. *All* young ladies should be off limits to the likes of him.

Lord Whittington pratted on, but she couldn't hear what he said because Lady Coldwell talked over him. The woman never realized when to stop riding her high horse.

"The dressmaker moans and groans and I know why. Her hideous red hair. Everyone knows red haired women act like fishwives. That's why I spend so much time civilizing the barbarian out of her. Red isn't the style. No, her hair is not acceptable. How do you expect me to get her married? She rarely leaves her bed chamber?"

The sound of feet on the floor above made her jump, scan the staircase. Getting caught by an eavesdropping maid would be an embarrassment.

"You can ease off the need to worry," her guardian said in a frosty tone "I have an offer signed and sealed for Miss Barrett. A genuine marriage contract."

Lady Coldwell did not respond, and the silence stretched. Must be shocked senseless. She could hear her silent judgments, 'how had the insipid, hideous Miss Barrett receive an offer?' She almost wanted to laugh until reality intruded. She might have to get married. Not that she didn't intend to get married. Only, she had been so sure she would find love like her parents.

His lordship continued to talk because Lady Coldwell appeared unable to do anything other than sputter. "Apparently our neighbor, Lord Silverman, met her at the last ball or musical or wherever you ladies trot off to each eve. He is more than interested. He has committed."

"Surely you mean Lord Silverman asked after my

Emily?"

"No, Lady Coldwell. He asked for Miss Barrett's hand in marriage. Told me he liked her conversation. I guess she isn't as tedious as you believe."

The sound of his boots and her shoes as they walked toward the door had Elizabeth on the run. Lord Wittington had a way of shooing Lady Coldwell out of a room. She fled up the servant's staircase to her bed chamber.

Lady Coldwell might believe her insipid, but some unknown man liked her conversation. She opened the door to her sanctuary and gulped in air. Once her agitation wound down, she walked sedately to her desk, arranged her gown and primly sat on the chair. Made sure her body showed off her assets as she had been instructed. Next, she tried to organize her interior dialogue. Long minutes later, a knock sounded at her door. Forced herself to create a prim-and-proper face as Lady Coldwell charged into her room.

"Miss Barrett. Do join me in my sitting room." The stairs made the over large woman wheeze out the words.

"I feel the onset of a megrim. I shall have a snooze after I finish this last thank you note. I'm honored for your invitation, Lady Coldwell and," she paused and deliberately emphasized the next words, "I know you would not be pleased if I were indisposed this evening. We are scheduled to attend Lady Attaberry's ball." She turned away from the chaperone and folded the blank piece of paper in front of her. Acted as if she were finishing a letter.

The woman huffed and puffed but left within moments. She realized her actions were boorish, yet she needed time to ruminate on what to do about this predicament.

Her father's sister refused her a roof when she found out her blunt happened to be tied up in a trust. The funds would not be available until she turned into the age of a crone. Those had been her solicitor's exact words. She wondered how old she would be before she became a crone.

She smoothed the folds out of the stationery, unstopped the ink bottle, and wrote—Questions for Lord Whittington. How much is my dowry? Is my dowry different from my trust? Could she ask him about the age of a crone? No. She wouldn't write the improper question on the paper.

She had a dowry because Papa mentioned the amount as they sailed into England. They had crossed the sea from Boston to hunt for a husband. He said her aunt would guide her. Her aunt had not been inclined to help. Yet she needed to believe she could find a true gentleman so her life would work out. Her father said the most important quality in a man would be kindness. She wrote, how kind is Lord Silverman?

The thought of her dowry reminded her of Miss Teasdale. The youngster, barely out of the school room, had a long, horse-like face, with buck teeth and cheeks covered in pimples. She giggled incessantly in a high-pitched tone which made one want to gnash one's teeth. People commented about her large dowry. Everyone said it was vulgar to talk about finances. Only…the young lady had a gaggle of men follow her around as if she were beautiful.

A lightning quick notion made her realize Papa tied up the money in a trust so the cads and bounders who desperately needed to pay off their creditors wouldn't pay attention to her. *Thank you, Papa.*

Lord Whittington could be kind, even if he acted distant. He took her in after she made the rounds of English relatives. The solicitor, Mr. Cavendish, sent her to stay with his sister while he approached the man. He happened to be the fourth cousin on her father's sister's husband's side of the family tree. His acceptance of her meant he had a kindness not evident with other relations. She found most of the British were cold. Deliberate. Would cut you with a look or a gesture.

Tears of sorrow threated to spill. This would not do. She looked at her list. What else should she ask? Upper crust society men grew up alongside one another. Her guardian should have knowledge of the Duke's character.

She wrote—Do you think Lord Silverman would make a good husband? She would listen carefully when he responded to her question. She did not believe he would steer her wrong.

A signed marital contract meant security. She would not be forced to attend musicales where young ladies croaked out songs and ineptly banged on piano keys. Nor would she have her toes stepped on by boys who galloped around the room and thought themselves men.

She realized she could select a companion once she married. One of her choice. One she liked. Not someone like Lady Coldwell. Someone who would teach her the ways of the ton. She had always been one to fit in, didn't care to stand out. This made her hopeful until she thought about poor Papa.

Her goodly father had died a little over a year ago.

Her black mourning dresses changed to gray and recently she had been allowed to wear ensembles in soft, pale colors. Her moods changed as her wardrobe changed. The need to get out and about and find a way to get on with her life became a theme of sorts. Papa would not want her to grieve forever.

Someone tapped on her door. Her stomach twisted into knots and her voice sounded shaky when she called, "Enter."

A maid stuck her head inside the room. "Lord Whittington asked if you could join him in the library, Miss Barrett."

She thanked the maid, picked up the stationery with hands that shook and walked with determination toward Lord Whittington's athenaeum.

Chapter Two

Elizabeth sat artfully poised on the settee where the lady's maid had arranged her moments earlier. The headache came on, no doubt due to the walnut extract treatment the hair dresser gave her this morning in the garden. A tedious process, but the alternative—unpopular, red hair seemed worse!

Did Lord Silverman know he would marry someone with Irish blood? She shuddered at the thought and decided to go over her toilet once again as a distraction from her reflections. Lady Coldwell's voice rang in her head, "His Grace could jilt you if you make one misstep."

Her eyebrows and lashes were darkened with lampblack to give the appearance she had dark hair. The rice powder made her skin look translucent. A maid dusted her from head to toe with the cosmetic before squeezing her into an over long, over tight corset, cinching her already hourglass waist.

Her hair, tied up in rags earlier in the day, had been artfully drawn away from her face so one noticed her slightly slanted, green eyes. Her tall coiffure, anchored with a multitude of hair pins, had her mother's pearls entwined in her tresses. She tried to protest the use of the necklace, but Lady Coldwell declared, "Pearls do not stain, gel. No, they do not. You have to have adornment because you look plain. Yes. You are very plain. I do believe the Duke mistook you for my Emily. Yes. I do believe he shall be horrified when he eyeballs you."

She caressed the beautiful white silk evening gown. This dress was the latest fashion, created by a real French emigrant. Her deceased mother would be proud. Her heart gladdened when Lady Coldwell told her she now appeared 'all the rage'. Papa would be furious with the low cut of the dress and the dyed hair.

She sniffed back tears and remembered she had made the only decision possible. She could not continue to live with Lady Coldwell and her deadly fan. Her leg bore bruises from the smacks she received for all manner of transgressions. Her resolve to get away straightened her back and shoulders.

Her toes ached in the too tight slippers. Hunger pains sounded loud enough to embarrass her, but she dared not say a word. Lady Coldwell and her daughter, Emily, nibbled on delicate toast points spread with jam while she had hairs plucked and her corset tightened.

She eyed the small dish of comfits located at the edge of the table. *How delicious they would taste.* Her mouth started to water as she gazed at the sweet treats. Tried to figure out how she could snitch and eat one before anyone entered the room. *Will they leave a stain on my gloves?*

Steps thumped on the stairs and she realized she should have grabbed a sugared nut before the Lady's maid arranged her skirts. She fingered the glove off her right hand as Lady Coldwell charged into the room. The yellow feathers on her turban danced merrily. Miss Emily Coldwell followed two steps behind. The dutiful daughter smiled shyly. She would like to know her better, but her mother intruded.

Such a dear, sweet girl! Such a horrid mama!

Her chaperon looked very pleased with herself. "You, Mistress Elizabeth Barrett, have been given a betrothal gift." She held up a small ornamental box which was thrust in her face.

"Are you excited about the gift or because I will be leaving soon?" She blurted before she thought. Perceived from the furious look flitting across Lady Coldwell's face that she had committed another *faux pas*. She instinctively shrank inside and stopped herself. Straightened her back. *Father, I will make you proud.*

"His Grace, Geoffrey Froth, Duke of Silverman has honored you with a gift and you make light of the present?" The angry matron sniffed as she wagged the box in front of her.

She wished she had more backbone. Wanted to snatch the box from her heavy hand. "I meant no offense to either you or his Grace," she apologized as tears began to form in her eyes. She could not cry, or lampblack would streak her face.

"No water pots allowed," said her chaperon and pulled a thin square of cloth from her reticule. The handkerchief in question had been previously used.

She waved the hankie away, grabbed for the box. Reluctantly, Lady Coldwell released the item from her clenched fist. She opened the present and gasped in horror. The ugliest, dullest brooch lay nestled in blue velvet cloth. The cloth prettier than the tarnished pin. And the brooch definitely looked tarnished. As if the old trinket had been set aside for centuries, dug out of the attic, and then delivered without a thought as to how the gift would be received.

In her anxiousness to see, Emily stepped in front of her mother, her face lit with excitement. Her hands fumbled toward the gift as she said, "Well, show us Miss Barrett. What have you been given?"

Lady Coldwell smacked her fan hard across Emily's open palm and the shy girl winced in pain.

Before she could stop herself, she jumped up from the settee and stared Lady Coldwell directly in her eyes. This cold-hearted tabby hit her and her daughter with her wicked fan every chance she got. She snatched the brooch from the box with her ungloved hand and held the piece up. "Here. You have seen it first. Would you also like to *wear* it?"

Her guardian gasped which made her double chin jiggle. Then she straightened and hissed, "Your display of vulgarity knows no bounds. You know not how fortunate you are. The Duke sent you a gift. Show some gratitude."

The fan shot out, almost smacked her arm but she dodged out of the way. Her hand jerked away, and she backed out of the room and into the entry way. The older woman followed her. For some odd reason, she waved the brooch in her face in a teasing motion.

The mother-daughter duo followed the dull stone with their eyes. The brooch suddenly flashed with brilliance. Lady Coldwell's eyes locked onto the pin as she slowly lowered her fan.

Caught up in a torrent of raw emotion, she witnessed the flash, instantly negated the fact the brooch could be a magnificent jewel when polished. "Fortunate?" she scoffed. "I have been transformed into someone I am not? I have been given to the first man to request me? Fortunate, you say. I say, unfortunate." She waved her arm, convinced she could keep her chaperon and the current situation at bay.

The first curl unraveled from her coiffure, touched her naked shoulder. She tried to blow the errant strand backwards. This situation seemed disastrous. Her temper overtook her, and she found she could not stop herself from waving her arm around like a lunatic.

Lady Coldwell shoved her daughter aside and pointed her fan. "You do not like your gift, Miss High and Mighty? You are an ungrateful gel. An ungrateful gel. Yes, I say. Ungrateful." She proceeded to fold her arms across her massive torso as her reddened face glared in her direction.

She looked toward Emily and whispered. "Is this a token of affection?" She held the unsightly brooch out toward her. "Is this what you would give to someone you loved?" The brooch started to move in a figure eight motion. As if her hand were propelled by magic. She became powerless to stop the action. Words ripped from her soul. "I want to marry someone I understand. Someone I can care for and who cares for me."

Tears threatened to spill from her eyes which made her even angrier. Pain welled up inside her. Her father had loved and cherished her. He had taken care of her. Had been determined to find a gentleman who would provide for her. Arranged marriages were commonplace and convenient. But this did not mirror how she envisioned becoming betrothed.

If only…

If only she could be certain she made the right choice. This betrothal happened quicker than a coach with runaway horses.

Lady Coldwell's eyebrows were up to her hairline

as she eyed her suspiciously. "What do you want?"

She shifted the brooch in her hand, "I want to love and be loved by someone special. Yes. That is what I want—I want to love and be loved by someone special." The words poured from her lips as she swayed. Then her world slowed as she whispered the heartfelt words again, "I want to love and be loved by someone special."

Thunder crashed on her right side...then on her left.

Trumpets sounded...a touch from the tip of a soft, angel's wing feathered across her cheek.

A flash of teal...a flash of gold...a brilliant rainbow.

Her body swayed to the right...to the left...forward...backward...upward and sideways.

Voices laughed. Talked. Screamed.

Someone moaned with pleasure...another cried in pain.

Music far, then near.

Warm light...heat on her cheeks...coolness in her toes and fingers.

Icicles ran throughout her body, raced up and down her spine.

A faint breeze. Distant thunder. A million stars.

She fell to the floor with a thud, her head colliding with a hard surface. Noticed faces peering at her before total blackness descended.

Chapter Three

Elizabeth listened to the voices around her but couldn't manage to open her eyes. A pain stabbed her head, neck and back. What happened? Had Lady Coldwell pushed her? What a mean trick.

Someone rubbed her hand in a gentle motion. The comforting gesture had her determined to remain in this fog-like state. Part of her seemed aware of others around her. Another part of her realized she was somewhere she didn't recognize. Like when one first wakes from a fantastical dream.

"I observed her lips turn up so I'm sure she's okay." The man who spoke sounded peevish. Men were always inconvenienced when women didn't behave. She did not like to make people fret. Even so, she did not care to discover who talked. For once, she would be selfish and lay on the thick woven carpet and dream.

Another, more strident voice demanded, "Did you push her? Good God, Jeff. What have you done?"

"I did not push her. You know Liz. Always her way or the highway. She waved the brooch like a crazy person and landed flat on her back."

Another masculine voice spoke. "Jeff stood between us when she suddenly ended up on the floor. I definitely heard her say, 'You're fired!' Then somehow, she slammed her head on the ground. I sickened at the sound. A dull thud even though she landed on carpet."

She realized she lay on the carpet surrounded by a group of men. How unacceptable. Where were the smelling salts? Her chaperone? Heat in her cheeks indicated she would look flush with embarrassment. What if her dress had hitched up and showed her ankles? Oh my!

"Look, her face reddened." The exasperated voice didn't belong to Emily but…immense gratitude swept through her to discover a lady stroked her hand. Her modesty would stay preserved. Mayhap the maid? Only the maid had an accent. But then, so did this woman. She could not place the accent at the moment. And, it took effort to try.

She needed more sleep. The place before now had been filled with colors and lights and sounds. She continued to feel light as a feather and her body needed…well, she did not know what she needed other than a tonic to get rid of the pain. Mayhap someone to stop the men grumbling in the background. *Who is Jeff and why does the other man think he pushed me? Where did Lady Coldwell scuttle off to?*

"Clear this room immediately," came a deep voice located above her body and to the right. *A gallant man to the rescue.* She recognized the sound of feet as they backed away from her. At least someone thought about her reputation. She tried to open one eye wide and found the effort more than she could manage. Tried to open both eyes to no avail. *Mayhap this is a dream.*

The lady's voice sounded curt. "She's been unconscious for about ten minutes. What took you so long?"

"I'm on the other set and came as fast as I could."

The man sounded calm. Like Papa. He had to be a Gentleman. Large, warm, comforting hands touched her head. Little tingles of excitement ran down her back. Such a gentle, loving gesture! *Loving gesture?* Her eyes snapped open instantly. No gentleman should touch her and make her feel tingly.

He looked like no man she had ever seen. Her mouth opened in astonishment. This gallant male seemed big. And brown. Brown hair, brown eyes and brown forearms. Nicely shaped forearms. Muscles evident. His shirt sleeves were deliberately cut above his elbows. He showed skin. Oh my! She should swoon only she already lay on the floor.

What genteel man showed his bare arms? She looked closer and noticed they were firm and had little golden hairs. His skin had been tanned to a toasty brown. He had to be a man of nature. Someone from the fields or the docks. Her father's workers were men of nature and they always smelled bad. This man smelled—like an exotic, heavenly spice. She inhaled deeply and realized how shameful she had become to acknowledged baser instincts.

Feeling stirred in her nether regions and she realized she had to stop yearning for…for whatever elusive element laid slightly beyond her grasp. The man of nature held her head, lightly touched her skull with bared fingers. She tried to move away and groaned.

His fingers stopped in mid caress. "Don't move," he gently chastised her. "I need to make sure you aren't seriously injured."

His voice sounded soothing, filled her with warmth. The concern in his brown eyes made the knot in her stomach melt. Had she died and gone to Heaven?

This person actually cared about her as his hands gently plied her head.

"Nasty bump."

Oh, this is not good she silently lamented. Had no idea what to do in this situation. A lady always knew what to do. How did one chastise a man who used vulgar language and looked like a God?

Pleasant fingers probed, and delicious shivers coursed down her back.

"Your neck wasn't injured."

His hand started to follow the shivers and she flapped her right arm in protest. She was a good girl, she was, but even her precious Papa, who treated her like a princess, hadn't touched her back in years. Once again, she tried to move away from his liquid touch. This must have been what her mother meant when she said a man could set a girl on fire. She had warned her to avoid touch until marriage.

Her beautiful, Irish mother and staid, English father had been so happy together, yet they rarely touched one another in her presence. She now understood why.

The man looked directly into her eyes causing an irrational sensation to spiral downward from her throat. He gazed at her for long moments, shook his head and said, "Did my touch cause pain?"

For a moment, his sensual fingers and the twinkle in his eyes mesmerized her. Did he have some extraordinary power? Papa told her about men who could make women fall into deep sleeps. He had not been a proponent of mesmerism and neither was she.

"Why you scamp! I am in no position to defend my honor." She managed to get the words out even if they sounded breathless instead of the declaration of war she should espouse.

The debaucher's full lips turn down at the sides, bushy eyebrows drew together and, his eyes glittered with intense emotion. "I know this is uncomfortable for you. Your face and neck are flushed. Let me take your pulse before I continue the rest of my examination. You might have a concussion. There's a large lump on the back of your head."

The man gently took her wrist away from the thin woman with big hair.

Big, black, shiny hair. And…a blue streak of color? A feather artfully arranged. Mayhap a peacock feather? Those birds were brilliant blue. The face had an impish look and a gold ring pierced her nose. There was no doubt she no longer laid in Lord Whittington's mansion. The outlandish woman started to stand.

"Don't go," she pleaded. She could not be left alone with this man in a…she looked around and found herself in a small, unusual room. As she looked upward, she noticed light glowing from inside the ceiling. Curious and strange. "Where am I?"

The woman's eyebrows rose. Her question brought her close. "You sure you want me to stay?"

The woman sounded unsure and was partially undressed but she needed a lady by her side. On closer inspection, she realized she wore pants—like a man. What a loony dream. She questioned her sanity. Decided to close her eyes and try to go back to sleep but the gentleman's voice intruded.

"Your pulse is slightly elevated." His hand stayed on her wrist and she couldn't find the words to tell him to stop touching her. His fingers were like a branding iron, burning, hot, and decadent. This must be how

Sally Winslow acted with Johnny. She had been the fast one who told all the rest of the young ladies what to expect. Why, she'd even allowed a boy to kiss her lips. Everyone understood babies could be dropped down your gullet once your lips met.

She opened her eyes and tried to control her fanatical emotions. The man pulled a weird item from a black bag and put one piece of a silver hose in one ear and another piece of the silver item in his other ear. "I'm going to listen to your heart."

"How?" she asked, totally fascinated. Would her heart tell him she liked him? Oh no! She did not want him to know.

He started to move the black and silver gadget toward her torso, and she pushed his hands away, tried to sit up. Her head spun, and darkness once again enveloped her. In the fog she listened as the man and the woman talked about her. Part of her understood what they said, the other part of her became extremely confused.

"Does she always act like this?" Dr. Demfry asked.

"No! I've been with her for a few months and she's polite and professional. I stayed in the other room when she fired her manager-boyfriend. He's a real creep. The director and guard were in the hallway and suddenly Liz grappled with the lunatic for some piece of jewelry. Liz' was on the floor when the director called for me."

"May be why she's so skittish. If he pushed her, she may not feel comfortable around men."

"I got the same impression when she asked me to stay. Every time you touch her, she acts weird."

"Let's transfer her to the hospital and run some tests."

Elizabeth opened her eyes and focused on the lady with big hair. Once again, she allowed the woman to rub her hand in a comforting way. The blue streak didn't look like a feather. Appeared to be her actual hair. Impossible.

The woman spoke, "We called an ambulance to take you to the hospital. Need to run tests."

"People die in hospitals. If I'm going to die, I want to be in my own home."

"Sweetie, you won't die. We intend to find out if you have a concussion."

Her curiosity could not be stemmed. "What is a concussion?"

"You're joking, right?" The woman's eyes bugged out. The earring in her nose flared with her nostril and she could not help but be rude and stare.

She looked toward the large male. "Why does the doctor speak into his snuff box?"

The Doctor placed the rectangle into his pant pocket, knelt down beside her and asked, "What is your name?"

"I'm Elizabeth Barrett."

"How old are you?"

"A man never asks ladies questions of an intimate nature." She realized her voice sounded more like a plea than a command.

The gentleman rolled his eyes. Mumbled what sounded like, "never ask an actress her age." His eyes squinted, his nose wrinkled in an adorable way. He asked, "What is the date and time?"

"You know we live in eighteen twelve."

"Oh boy." The lady abruptly stopped rubbing her hand.

The Doctor continued with his questions. "Where do you live?"

"I reside in Boston, but I am here for the London Season."

The lady laughed out loud before she said, "California doesn't have a London Season."

She had to ask, even though they hadn't been formally introduced. "What is your name?"

The interesting woman looked at her as if the chickens roosted in her hair. "I'm your hairdresser, Tina Davis."

"I am pleased to meet you," she trailed off because she didn't know if she should call her a Lady, a Missus, or a Miss. She decided to use the term Mistress. An acceptable title. "I am pleased to meet you Mistress Tina Davis."

"Ooh La La. Mistress Tina Davis. Well, I guess I've taken a step up in the world."

"You are not a titled Lady, are you?"

Her question elicited a loud snort that might have been a laugh. "No. I'm definitely not a Lady."

Relief flooded through her body. "I don't know this California place, but England most definitely has a season and I am staying with a distant relative named Lord Whittington. Please have my guardian attend me."

Everyone stared at her. A big, burly man who had to be a stone overweight barreled into the room. "Who is Lord Whittington?"

Her voice rose an octave. "My guardian. I need him to attend me at once."

"The only one who is going to attend you is the good doctor," the man replied, looked at her with his head cocked to one side. A frown marred his thick lips.

When no one stirred she demanded in her most imperious tone, "Get my guardian, this instant."

Chapter Four

Everyone talked at once. Horror had her frozen on her back, listening. Elizabeth took in the room and the people who conversed in a strange language. Their English seemed familiar and at the same time different. Her gaze lit upon the inconceivable lights.

Men in the hall yelled at each other. This made her shrink inside. All the strangeness she witnessed had fear crawling under her skin.

Could I be dead? If so, why aren't Mama and Papa here to greet me?

She knew she hadn't landed in Hell because she didn't see any fire or brimstone. No heat. No pain. Well, her head had a mighty ache, so she did feel some pain but not the sort she expected if she ended up in the bad place.

She tried to get a view of the men in the hall from her place on the floor. Their shoes were different. Not London made. The carpet, the rooms lighting, and the wall color looked unusual. Where had she landed?

Panic filled her chest and she closed her eyes. Mistress Tina Davis talked slowly, cautioned her to stay calm. She thought about Heaven and the pearly gate. She opened one eye, peered around, and tried to locate a gate of some kind. Surely, she would see a gate if she were in Heaven.

Do I honestly expect to get into Heaven? She

hadn't been a saint.

Which left Purgatory. An in-between place where one rusticated and did penance for wrong doings while on earth.

The debonair gentleman doctor smiled a handsome smile before he said, "Don't squirm."

Two men carted in a contraption with wheels. She allowed them to place her on the movable bed but when they tried to tie her in with thick cloth straps, she screamed like a banshee. She had seen them strap Lady Sexton into a white coat with many ties. The old lady had talked to dead people as if they were real. When she returned from Bedlam, she didn't look herself and never spoke again.

The doctor took a peculiar device out of his bag and asked everyone to leave the room. She stopped mid-scream, gulped air. "Mistress Tina Davis needs to remain. She must stay. I need her to be by my side. Please let Mistress Tina Davis stay." She held on to the other lady's hand as if she were a lifeline.

The young lady reminded her to breathe in and out and made statements about peace and love. Her voice eventually soothed her, and she calmed while listening to the murmurers and mutters.

"I'll stay as long as you need me." Mistress Tina Davis patted her hand in a reassuring gesture.

"Thank you." She hoped the woman meant what she said. Tried to focus on her appearance. She looked a few years older than her and also had tanned skin. What lady would allow sun to turn her vulgar brown? A sign of bad breeding to be sun kissed. Made one appear…well she wasn't sure what, but she understood freckles unsettled many a gentleman.

She placed her left hand over the nice Mistress Tina Davis' hand and involuntarily gasped. "What has happened to my fingernails? They are beautiful and...they are painted!" Shock made her reel until she conjured up a memory. A memory where she sat in front of Mistress Tina Davis and had tips put on. She recognized everything and nothing. This had to be Purgatory!

Mistress Tina Davis shook her head and whirled her finger around her ear in some signal to the Doctor. Her entire body stiffened because of the odd gesture.

"You are going to be okay." The manicured hand with blackened fingernails came down upon her forehead.

Could she be in the intake room? How perfectly sensible. They had to evaluate her and her life. Decide what her punishment would be for the way she had lived. The Powers-That-Be might allow a woman to touch her without gloved hands while in mixed company. And black nails. Could this sweet lady be a demon sent to tempt her?

Her body started to shiver and shake and Doctor Demfry said, "She's going into shock."

She didn't understand. Her body quaked, and fear made the pressure on her chest increase. *Where am I? What is this place?*

The doctor plucked more instruments out of his bag. "I don't want to sedate her with a head injury, but she's in shock." He placed a black strap on her arm and pumped a small black bag at the end. "Her blood pressure is extremely low."

A sudden prick, like a bee made her kick her legs in panic. Lassitude eventually washed over her, and her body slackened.

"Promise me you won't leave me Mistress Tina Davis." The sound came out in a strangled plea and the concerned lady nodded her assurance as she continued to pat her hand in a soothing manner.

She had no control of her body. Every appendage became as limp as overcooked cabbage. The terror and dread drained from her. She remained helpless as two men strapped her on the bed, then rolled her down a long corridor. Mistress Tina Davis stayed within eyesight. Mayhap this was how you were greeted when you didn't get into heaven. No one ever explained what to expect in Purgatory.

Next, the bed magically rose upward, and they slid her into the back of a boxed contraption made from materials she had never before seen. Mistress Tina Davis sat by her side during the ride. Banshees wailed overhead once the metal doors shut. Uneasiness made her keep her eyes open even though sleep tried to descend. One of the men leaned over and asked her questions but she refused to answer. Would not give in to temptation. Wanted to believe she had not been a bad person while alive.

Came up with a plan of sorts. She would review the Ten Commandments on her way to this place called Mercy Hospital. A great name for Purgatory's reception area. Why else would they have banshees wail upon arrival?

Thou shalt not kill. She had never considered killing anyone. Then she remembered Johnny. She wanted to drown Johnny when he put a snake down her back. Would God count a childhood incident against her?

The overhead wails stopped, the back portals on the conveyance opened and the strangely dressed men rolled her bed into the open air. Sun streamed from a brilliant blue sky. She looked on in awe as the doors to the overlarge mansion magically opened.

Doctor Demfry waited for them, said he would continue the examination. This certainly looked like a place where you were required to confess one's sins. The magic doors slid shut behind her and a shiver snaked down her back.

The stench of death filled her nostrils. Death had a funny smell. Made one want to throw up. Her mother had the same odor when she died. Would her mother come greet her? Oh, how she wished some relative would arrive to help.

Doctor Demfry walked over to where she lay. "How do you feel?"

She whispered, "I cannot lie. I am fearful." She looked around and asked, "Where is Mistress Tina Davis?"

"She has your insurance cards and went to check you in. Someone gave her your purse. I plan to run tests so we can assess the situation."

Oh no! They would find out she wanted to strangle Johnny over the snake incident. How could you hide a vengeful thought from God?

The gallant man patted her hand with tenderness. "Calm down. The tests won't hurt."

Well the good and mighty Doctor could say test wouldn't hurt because he selflessly cured people of all manner of ills. She, on the other hand, liked the way her ankles looked in black boots and satin slippers. She loved the comforter on her bed, and everyone knew one sinned when they fell in love with an object. Those tiny rosebuds were so beautifully crafted. Then, in London, after Papa's untimely demise, she had ordered silk under clothes. They were decadent. Unfortunately, she had insisted on more than one pair!

This train of thought made her assess how she dressed. A blanket had been laid over her body. How had she failed to notice what she wore? Mayhap she had the garment she died in. Her last memory had been her argument with Lady Coldwell. Her rigging consisted of an exquisite silk gown. The material she wore underneath the blanket did not have the itchy layers of undergarments. Where were her undergarments?

Mistress Tina Davis walked over and punched Doctor Demfry on his arm. "Did you make her nervous again?"

He chuckled. "Liz doesn't get nervous, do you?"

"Who is Liz?" She tried to see if someone else had joined them. Could Liz be one of God's minions? Her mother always said women were dirt on earth but ruled in heaven.

"You're Liz." Doctor Demfry frowned and shook his head from side to side.

"I'm Elizabeth Barrett, Doctor Demfry. We met at the other place." She tried to be polite.

"I met you over a year ago. You told me to call you Liz."

Did he try to make her forget all her decorum and add another black mark to her slate? Her mother warned her. Angels recorded all manner of sins. "My name is Miss Elizabeth Barrett and I expect you to use my correct name when you address me."

She did not like the hurt look upon his face, nor the fact Mistress Tina Davis hissed like a cat. "I wouldn't piss off the man who happens to be your biggest fan."

She didn't respond because she had no idea what her acquaintance implied. The words registered a few moments later, but she had already been wheeled into a room for her first test. Two women helped her off the rolling bed and placed her on her back so she could be viewed by a huge white machine. Someone named Mister Technician explained the 'procedure' to her which made her jingle-brained.

She remained quiet and realized by being silent, she could reason. In this place and in this body, she had access to a lot more information inside her head. Other situations and experiences.

Forcing herself to remain calm, she examined her fingers. Realized they were not bit and gnawed on. The nails were polished and perfectly shaped.

Her hands were no longer reddened from the help she had given mother with the wash. Her long, tapered fingers looked lovely. As if she were the Queen. Even her teeth seemed different.

She experimented. Ran her tongue around the inside of her mouth and noticed the crooked eyetooth had become straight. Even. How delightful. What color yellow would they be? Amber or pale? She'd seen as many variations on teeth as there were faces. Some Londoner's even had black teeth.

Mayhap they would have a staring glass in this place. Curiosity about her looks could not be stemmed. She hoped to see herself once they finished the test.

And the test. No chalk necessary. No memorization of numbers. A machine scanned her body. Sounded loud to her ears. The nurse told her the readings would be accurate. She believed this to be true.

The notion came to her in an instant. Purgatory did not meet her expectations. It surpassed them.

Chapter Five

Elizabeth woke when she heard a commotion outside her door. She noticed Doctor Demfry blocking the entryway from the angry man named Jeff. He had to be demonic. All those indecent words she did not personally understand flew from his lips, along with spittle.

"I demand to see Liz. Nothing's wrong with her except theatrics."

"I'm not sure Miss Barrett wants to see you." The doctor looked calm, yet his demeanor appeared forceful. Oh, how she liked a strong, determined gentleman.

The other man could not be called a gentleman. He tried to push past Doctor Demfry who stepped in front of him, blocked his way. Then a slew of vulgarity streamed from the man's mouth. By the bitter tone, this man was not a nice person.

Could he be the Devil's follower? A demon who would try to get to her before a decision could be made? London had been left behind. This other place, outside of her time, had a chamber pot which seemed beauteous. She had flushed the toilet numerous times before Mistress Tina Davis forced her to stop.

She slept through the night on a soft, comfortable bed. No smells. No lice. No feathers poked through the material.

Mistress Tina Davis stood up from the bedside chair and leaned over her. "Did he hit you?" she demanded.

"I…I do not know." She touched the warm blanket on the comfortable bed to give herself a sense of security.

"Come on, you know. Why do you feel like you have to cover for that bossy prig? Battering could happen to anyone. You won't be the first one nor the last one to complain about being slapped around."

"I do not know how I came to be on the floor. First, I argued with Lady Coldwell. Then I lay in the ante chamber where we met. I believe I died. It's the reason why I am here."

Her acquaintance rolled her eyes. "Why am I so flexible?" she muttered before she glared. "The knock on your head has done some serious damage. Didn't the psychologist explain you are not from the past and Lady Coldwell doesn't exist? For Pete's sake, stop staring at my nose ring. You make me feel like a freak."

She digested the words and said, "You do have a strong heart Mistress Tina Davis. I would not have known what to do when I got here if you did not guide me. The knock on my noggin is better and I thank you for asking. This comfortable bed helped." She noticed the woman rolled her eyes again.

"I do have a question or two about the woman who said Lady Coldwell is not real but first I need an introduction to Mister Pete. You are not hunched at your back or hairy like the monkey boy, so you are definitely not a freak. I only…" She trailed off with embarrassment. Noticed her companion started to steam up like a kettle. Looked hot and ready to boil. "Jewels

183

in the nose are new to me. I have a lot to learn. Under your tutelage, I promise to learn quickly."

"My tutelage? Monkey boy? Geez! Listen up missy, you need to learn, and I plan to teach you. Tell Doctor Demfry that Jeff is not allowed near you."

"I cannot interrupt two gentlemen as they talk."

"They are not talking, they're fighting, which will get physical in a moment. You have to tell the doctor you don't want Jeff around." Tina walked around the bed, pierced her with an intent look. "You don't want him around, do you?"

"The man in the hall with his face the hue of a tomato? No. I do not want him in my room."

"Doctor do not let him enter," the woman called out as the two men stood face to face near the door. They bumped each other with their chests. Both men refused to move. She walked quickly toward them, faster than a lady should, but she must have deemed the situation dire. "Liz refuses to see Jeff."

"I don't remember telling you, you could address me by my first name. I am Mr. Ledger." He pushed his way into the room and the doctor darted around to block his path, so he couldn't get closer.

Her heart beat faster but she could not continue acting cowardly.

"Get out of this room Mister Jeff Ledger. You are not needed nor are you wanted. I have Mistress Tina Davis to look out for me. Doctor Demfry believes I need peace and quiet. You are not peaceful nor quiet."

She experienced a moment of appalled disbelief when Tina stuck her tongue out at Mister Ledger and blew in an age-old gesture used by recalcitrant children. Another part of her, the part trying hard to be a Lady, found the action comical and she could not contain her mirth. Once she started laughing, she could not stop.

The doctor quickly ushered the stunned Mr. Ledger from the room as her champion yelled at his back. "She gets hysterical with you around, you big jerk."

She continued to laugh. "Thank you. You definitely helped me with my problem. I thought for sure I would have to go with him."

"Over my dead body! I'll make sure he stays away. In fact, the lawyer stopped by while you slept and asked me if you wanted to file a restraining order."

"I know not what you say."

The woman put her hands on her hips and glared. "You clearly believe you're from the last century. This is twenty twelve and woman in our time don't allow men to batter and bully them."

"I'm in twenty twelve?"

"Yes. We no longer wear corsets, women earn their own money, and have the right to vote!"

"We do? Oh my." Overwhelmed at the responsibility, she sighed loudly, clasped her fingers together in her lap and paused a moment to think. Her brain had all this other knowledge but voting? Why would a Lady even want to vote? Then a memory surfaced of her in a booth pulling a lever.

The doctor entered the room. "I'm going to discharge you. The tests show you have a slight concussion. I'd like to keep you here for another day, but the insurance company won't pay. Doctor Stoneherst said you have reasonable memory lapses because you televise a show from the eighteen hundreds. You've also suffered a head trauma. I need you to answer one question. Did Jeff Ledger hit you?"

185

"I do not know if Mister Jeff Ledger hit me," she said truthfully. She tried to figure out the rest of his words. He spoke quickly, and she could not grasp all the verbiage. Her brain had to translate so she understood. And her mind translated when she concentrated. The language appeared to be the same yet different. And, the memories in her head belonged to…well, she did not want to think too deeply. Some of those memories did not become a Lady.

Her companion interrupted her rumination. "Stop with the Mister and Mistress. Your manners are hard on my nerves."

"What shall I call you?" She was befuddled. Confused. Yes, confused would be the right word to use here in Purgatory.

"You need to call me Tina. I swear I will not answer to Mistress Tina Davis."

A lanky man walked into the room and threw a large bag at Tina which fell on the floor. Articles of clothing spilled from the bag. "I'm tired of everyone else being first. Here's your junk. I've sublet the apartment and I'm ready to head out of town. You can come, or you can stay and take care of Miss High and Mighty." He pointed at her.

Why would he point at me?

She spewed before she could think. "Why you lily-livered, no good lout. We are in a pickle and you come to make demands of our good-hearted Mistress…of Tina. She is fair and good and has a faithful heart."

"Yeah, she has your best interest at heart. As for me, I'm outta here." The man stomped from the room.

She wanted to say more but caught her tongue. The body she lived in talked first and thought afterwards.

The impulse to be rude had been an instantaneous reaction, so unlike herself. She generally thought about what she would say before she mouthed a word. In fact, she never stated her opinion. Once in a while her Irish would come out and she paid consequences. Like now! Tina sat slumped in a chair they called plastic as tears ran down her cheeks.

She climbed over the bar used to keep her in bed and did not care if Doctor Demfry gaped at her unladylike gesture. She knelt beside her friend and patted her on the back. "You and I are in this situation together."

"Yeah? Well, I don't have a place to sleep tonight."

"You can stay with me." The words were out of her mouth before she knew her own intentions. "I do not know where I maintain my accommodations, but I believe I have some form of..." her voice trailed off.

Tina said in an incredulous voice, "You live in a frigging mansion."

"Then you are invited to my frigging mansion to stay with me. Who else resides in the frigging mansion?"

Doctor Demfry chuckled.

"I am sorry this is so comical to you, Doctor Demfry, but I cannot remember who lives in the frigging mansion."

"You can call your home a mansion. Not a frigging mansion." He continued to smile as he took her hand and helped her up from her friend's side. "You have a maid and a gardener and about seven bedrooms. You even have a guest house."

"Have you seen this mansion?"

"Yes. You give a staff party every Christmas."

She clapped her hands. "I am so glad we still have Christmas." Yes, this had to be Purgatory. In Heaven, celebrations would go on daily with Jesus and the angels. This place had many luxurious items, but people didn't get along here. The man-boy had been furious with Tina. Jealous. And everyone knew jealousy was one of the deadly sins.

Her mother mentioned Purgatory could be viewed as a place to pay for the lessons one did not learn when alive. The man-boy needed to learn Tina's value. Her mother also said everyone lived in mansions. She lived in a mansion. Vowed to be good so she could get into Heaven when the time came.

"You don't have to take me home with you," Tina interrupted.

"Oh yes I do. I must have a chaperon. You shall be my chaperon."

Doctor Demfry and Tina exchanged a strange glance, but she pretended not to notice. "I am here in the year of Purgatory which is in twenty twelve. I will uphold the values taught to me by my mother as a wee child. You shall be my chaperon and teach me what I need to know. Why, you are much better than Lady Coldwell and much more congenial."

"Thank you, I think."

Doctor Demfry put his hand on Tina's back. "Are you going to be all right? I assume that man is now your ex-boyfriend?"

"He's in the past. Definitely an ex! Can you believe he dumped me because I stayed with Liz overnight? The A-hole is a pathetic excuse for a man."

She picked up her friend's hand and held both of them closely. "I would say those soothing words you said to me yesterday, but I forgot exactly what you said."

"I'll teach you how to meditate."

"I should love to learn how to meditate. What is meditate?"

The doctor interrupted them. "I hate to be the bearer of bad news, but a slew of reporters have camped outside the hospital since your arrival. The Director is on his way here and wants you dressed and ready to run out the back entrance."

"A Lady never runs."

He grinned, and her chest did a pit-a-pat and a lurch. "The paparazzi will make a Lady such as yourself run."

"What is paparazzi?"

"Vultures. They want to pick your bones clean. Here," Tina told her, "you can wear some of my clothes."

She held up a teeny scrap of material. "How do I put this on?"

"Geeze. Do I have to show you?"

She nodded, hoped she would learn quickly so she did not have to treat her as a Lady's maid.

Tina sighed. A long, loud sigh. Squared her shoulders, looked as if she had made some type of decision. "I promise to stay with you until you get your bearings back."

"Were my bearings stolen?"

Tina giggled as she motioned her toward the bathroom to help her get dressed. She balked at numerous outfits until they settled upon a pair of leggings, jeans, and a long-sleeved top.

She didn't want to be critical, but she had to tell

her chaperon, "You dress immodest."

"In this time and place, we show our gifts from God."

"Gifts from God?"

"I'll have the chauffer drive by the beach on our way to your home. You need to see how this century looks and behaves. Then you might snap back." She pointed at her head.

"I do not want to snap back up here. I only want to go forward." Purgatory did not seem so bad, yet she did not want to destroy her chances to enter heaven. Magic lights switched on and off at her touch, people lived inside televisions, the water tasted drinkable, and toilets flushed. What would Heaven look like?

Once she had listened to a preacher in the streets crying, "Hell on earth." Mayhap earth could be a bit Hell like with sewage in the streets and women like Lady Coldwell. But now she resided in Purgatory. Soon she would be in Heaven. She put on her new clothing without another sound. Decided to listen to her chaperon and learn how one should act.

They exited the hospital and were instantly surrounded by men with large machines. The machines were pointed at them. "Are those weapons?" she asked a man who stepped between her and her chaperon.

"What do you know?" the man asked her.

"I know not what those machines are. Please explain."

Tina managed to grab her hand, pull her forward. The sound of whirls, clicks, and other odd noises made her skittish. She decided to smile. Her mother told her nothing could harm you when you smiled and acted pleasantly. *I'll pretend I'm the Queen.* Elizabeth straightened her back, smiled politely, nodded and sauntered sedately toward the long, shiny black conveyance.

They waded through the crowd of demons. Lucky for her, none of them touched her skin. Tina shielded her with an overlarge bag used like a weapon, hissing and shooing as they plodded through the screeching fiends. A door opened once they neared their destination.

"What type of carriage is this?" she asked as she got shoved into the contraption.

The man in the seat facing her looked at her chaperon. "She still believes she's in eighteen twelve?"

"No, M' Lord. I realize I am in twenty twelve," She tried to figure out how to seat herself in a modest position. "Mistress Tina...I mean Tina will be my chaperon and she will teach me about this time period. I understand I have passed the tests given to me in the hospital. I plan to cooperate."

The man thrust a bunch of bound papers at her and barked, "Do you think you will be able to memorize your script?"

She lovingly ran her hand over the thin sheets of paper with words printed on each page. "I can do anything with the help of my faithful companion."

"Okay Miss Side Kick. You are now responsible. Help her memorize the script. We'll pay you double your current rate. Liz needs to be on set tomorrow at six a.m."

"Doctor Demfry said she shouldn't go back to work until he released her. Today, he released her to go home. Not to work."

"When is the damn Doctor going to examine her

again?"

She gasped. The man across from her condemned the good Doctor.

"He said he'd make a house call tonight."

"Make sure he releases her," the man snapped as the conveyance stopped. He peered at her with a funny, steely gaze until the driver opened his door. He got out without another word.

Tina waited until the man left, then opened a little box in the back, took out two small bottles and quickly drank them in big gulps. She looked away to preserve her chaperon's dignity when she smelled the medicinal brew. Next Tina started to push knob-like protrusions. One opened the glass between them and the man with a cap who she thought to be the driver. The other knob opened the top of the roof. Rays of glorious sun shine beat down upon them.

"Let's stand and I'll show you your new world."

She had never felt further from acting a lady than she did right now. Even so, she stood on the seat and glanced at her surroundings. The atmosphere smelled different. Streets were burdened with vehicles called trucks, motorcycles, and cars. Her new friend and faithful chaperon pointed out all the oddities when she asked questions. And she had many questions. Dandies now covered their bodies with tattoos instead of watch fobs. So many colorful sights. Carriages were passé and nary a horse did she see. Demons were called Paparazzi and they followed her every move. She smiled and waved.

This would be her last chance to stop petty behaviors and gain entrance into Heaven.

Chapter Six

Dr. Demfry abruptly stopped his rusted-out vehicle in front of the mansion gates. A throng of Paparazzi blocked the entrance to Miss Barrett's home. He got out of the car and pushed his way over to the call box. Had to elbow journalists as he went, refused to answer their meddlesome questions.

Buzz. Buzz. Buzz. He did not get a response.

A tall, muscular blond man dressed in jeans and a cotton button down shirt told him, "They turned the buzzer off. Too many reporters wanted interviews."

"That includes you?" He realized he sounded surly, but he didn't care. As any good doctor would, he needed to check on Miss Barrett. Wanted to make sure all the commotion hadn't caused her more confusion.

"Nah, man. You're her doctor."

He didn't feel the need to respond.

The big guy stuck out his hand to shake. "I'm her brother."

His up-raised eyebrow and the fact he backed away had the man say, "I'm her brother even though we don't look alike."

"No. You don't." He quickly walked back to his car and hit the button to unlock his doors. The big guy slid into the passenger seat and a reporter opened the back door of the teeny car and wedged himself in. He slammed his door, hit the lock button before another person could get into his compact car.

"Hey, Doc. Why do you drive a piece of shit like this?" The reporter demanded as the camera came up over the back seat and pointed at his face.

He calmly pulled his cell phone from his pocket and dialed nine-one-one. When the operator answered he said, "I'm at two hundred eight Canyon Road and I need assistance. A deranged man is in my back seat and another fellow entered my vehicle without my permission. I believe they want to take me hostage."

"We have officers on the way. Please stay on the line while I…"

He disconnected. "Get out," he told the two stowaways.

The man in the back seat scrambled from the car as soon as the doors unlocked. The big fellow looked at him placidly, hit the door lock and said, "I hope you have my sister's newest cell number. She seems to change phones every few months."

"You need to be out of here before the police arrive."

"I need to make sure Liz is okay. Father sent me. She's all over the news. Does she believe she's from another century?"

"I will have you arrested." He used his no-nonsense tone.

The man pulled pictures from his shirt pocket. The snapshot showed a much younger Liz who stood next to the man in his vehicle. The next photo showed them together on a swing set. His arms were out like he had pushed. Her face radiant.

"My sister doesn't remember me yet. Someone named Tina screens all the guests. She cut off the buzzer because so many reporters and tabloid magazines make claims."

"Tina thought you lied?"

"I didn't speak to her. I told the crowd," he pointed to the seven or eight people milling around in front of the property, "I'm with *The Sun*."

"What type of publication is *The Sun*?"

"The sun happens to be a large fiery orb circling the earth." The big man laughed, and he realized this man had a similar sense of humor. The type of humor Liz had before she bumped her head. Then again, he didn't personally know the actress. She seemed like a beautiful, hard-working woman with a ladder to climb. Way too ambitious for the likes of him.

He had been insulted when she demanded he call her Miss Elizabeth Barrett. Recognized the fear in her eyes and suddenly realized she seemed out of touch with reality. They had a solid work friendship which her manager, Jeff, tried to squelch. Everyone on the set would be relieved with the SOB out of the way. Miss Barrett would be better off without him.

He gazed at the guy with the pictures who wanted to get into the mansion. And for some strange reason, he felt the need to protect the actress.

He had experienced a moment of connection when she laid on the floor in her dressing room. He amended his thought. He had lusted after her injured body. Pure, unadulterated sexual attraction. Warmth wash through him when her luminous emerald eyes peered up at him, beseeching and helpless. Then she called him a scamp. Her words snapped him back to reality. He shook his head and realized he had *always* had a slight crush on her. The way men do around beautiful, successful women. So how had he become enamored by the innocent version of the actress?

"I have no way to verify you're her brother. I'd like to help you but, in this situation, we will wait until the police show up." The words came out harsher than he intended. He had to remember Miss Barrett was his patient, not some nubile young lady who needed to be saved.

"I understand. I have my driver's license from our home town, and we have the same last name." He turned slightly in his seat so he could get the wallet from his back pocket. Produced a license from El Paso, Texas. The name read Brian Barrett.

"This doesn't confirm your relationship. I'm her doctor, not her personal confidant and Barrett might be her stage name."

"I waited for Jeff to show up. He might not let me in the front gate because I intend to knock out a few of his capped teeth." His fist clenched. "The reports speculate on their relationship. Did he hit her?"

The police cruiser pulled up and he got out of his car to talk with the officers. So did Brian Barrett. After a short conversation, the reporters were told to move away from the gate. He decided to give Brian a ride up the steep drive after the studio confirmed their relationship. "I have my eyes on you. The cops will be back after they circle the block. If you are not who you say you are, I'll make sure you're arrested."

"I'm glad my sister has someone like you on her side. Jeff," his voice trailed off as he bit his lip. Asked in a quiet voice, "Will she be okay? I've never known Liz to be unsure of herself. The reporter who jumped in the back of your jalopy told me she seemed camera shy.

Impossible in her industry. He also stated she asked him a weird question. Said my sister sounds crazy."

"My lips are sealed until I know who you are." He would not tell this man her story until he checked their relationship. How he'd be sure without his patient acknowledging him seem insurmountable. Maybe the studio had his picture on file.

They parked near the double front door and knocked. Tina answered, her impish grin inviting until she looked at Brian. "Who's the big boy?"

Brian thrust the pictures in her hand, along with his driver's license. "I'm her brother. Father told me to get my ass to California and check on Lizzy." He pushed past the open mouthed hairdresser and started calling out. "Liz. Lizzy. It's Brian. Where are you Liz?"

The doctor noticed movement at the top of the stairs. His mouth went dry as the sunlight from the skylights made Liz appear like an apparition from heaven. At first glance, he thought she resembled an angel. Light streamed through her diaphanous nightdress, leaving an imprint of a perfect figure. Sensuous instead of angelic.

"Good God sis. Put some clothes on." Brian rushed up the stairs and Tina ran after him as she waved the unseen pictures at his back.

He realized he probably had a sappy grin on his face, but he couldn't help his expression. She had covered up only…she looked more provocative than if she wore daisy dukes.

Tina hissed, "I told you your outfit looks indecent. Put those shorts and T-shirt I gave you back on."

He tried not to stare but couldn't control his base emotions. The woman had an expression of total ignorance on her beautiful face. He could tell she didn't understand because of her slack-jawed chin. Innocence never looked so seductive. Her long red hair streamed around her face and down her back. He wanted to bolt up the stairs. Touch her. Smell her. Be with her.

The long pale peach robe matched her skin tone. He could see teeny feet peeking from beneath the robe and one slender hand went to her mouth as she nibbled on her fake fingernail. How he wanted to be her fingernail. Couldn't help but notice the outline of her body. She had a pear shape, long legs, and looked busty. Her nipples were covered. Barely. Would they be dusty rose, pale peach, or brown?

His pants tented without his permission and he wanted to turn away. Like a car wreck, he continued to stare. Knew better than to gawk but some part of him felt compelled. She exuded sensual innocence which didn't make sense. She's an actress for God's sake. One who had been around a casting couch.

Her brother stood on a lower step and yelled at her.

Tina screamed at Brian and suddenly the sound of a hand hitting flesh created complete silence. Tension vibrated in the air.

Tina had slapped Brian in the face.

The hairdresser hopped up to the top stair and stared Brian in the eyes, her hands flapped at her sides, like a windup toy. Without thought, he bolted up the stairs, two at a time and managed to get between the two of them.

"Let's all calm ourselves," he said in his bedside voice. He took the balled-up pictures and driver's license from Tina's clenched grip and held them out to Brian.

"She hit me." Brian held a large hand to his cheek as he gaped at Tina. "You hit me."

"Yes, I did. You tried to put your hands on my," she looked at Liz. "You can't touch her. I'm her chaperon."

Brian stared. Then glared. Then guffawed. "Chaperon? She hasn't needed one of those since she turned two."

Tina sniffed. "I'm her chaperon and I say no one gets to see her dressed like this."

"What is wrong with the way I am dressed? This is the only item in my closet that covers my ankles." They all looked at her bare feet and he heard himself groan.

Her brother stopped looking amused and snatched the photos and driver's license out of the doctor's hand, placed them in his shirt pocket.

Then he turned to Liz. "You told me if you came to Hollywood you would not embarrass father with nude pictures. Your outfit leaves little to the imagination. More than a brother wants to see. Every man in creation will lust after you."

"I have a brother?" She looked at him as if he would be able to confirm Brian's identity.

He had to clear his voice before he could speak. "Let Tina take you in to change your clothes. Then we can talk."

Tina glared at both men, grabbed Elizabeth by the arm and snapped out an order. "Come on, missy. We need to get you dressed so your so-called brother stops his ape shit crazy act."

"He looked more like a mad dog than an ape when he charged up the stairs. Did I ever tell you about Lady Jensen? She had an apple on her hat and Lady

Trenton's monkey came and snatched the piece of fruit off her head." The two men didn't hear the rest of the story because Tina slammed the bedroom door behind them.

Brian turned to the doctor, "She's nuts, isn't she?"

He couldn't respond. "She didn't recognize you, so I have to ask you to leave."

"I'm not leaving." The man pulled his cell phone out of his hip pocket and punched in a code. "Dad. You have to come to California. Something is dreadfully wrong with Liz." The doctor could not hear what the other person on the phone replied. "The situation is bad. Your daughter is half naked." This time the response wasn't coherent, but Brian held the phone away from his ear as his cheeks reddened.

"I know you have a sermon to give but my sister is confused, and you need to let bygones be bygones. You always preach forgiveness so start forgiving your daughter because she became an actress." Loud comments came from the cell before Brian hung up. "Dad will call back when he makes flight arrangements. I plan to stay in the blue room. The room I always use when I visit." The large man exited the stairs and stalked down the hallway to the right, went into one of the doors and started to bellow. "Whose stuff is on my bed?"

Tina appeared in the hall. "Get out of my room, you nosey, no-good scum bag." She ran past him, almost pushed him off the last stair, charged down the hall as Brian poked his head out of the door. For the first time in a long time, he didn't know what to do.

Miss Barrett bolted out of her room wearing shorts and a T-shirt. Her shapely legs disappeared into the

room where he heard Tina and Brian arguing.
He decided to follow so no one got injured.

Chapter Seven

Doctor Demfry looked toward the mansion as he unloaded the last bag from his car. How had Tina convinced him to live in Ms. Barrett's guesthouse with Brian? The studio had a noose around his neck. One they slowly tightened. Tina happened to be the newest agency member to apply pressure.

Student loans had him in a financial predicament. Made him take the part time gig for the studio while he set up his clinic. Yet, his finances did not generally stop him from saying no when someone became unreasonable.

Brian and Tina's snipe-fest made him rethink the word reasonable. He couldn't leave the two of them alone together. Feared their argumentative behavior toward one another hurt Elizabeth's ability to heal. Nobody felt comfortable because the two young adults acted like children. Slung words like arrows at each other.

Brian met him at the door. "My father's flight will be here tomorrow. I hope Liz takes one look at dad and returns to her normal, feisty self. Did you hear her when she said, 'I'll let this body think about you?'"

He shuffled away from the entrance and picked up two bags left on the door stoop and hauled them into the doctor's assigned bedroom. Dropped them on the floor with a thud. "She made cockamamie comments like, 'my body recognizes you as my brother even if I don't know you.' What the hell does that mean?"

He was as confused as Brian, but he didn't intend to show his feelings. The studio verified his relationship with her. They also wanted an up-to-date report on unusual behavior. He wasn't prepared to be the one to put the first nail in her coffin. Wondered if Ms. Barrett had dissociative identity disorder. They were sending someone over tomorrow who would do an initial psych evaluation.

The actress appeared to have two distinct but different personalities. The woman called Elizabeth seemed timid and thoughtful. Not that Liz couldn't be thoughtful—she could when her own ambition didn't get in the way. She *had* fought for the rights of the writers and he had admired her for her tenacity. The current inhabitant wouldn't fight for any cause unless the cause related to her virtue.

"What's with the frown?" Brian's arms crossed his chest.

He pushed past the man's bulk when he didn't move out of the way. "I notice differences in personality between Liz and Elizabeth. She refuses to be called Liz."

"Yeah, what's up with that?"

"I'm not sure." He picked up the pants he had laid across the king size bed earlier and strolled toward the walk-in closet. This guest bedroom had more room than the entire apartment he vacated. He realized he gave up the lease quickly. Living over a meat market wasn't the impression he wanted to give clients. While he hung up his clothes, he thought about his work at the studio and how he balanced the job with his clinic.

Brian stood at the closet door, eyes upon his every movement.

He contemplated his words. "Tina asked us to have dinner by the pool. Can you manage to sit and talk without starting World War Three."

"That Tina." he laughed, placed his hands on his hips dramatically as a grin spread across his broad face. "She's the bossiest person I've ever met."

"You purposely rile her."

"If I weren't a preacher's son, I'd probably date someone like her."

He didn't understand. "You're not making sense. She wears the punk look, but who under thirty doesn't in this day and age other than you and me."

"You have a point. I don't see any tattoos on you. No piercings or baggy pants. I wouldn't be caught dead in baggy pants."

"But what does your choice of clothing have to do with being a preacher's son? We all choose what we wear."

Brian started rapping about choices and they laughed together. He pointed toward the door. "Let's head over to the patio. I can finish unpacking later." They walked on a manicured path leading to the pool area. The doctor liked the sense of peace the landscape provided. "This is a magnificent estate. Did your sister purchase the property as an investment?"

"Liz handles all her own finances. She's great with numbers and told me she would be an accountant if the Irish rebel in her hadn't insisted she become an actress. This happens to be her first investment. I helped her scout locations and we got a great deal from an aging, drug addict who needed money. I advised her not to allow Jeff Ledger to live here since he didn't have any money of his own to invest. The guy went through cash like most men go through disposable razor blades. And...he acted like a pompous ass. I can't figure out why she dated him. Maybe she thought she could manage him."

"Tell me more about her relationship with your father."

Brian laughed out loud. "You sound more like a psychiatrist than a medical doctor. Their relationship is complicated. Our mother was a card-carrying conservative. Ran the church with an iron fist all the way up until she ran off with the assistant pastor. Lizzy looks like mother. Consequently, my hard-headed father has never been her biggest fan. Saddled her with responsibility and kept a tight rein on her as if she were a horse. They fell out when she told him she planned to move to California. Haven't talked in years."

"That might explain some of her behavior."

"How so?"

He opened the gate. The gardens, and the poolside area butted up to an outdoor kitchen. He spotted his client and Tina. They sat at a wrought iron table and chatted like best friends.

"We can discuss your sister later. Now we need to be polite and make small talk. I want Elizabeth to feel comfortable. No arguments with Tina. You might want to tell some humorous stories about your childhood and this hard-headed father, so your sister can be prepared when she meets him."

Brian nodded affirmatively then walked up to Tina and said, "Why the blue streak? Did you want to be a Smurf when you grew up?"

He groaned. This would be a long evening.

***

Elizabeth laughed at her brother's joke. As she looked down at her bare legs, she disliked how she felt. Purposely sat at the wrought iron table instead of lying on a lounger like her chaperon, so her appendages weren't so noticeable.

The doctor sat next to her. He wore pants called shorts and his strong, muscular legs were covered with golden hairs, as were his shapely arms. He appeared to her like a large, huggable toy she wanted to squeeze. Immediately her face turned hot with shame.

He noticed her blush when she looked at his legs. Decided to ask her clinical questions so she would feel at ease. "Do you mind answering a few questions?"

Her body tightened and she wondered at her strange reaction to his simple request. Before she could stop herself, she replied. "Depends on the question." Her tone sounded deliberate and held a taunt note, so she rushed to say. "I'm sorry to act churlish, Doctor Demfry. I know I come across as obnoxious, which is not my natural inclination, but this body I inhabit has a quicker wit than me."

"I wanted to talk to you about the other personality. When did you notice someone else resided inside you?"

She laughed. "You know perfectly well I lived inside of my own body from the day I was born until I came to this time and place. I've ruminated about my experience. Realize I waved a betrothal brooch in the air when…" As she shook her head, she tried to remember exactly what happened but couldn't. "The incident happened so fast."

"You were betrothed?"

"Someone asked for my hand in marriage and my guardian believed the arrangement a good idea. The man held a title and I was an up-start American. The offer seemed better than I hoped to receive after Papa's death. Why do you look so confounded? Have you made an offer for someone to be your goodly wife?" She realized an unfettered man would find the question unseemly. Even if he had an eye for one of the ladies, her interest was too personal and improper.

"I finished my internship eighteen months ago. Haven't had time to think about a wife because I've been busy building my practice."

"You have much to offer a woman, Doctor." She wanted to slap herself for being so forward. Her cheeks heated, and the kind doctor looked away, which gave her a reprieve.

"This other voice you hear in your head. Is the voice inside your head or is it your voice?"

"I know not how my mind works. Let me sit here and gather my thoughts before I respond." She noticed he stared, and her cheeks burned with embarrassment. Purgatory and Earth were similar. Challenges as to how one should or could behave were complicated. Right now, she could be drawn into temptation by him. Did someone evil want her to engage so she would fail? Require her to stay here in Purgatory longer? She understood the good doctor happened to be one of her assessors. If he realized how she responded to his presence, she would never get into heaven.

"I felt strongly about the way Lady Coldwell treated her daughter. I do believe I railed against her, yet I can assure you I did not mean her any harm. It started with a loud crash of thunder and I felt myself fall upwards. Viewed glimpses of lights and sounds and a wondrous scent which cannot be described. An angel touched my cheek. A few minutes later, I'm in the ante chamber of Purgatory. You took me for my entrance examination. I am so glad I passed. I didn't relish the thought of going to hell."

"You believe you're in Purgatory?" His voice sounded high pitched.

She witnessed the pupils of his eyes become bigger as his face scrunched up with concern. "I am in twenty twelve. The year of Purgatory. Like B.C. means before Christ. Didn't know Purgatory had a time frame until I arrived. This is the same body with some differences. The new, improved version of me. My teeth are white. And look how straight they are?" She opened her mouth and swished her tongue around so he could see her teeth.

He flinched.

"I'm sorry, Doctor. I thought I could show you because you are an examiner. Did I act overly bold?"

He shook his head, continued to stare at her. Made a hand gesture as if to say go on. She decided to continue with her story. "I've looked in the staring glass and I am the same but different. But I have already told you. I found out I can swim, and I like to exercise. Who would have thought a lady would like to perspire, but Tina tells me I have to keep in shape. She had me work out to a...video. My body could trace the movements. Seems like a part of me knows what to do if I stop my thoughts and let myself be free. I can even access memories."

The Doctor's face blcached like a whale's underbelly.

"Are you okay? You don't look up to snuff."

"Dr. Stoneherst arrives tomorrow for a thorough examination. You met her at the hospital. She plans to ask you questions and I want you to answer her truthfully."

"Oh, I cannot lie. You will put me under the scanner again and discover the truth faster than I can snap my fingers." Then she had a strange notion flit through her head. "Doctor, I'm confused. How come I had a mother and father in eighteen twelve and no siblings but here I have a brother? I do not understand. I believe I traded places with someone who is me but not me."

"You don't recognize Brian as your brother?"

"No. He's my brother. I have memories of him tugging my pony tail…" she didn't know how to voice what she understood. The memories in her head belonged to someone called Liz.

A loud cry and a splash had her turn around in time to witness Tina's head surface. She sputtered water and screeched, "I can't swim." Her head went under again. She floundered in the deep end of the pool right where Brian dumped her.

Her head bobbed up, then went down.

Brian waved his arms and jumped in as he shouted, "I'll save you."

Tina somehow maneuvered so she held his head under water. Then she swam toward the edge of the pool where Dr. Demfry and Elizabeth sat, but not before Brian grabbed her foot. Tina paddled and paddled but didn't go anywhere.

"My brother likes her." She didn't know how or why she knew but she recognized her brother was captivated by her chaperon.

"Do you think I should rescue her, or rescue him?" He asked, a smile on his lips.

"Let them figure out what to do. I believe we should finish our conversation."

Chapter Eight

Doctor Demfry drove Brian to the airport in Miss Barrett's plush Mercedes. The young man appeared nervous. He couldn't seem to get comfortable in his seat and constantly changed the playlist.

"I need help when I explain Liz's situation to Dad." Brian switched off the streamed music.

"Maybe Dr. Stoneherst can help. We did leave your sister behind for an initial evaluation."

"Yeah. And did you see how bossy Tina acted. She demanded Maria make the menu exactly the way she said." The big boy huffed.

He experienced a sense of relief. Tina ate healthy and insisted the menu reflect a balanced meal plan. No more bags of flaming hot cheese puffs for dinner. He did not plan to tell Brian his sister suffered a stomach ache because of him. "The maid needed direction and your sister doesn't know enough to direct her."

"Pull into the pick-up lane ahead," Brian shouted and pointed. He wasn't surprised when they pulled up and found a man dressed in black with a sour expression on his face. The preacher carried one small bag. Did he only plan to stay overnight?

Brian greeted his dad with a nod and opened the back door, so he could get in. The preacher climbed into the backseat and so did his son. When had he become the chauffeur?

The older man barely nodded a hello to Weston before he started to speak. "Is your sister prepared to stop this acting nonsense? Has she told you she wants the Lord's forgiveness for making an old man worry? Has she figured out evil begets evil?"

Brian fiddled in his seat and did not interrupt the long, frenzied tirade. Finally, the man took a breath and Brian said, "Father. The situation is serious. Lizzy has a concussion. She's acting strange." His voice trailed off.

"Quit blubbering and talk." The preacher slapped the back of Brian's head.

His blood boiled. He had to bite his tongue to keep from mouthing words he would regret.

"Liz believes she is another person called Elizabeth and she swears she's from the year eighteen twelve." Brian explained.

The man in the back did not respond with another tongue-lashing. He pulled a bible from his carry on, started to pray. A loud, lengthy prayer. The hour-long devotion ended as they pulled up to the mansion.

"So, she lives in a house bigger than my church. I shouldn't be surprised. She always wanted the best. Like her mother. Flowers on the altar. Cushions on the kneelers." He threw his hands in the air. "Sinners need to feel the pain they cause the Lord. I do believe she is tainted with generational sin from her mother's side of the family."

Brian's face turned white. "She put a roof on your church and gives you money to live on. More than I can say for your parishioners."

"This is her penance and cross to bear. I feed homeless people and," his chest puffed out, "I put the fear of God into my congregation."

212

He agreed. Most people would be afraid to approach this man's collection plate. No one wanted to get hit over the head with a bible. He called Tina on his cell phone. "We're outside. I have a door opener but I'm afraid the Paparazzi will stampede the gate."

The preacher bellowed, "I'll take care of these Godless men." He got out of the car and started to preach. Sounded more like a rant. Held the bible over his head, waved the book like a weapon. The doctor realized he could hear his voice ricochet the entire length of Canyon Drive. Canyon Drive happened to be a long street.

"Don't look a gift horse in the mouth," Brian said as the reporters scattered. They drove through the opened gate.

"Your father made those lookie-loos back up." Checking the rear-view mirror, he discovered the preacher swatting at a camera. Liz' reputation would suffer.

"You can't argue when Father's on a roll. He's gotten worse over the years."

"Are you sure he's sane? I detected spittle flying around the back seat." He looked in the rear-view mirror and saw the man point and screech. He touched the remote and the wrought iron gate started to close behind them. The thin, aged preacher slipped through the crack, still shouting bible verses as he tried to convert the men who snapped pictures and took videos. "I wonder if this will end up as a YouTube sensation tomorrow."

Brian laughed. "Deranged father visits deranged movie star."

"Is that what *The Sun* would say?"

"*The Sun* would say embittered man spews hatred on unsuspecting population who deserve no better than they get."

"How do you really feel?"

"I hoped father would show some concern about his only daughter. Instead, he's on a tirade. Could be exactly what Lizzy needs to remember who she is. Father will preach at her. Generally, she laughs in his face. Once, he locked her in her room and gave her bread and water for a week. She snuck out the window each evening and went next door. Mrs. Wimple fed her. Said the two of us needed a mother."

The car door opened, and the preacher took a seat in the back. He gulped in large amounts of air as they drove up the shrub lined drive.

He couldn't help himself. Looked over the back seat and told the older man. "Takes a lot of energy to get people to hear what you have to say."

The man finally noticed him. "I do believe we have a man of God among us. Take note Brian. This is the type of person who will enter Heaven."

He hoped the man didn't see him roll his eyes as they continued to move toward the house. The preacher leaped from the car before they came to a stop and stood, gaping at the large Spanish style home.

The monstrosity looked beautiful. Terra-cotta colored stucco walls and brilliant red roof tiles. Blue shutters lined every window as did flowerboxes showing colorful blooms. The green creepers had delicate yellow flowers he could not identify. Those creepers climbed the foundation, clamored toward the second story. The over-large double doors were made of wood with iron hinges and had knockers in the shape of arms with hands.

He looked at the rolling green lawns spread out as far as the eye could see. Trees were planted strategically, and the drive circled a fountain in front of the house which allowed cars to park. The foot path to the left went to the detached three car garage, as did the driveway. The guesthouse stood off further back, behind the garage. He didn't want to drive far and have to run back so he parked near the flowerbed closest to the entrance.

Brian didn't knock but opened the front door and walked in. His father caught up with his son. The Spanish tile and cool, refrigerated air made him realize he had started to sweat once her father's monologue in the car began. The stairs, where Brian and Tina had their little spat, rose majestically in front of them, hallways and rooms off to the right and left side.

"Anybody home?" Brian yelled as his father stood, slack jawed.

He pointed to an intercom system near the front door. "The gadget is here for a reason."

"I know but Tina gets pissed when I yell." Brian grinned.

His father's face twisted into a deep frown accentuating the downward slash of his mouth. "Watch your language, son. I do not want to be up all night praying for your soul. I have enough on my plate with your sister's decadent lifestyle."

The click-clack of sandals on tile and laughter apprised them of Tina, Elizabeth, and Dr. Stoneherst's appearance. Tina rounded the corner and beckoned to them, "Come into the sun room and have lunch. I had Maria prepare salads, sandwiches and iced tea." Then she looked at Brian and said with a straight face. "I know you like to drink. Should I bring in a bottle of fine wine or hard liquor? What's your preference today?"

Brian blanched, eyed his father who stood rigid as he stared at his daughter. No one changed position or spoke. Mr. Barrett finally held out his arms and told his daughter, "I am sorry we aren't on speaking terms. Please come and pray with me."

She rushed into his open arms. "Mr. Barrett. I am so sorry you and your daughter don't get along. As long as I'm in her body, I'll try to be polite and," her voice cracked, "respectful."

The preacher's harsh features softened. "I'm surprised you didn't laugh at me and tell me to go stuff the collection box with money. That used to be your favorite expression." The older man tentatively held his daughter in what looked like an uncomfortable embrace.

"Father, I have to confess I did want to laugh but only because Tina teased Brian about what he drinks. Those two have taken an instant dislike to each other. How queer." She backed out of his arms and placed her hand in his, tugged him forward down the hall. "Come. We'll have lunch and then I can show you around. This house is crazy big."

Brian mouthed, "Crazy big," at Tina who shrugged.

He smiled. Elizabeth picked up odd phrases. She cussed last night, and he had to tell her the word she used was vulgar. Enjoyed watching her color to a tantalizing hue.

Her father put his hand out to stop his daughter

before she sat. "You look well, my dear child," he stepped back and scanned her from top to bottom.

He, too, scrutinized her chosen outfit. She wore a simple white cotton dress. One he assumed cost a fortune. The garment had delicate sleeves with superfine stitches made into a rose pattern. Her dainty gold chain held a pink rose pendant, as did the earrings and golden bracelet. The outfit came to mid-calf. You could see strappy summer shoes encasing delicate feet. His heart stopped when he noticed her toes were the same exact color pink as her pendant. Even his mouth went dry.

Her father accepted what she wore because he did not comment. He asked her in a soft voice, "What is this about you inhabiting Liz's body? You are Liz."

"I'm Elizabeth. I'm from eighteen twelve and I've finished my psychiatric evaluation with Dr. Stoneherst. She plans to tell us what she suspects but I'll give you a hint." Her green eyes sparkled with humor. "I'm a time traveler. Isn't that delicious? I can't wait to let the Paparazzi know. They will be relieved, and this will explain my knowledge of another time."

The preacher opened and shut his mouth but for once, he did not say a word.

Dr. Stoneherst interrupted. "Let's go have lunch and then Elizabeth can give her father a tour. I believe she put him in the green room. I'll have my secretary bring over a change of clothes and I'll stay in the pink room. Such a fun, childish décor but totally feminine and, as she mentioned earlier, delicious."

Elizabeth guided her father into the sun room and helped him into a comfortable, overstuffed wicker chair. Served him before the others had a chance to settle in.

"Can we pray together later, sir? I want to thank God for bringing me to the year two thousand and twelve. I'm glad I still have a chance to redeem myself and get into Heaven. Can you believe I thought I lived in Purgatory?"

The preacher choked on his iced tea. "Purgatory?"

"Yes. Silly me. Dr. Stoneherst explained what happened. I waved this ancient brooch around. Someone borrowed the piece from a museum. There is a legend that goes along with the jewel. The myth says the piece is a portal element that allows one to travel through time. The studio can negotiate with the museum, so I have a chance to go back. I don't want to go back to the past right away because this place is so modern but I'm sure Liz wants to return because," she laughed, "this place is easy on ones' eyes. Can you believe I'm an actress? Scandalous. Utterly scandalous."

The preacher nodded agreement.

Brian looked at Tina, who shrugged.

Elizabeth smiled at him and fury rose up from the pit of his stomach and into his throat.

Dr. Stoneherst asked, "Can I pour anyone else a glass of tea?"

He couldn't keep his mouth shut. "I think I need a stronger drink than tea. Then you, Dr. Stoneherst, can explain what in the hell you are doing to my patient."

Chapter Nine

"This is a debacle. Elizabeth believes she's a time traveler. Why the sudden shift in perception?"

He didn't give the director a chance to continue. "She believes the story because of Dr. Stoneherst. Your specialist is a quack. Told Elizabeth she would help her travel back in time."

He didn't want anyone to hear him as he paced the patio and ranted into his cell. Glaring at the placid pool of water, he wished for peace and calm. Asked questions over and over again even though he sensed he wasn't getting the truth. "Why did Dr. Stoneherst concoct such a far-fetched story?"

The director evaded his questions. "Her fool boyfriend started this debacle. Jeff Ledger went to the press with a preposterous story about Cupid's brooch. Said the item is a time travel device. He laments and moans and groans and says he wants the real Liz back. He's making money on her tragic situation and," the voice on the other end of the phone rose to a wail, "he's sued the network and Liz personally for breach of contract."

He could care less about the lawsuit. Everyone in Hollywood had one. "I don't give a rat's ass. You have lawyers to take care of those problems. I care about my patient. Why did you send this psychiatric whack-a-doo over here to evaluate Ms. Barrett?" He forced himself to inhale deeply. The situation had reduced him to name calling. *I am a professional.*

The director coughed or laughed.

Weston hated when his temper got away from him, plopped on the lounge chair and glared at his cell. Waited. Finally, the other man spoke.

"I have Liz scheduled to be on set tomorrow morning and I want you and Dr. Stoneherst with her. She can recite lines. Tina says she's memorized her script. I have to put the rest of this season in the can. If Liz needs to believe she's a time traveler for me to get her butt back on set, then so be it. I have a lot of money invested in this production." The director's voice cracked every time he mentioned money.

"Look you jackass. She has a concussion. She'll be okay in a week but if you push her into going back to work too soon, she might not be able to memorize lines. So...," he paused, reminded himself to remain calm. He had to convince this man. "If you want to keep the show on the air, you will give her the break she needs." He hated how the studio treated her like a money-making machine.

"You don't understand Doctor. Jeff put us behind schedule. He sued. Threatened to shut us down. And he may be able to. I need Liz on the set in the morning and Dr. Stoneherst found a way to get her here. You didn't."

"Did Dr. Stoneherst tell you her father intends to stay by her side until the demons are expelled?" Weston's hands shook. *How had this gotten out of control?*

"What demons?"

"The ones ensnaring his daughter's soul. You need

220

to figure out how to get Dr. Stoneherst to convince her father to back off. He's the threat. He told her being an actress is scandalous and your favorite actress agreed."

"What in the hell are you talking about?"

He could hear a thud, a whoosh, and other strange noises. Wondered if the director's temper had him in a destructive mood. Decided to talk softly. "I want you to know her father may convince her that she's full of demonic influences. He could ship her off to an insane asylum or his church, which is pretty close to an asylum. He has demons of his own and he's not stable. Brian appears to be the only normal person in her family and he's not exactly right. He purposely aggravates Tina. It's like I'm stuck in the middle of a bad sitcom."

"Do you want out? Is that why you called?" The voice on the other end of the phone sounded frantic.

"No. I want what is best for my patient. Miss Barrett *is* my patient." He realized his voice carried too much venom.

"Then have her on set tomorrow at six a.m." The phone cut off.

He had the urge to fling the cell into the pool. Jerked when Tina cleared her throat.

"You're the only one who actually cares about her, aren't you?" The words were whispered, even though they were the only two on the patio.

"I know you care about her, Tina. Your actions speak louder than words. Her brother also cares. We have to make sure she isn't harmed." He tried to calm down. They had to protect Elizabeth.

"What should we do?"

Determination to do right calmed him. "We go

with her to the set. I'll have someone else see my patients. I plan to stick by her side until she regains her memory. I don't want anyone planting false hopes or conspiracy theories. Time travel indeed."

Tina sat on the edge of a lounge chair. "She's memorized her lines and I convinced her to take a nap. I guess women from her century did 'lie-abouts' back in the day. Her father and brother are engaged in a shouting match in the den. Dr. Stoneherst sat her fat ass in the music room behind the piano. Pounds on the keyboard without a care in the world. That crazy shrink is up to no good."

"I need a plan before we have a discussion with Dr. Cray-Cray."

Maria came out the sliding door carrying a tray of iced tea. "This will help. Long island iced tea. Good for the nerves."

"Are you afraid we will storm the music room?" Tina asked the maid.

"No. Develop your contingency plan before you step into the lion's den."

He took the drink and thanked Maria. Gulped the entire glass in four large swallows. "Let's go face the music."

Tina took a big swig from her glass. "You mean beard the lion."

The music drifted toward them before they walked through the door. Brian sat on the sofa staring into space. He looked dazed. Anyone would be dazed if they had to listen to the father's rants. The music sounded light and cheerful. Dr. Stoneherst nodded to them as they entered but continued to play until the tune came to an end.

"What brings you two gloomy Gus's to the door?" She said as she got up from the piano bench and sauntered over to a chair.

"We came to talk about my patient." He didn't want to sound like a tyrant, but he felt tyrannical. Promised himself he would put a stop to all this nonsense.

"Good. I need everyone to cooperate. You see, I believe Elizabeth's head bounce made her delusional." She held up a hand to keep everyone from talking at once and pointed to the sofa and chair. "Have a seat, Tina, Doctor."

Tina and Weston stood like statues until she said, "Please. We need to talk about our strategy."

Tina sat in the middle of the couch, next to but not touching Brian and he scooted into the spot next to her. Wiggled his bum on the cushion and Tina scooched over so he would fit. Brian squirmed when his leg touched Tina's.

"I like the seating arrangement. Very Freud. You appear to have aligned against me."

"We wouldn't have to have this conversation if you hadn't gone off on a tangent." He leaned forward so he could see past Tina and asked Brian, "Where is your father?" He didn't need *another* complication.

"He decided to settle into his room. Needs to pray for us. Especially her," he pointed to the woman who had a smirk on her face.

"Will I have to sleep with the door locked? A loaded gun at my side?" She laughed, clearly enjoying herself.

"I'm glad you find this situation funny. I find you…less than professional. Time travel? Really?" He crossed his legs and made a mental note to keep his hands in his lap. His cell beeped, a text message no doubt, but he refused to take the phone out of his shirt pocket.

"I don't believe in time travel any more than you do, doctor. I've given my patient a way out. A way to be Elizabeth for a while until Liz has enough confidence to return."

"You mean she has a split personality?" Tina's eyes flooded with tears.

"No. She doesn't have a dual personality and she isn't crazy. She has a confirmed concussion. The concussion coincides with the termination of her boyfriend slash manager. A highly stressful situation. Her ex blathers to the press about Cupid's brooch. Believes the antique is a time travel piece. Liz told a reporter from Entertainment," the lady's voice changed to a high, thin pitched sound before she said, 'she hailed from eighteen twelve.'"

Her mimic fell flat. He realized he glared while Tina gasped, and Brian started to stand. Tina pull Brian's pant leg, so he plopped back onto the couch.

"How did you convince her? She no longer believes herself in Purgatory." He hadn't been successful when he tried. Yet this smug doc spent three hours with her and changed her mind. He had noticed some differences. Elizabeth continued to act like someone from another century only she seemed to accept her current situation. The entire ordeal confused him.

"I explained how she arrived on a Monday. Today is Thursday. We are on a different date than the initial time she arrived. Everyone knows purgatory has no time constraints."

Tina fidgeted with her earring. Brian put his hand on her knee to keep her leg from jumping up and down. He purposely unclenched his fists, contemplated how she knew exactly what to say. Crossed his arms over his chest as he pondered her response.

Tina broke the unnatural silence. "I didn't realize there were no time constraints in heaven." She flicked Brian's hand off her knee.

"No one knows for sure what's on the other side. But I used simple logic."

Tina put her hand in her mouth and made a gagging motion.

The doctor crossed her legs, tilted her head, and grinned like she had won a prize. "Our actress is a logical woman. Has taken an outdated story line and made *Times Past* a popular televised series. She's done a brilliant job of marketing. At first I thought this was a strategic move to up the ratings." She laughed like she had made a joke.

He wanted to physically grab her and shake the smirk from her face. Instead he laced his fingers together in a fist in his lap.

Dr. Stoneherst didn't notice the wall of stoic silence sitting in front of her. "The incompetent boyfriend, her concussion, and the time travel story created new viewers. Individuals who are engaged in the show. Fans clamor for more episodes. And, dear, precious Liz," she sighed, "has gone from a moderately successful television star to a full-blown 'actress.'"

The air quotes she used pissed him off. The psychologist laughed loudly and mocked him by lacing her fingers together and dramatically placing them in her lap. For the first time in his life, he had the urge to slap a woman.

"I'm waiting for one of you to cover your eyes, one to cover your ears and one to cover your mouth," she said. "Stop making this a tragedy and have a little fun. This couldn't have been planned any better."

"Your inappropriate cracks, Dr. Stoneherst, aren't appreciated. I don't like to be made fun of and neither do Brian and Tina. We are worried about Ms. Barrett. You indicated you believed this was a publicity stunt. I assure you this is no performance." He stood, walked past the irritating shrink and stopped by the piano. He would not allow this fraud to harm his patient.

"Dr. Demfry, this is not a publicity stunt." The doctor's face changed. She looked hard and at the same time she looked...he couldn't explain what he saw on her face, but he became unsettled by her expression.

She shifted in her chair, so he could no longer see her features.

"We have an actress who cracked her head on the floor and woke up confused. Jeff yelled at her and no one understands how she ended up on the ground. We still can't prove he pushed her. I suspect he might have. She's afraid. I know I would be if I thought someone would attack me." Pointedly she turned and glared at him.

He did not like the veiled threat.

The doctor turned and faced Tina and Brian, said, "You know Jeff will continue talking about the brooch and mystical properties. I'm sure in all the confusion, Elizabeth became..."

Brian finished the thought. "You think Liz is a fake."

"No. She believes what she says."

Brian put both arms on his knees and covered his head with his hands. "Okay. So, she became stressed and some part of her made up a story. This allows her to be someone other than the overzealous career woman people believe she is?"

"Bingo. We have a winner." The nasty smile on the therapist's face became more pronounced.

He disliked the sarcasm. Realized her analysis made sense only...he couldn't make himself agree with her. Decided to ask another question. "How will you control her father?"

"I need your cooperation. Her father could convince her she has demons inside. He told me, and I quote, 'the devil made her do it.'"

Brian opened his mouth as if he would defend his father.

Dr. Stoneherst held up one hand. "I go to church and my church is not about hell and damnation. We worship and fellowship. My God is loving. Gentle. And I don't believe in demons even though I've had a client who needed to go through a formal exorcism. The ceremony gave her peace."

Weston threw his hands in the air, walked past her chair, sat down again and gave his best intimidating look. "First time travel, now exorcism. You are one of a kind doc."

She ignored his sarcasm, pointed to Brian. "If your sister needs an exorcism, your father will be required to do one. My experience tells me we should let Elizabeth be Elizabeth for a week or so. Have her say fewer lines than normal. Allow her concussion to heal. We give her the brooch and she emotionally travels back in time. Liz will reappear, and the set can return to normal."

Elizabeth becoming Liz didn't cheer, him. In fact, this terrified him.

Chapter Ten

A month passed since she came to be in twenty twelve. Elizabeth had numerous consultations with Dr. Stoneherst and even did a hypnosis session. Papa would be astonished to find mesmerism worked. She realized she was not in Purgatory.

Understood in a deep recess of her heart that the brooch brought her here to this time and this place. She also comprehended she could only talk about this subject with Dr. Demfry and Dr. Stoneherst. Everyone else wanted to label her with some form of mental instability.

"Liz," her manager called. "Please take your place on stage."

"Elizabeth. Please remember to call me Elizabeth." She hated how everyone called her Liz. The shortened version of her name sounded tawdry and familiar. Too familiar. They didn't even use Miss or Mistress. Now they called women Ms. and women's liberation had seriously ruined men.

She shook her head as she thought about how advanced technology had become and how uncouth men were. They no longer held doors open unless you could pave their way to a better place using money. Tina assured her men 'wanted a piece.' She did not know a piece of what, but she noticed everyone seemed to want some favor from her.

Her producer needed her to make him money.

The paparazzi needed her to sell stories.

And, reticules were now called a purse and young men expected older woman to pay.

She loved how Tina shared her knowledge. Had explained, in detail, the lawsuit that no good scoundrel, Jeff Ledger, had perpetrated. Dr. Demfry told her not to worry. Her heart did a pitter patter when she thought about him and his kindly manner. He explained to her she would have to go to court and talk about her private life. How a Lady had to participate in such a tragedy confounded her.

She stood in place and acted out the scene without a mistake. Acting meant a great deal to the body she lived in.

The Director called cut. She had had a few words with him when he wanted one of her suitors to kiss her on the lips. Stood steadfast in her refusal. Only allowed the man to kiss her wrist. The acceptable way people conducted themselves in the time period of the show.

That wrist kiss hadn't rocked her world the way Dr. Demfry did when he stood close. She liked that term—rocked her world. Her foundation rocked and her world turned when she landed in this century.

Her friends were genuine. She even liked the easy-going camaraderie from her fellow actors. Who would have believed an old-fashioned gel such as herself would like to go to work each day? She loved her job. The only option opened to her before had been marriage and the production of progeny.

She glanced downward at her dress. Cherished these costumes. They were better than modern clothes. Made sure the show had the young ladies, such as herself, wear acceptable day dresses. The married ladies were allowed to bare their bosoms. She confided to the wardrobe man how women who hung on the fringe of acceptability wore dampened cloth to show their figures. They liked her ideas and some of her witty script changes.

Doctor Demfry walked onto the set. She sensed the minute he arrived because she forgot her lines. How he unsettled her.

She glanced in his direction. The man never thought her cheap because she acted. That, too, had changed. Actresses were vetted and petted and invited to the White House. Back in her time, when the Prince of Wales became the Prince Regent, he had to denounce his involvement with an actress, so Parliament would give him funds.

Her brother stood next to the doctor. He looked so handsome in his dress pants and shirts. She didn't know why Tina made disparaging remarks, then eyed him the same way she eyed chocolate. Then again, she probably eyed the good doctor like Tina eyed her brother.

As she walked toward her brother and the doctor, she noticed the faint smell of clean skin. Dr. Demfry carried a husky scent with a dash of spice. She smiled and greeted them. "What a fine day today. How goes your life?"

She loved to hear *his* voice, so she always asked a general question and looked directly at him. Bold to be sure but this body made bold moves. He talked in a low, deep bass that rumbled and sent strange flutters throughout her insides. She had a mad crush on the man. Why his warm gaze sent shivers straight to her nether regions.

"A fine day indeed. The California sun shines so bright and hot, like the tempers of the men who head up this studio. I hear you went on Ellen and spilled the beans."

"I did not take beans with me, Doctor Demfry. I took avocados. Those big green fruits are so delicious. I had to share some from my backyard. Ellen acted grateful and after the program, we sat together and had a delicious meal. She prepared a chopped salad."

"You also talked to her about the past." His voice seemed gentle, yet she could tell by his expression she disappointed him. She hated when he gave her that look.

"I told her my televised series wasn't exactly like the past."

"Yes, I listened to the interview. The Executives want you to stop the talk shows until after the trial. Jeff filed an injunction, so we have to close the show for a while. Said he came up with the idea for this program. Now he wants a slice of the pie."

"I didn't know we made pie?"

"Ms. Barrett, Jeff Ledger wants money. Cash. A way to pay his bills."

She laughed. "I hired him long after I took this job. Brian and I found the paperwork last night." She looked at her brother. "I'm so glad you decided to stay and keep track of all my financial obligations."

Brian didn't smile. "You used to relish your financial obligations. Now you want me to tell you what to do. I don't feel right about this, Lizzy." He tugged on one of her curls which took the sting out of his words.

"I know you are all worried about me. The

producer plans to shoot my scene with Cupid's Brooch tomorrow." She smiled even though she didn't feel like smiling. She loved her brother. She loved Tina. She loved the man who Liz refused to call father—the man who had changed the most during her stay in this body.

Liz would be surprised when she came back and found out she had mended fences with the irascible old coot. But most of all, she wanted to feel Dr. Demfry's arms around her, holding her, comforting her. The thought made her launch herself onto his chest and weep loudly.

Strong arms wrapped around her. "Whoa. What's wrong?"

"I've become a watering pot, haven't I?" She sobbed louder. The man held her until she became calm. Somehow, she managed to feel comforted and full of tension at the same time. The Liz part of her brain understood this much better than she did.

Dr. Demfry smiled, his endearing lopsided grin, and brushed tears from her cheeks with a warm thumb. "You don't have to do the scene with the Brooch."

She didn't? Hope surged through her until she realized Liz might not want to stay in eighteen twelve. All this luxury would be gone. Air conditioners, warm showers to start the day, and chocolate covered marshmallows. She didn't want to give them up either, but morally she had no choice. How she would miss her long conversations with Dr. Demfry each night by the pool. She could talk to him, no matter how trivial the subject.

She stepped out of the doctor's embrace at the sound of feet approaching. The stage manager appeared. "Your fan base has doubled. The studio executives haven't pulled the plug on the show. But I'm worried. We received a Cease and Desist Order which means we can't shoot your brooch scene tomorrow."

Dr. Demfry asked for details and she listened with half an ear. They would have to go to court tomorrow. This gave her one more day with the man she loved. Loved? Oh no. She could not love someone she had to leave.

Dr. Demfry's brow crinkled with worry as he talked to her manager. The urge to reach out and brush the errant lock of hair from his forehead had her hand move upward before she controlled herself. Liz would have touched him. In fact, Liz would have called him by his first name. She blushed when she said his name to herself. Weston. His name had such an old fashioned yet modern ring.

Today's women experimented with their bodies. She denied herself this pleasure which made sleep impossible. Her body could not be virginal. She didn't dare ruminate about something so intimate. She'd seen bold inventions—planes, trains, and exercise machines. Used the exercise equipment on those nights she couldn't sleep. She now had 'ripped' legs.

Funny how great the inventions were and how people had not changed. Many scoffed at her idea of arranged marriages, but she had witnessed happy ones. People today gave in to indiscriminate encounters with each other and married many times. Part of the sexual revolution. Revolution seemed the right word.

She wanted someone special. Someone who thought her special. Tina confessed she liked that concept one night when they sat by the pool and drank wine. Modern life confused her.

Her body wanted Dr. Demfry. Would he find her special? She didn't dare consider the thought because she had to travel back to eighteen twelve. Would never start a dalliance. Liz wouldn't give the good man a second look. Why, she took up with Jeff, *the bounder*. Hollywood had a million men like him. They knew what to order and what to wear but they had no depth of personality. How had her twin soul missed his lack of depth?

She shook her head to clear her thoughts and decided to ease Dr. Demfry and her manager's worries. "They won't pull the plug on the show. My so-called mental instability makes the studio money. Who do you think set me up with Ellen? I had to sneak away with Dr. Stoneherst so Tina couldn't stop me. Dr. Stoneherst only does what the Studio Executives tell her. Do you know my viewing audience is larger than ever?"

Brian chuckled. "Now you sound like your old self." His grin faded. "Lizzy, you need to stop hiding from Tina. She panicked yesterday when you left without notification. Insisted you had been kidnapped."

"I know. I didn't mean to worry her, so I left a note." Guilt gnawed at her innards like a dog gnaws a bone. Why had she listened to Dr. Stoneherst? The woman planned to propel her career stepping on the backs of others. She detested her type. Like those ape leaders of the *ton*. They all jockeyed for a position by harming one another. Dr. Stoneherst did the same. The behavior sickened her. Human nature had not evolved.

She inhaled like Tina taught her. Next, she changed the subject. "I know how to look at numbers. Papa let me help him from time to time in the past, but he considered my intelligence unladylike. Our numbers have grown. This show is a success. No one cares whether I act like a lady or not. In fact, this studio encourages me to act on impulse."

"Like hiding from your chaperone?" The doctor gave her his concerned look. Then he said, "I care. I care about you. I want you to act like a lady. Please don't run away again. The Ellen show may be brought up in court."

She believed the doctor when he said he cared. Why oh why had she listened to the psychiatrist? The odious woman poked fun at people. A trait she did not care for. Selfish and mean spirited.

"Tina told me I have to take care of myself because no one will take care of me. Dr. Stoneherst had the studio's blessing, so I followed her lead. I am sorry, I've learned my lesson."

The good doctor put his warm hand to her chin and lifted her head gently. "Tina, Brian and I have your best interest at heart. If you don't want to do the scene with Cupid's Brooch, you don't have to. You can decide after tomorrow's hearing." He shifted to the left, to the right, looked as if he made some decision and said in a no-nonsense voice, "You don't have to do the scene, if you don't want to."

For a moment his eyes pleaded with her.

"I understand if you want to act professional but Elizabeth," he paused, "I will support you no matter your decision."

She wanted to cry. The right decision would give Liz the opportunity to return to her old life. Unfortunately, her time in paradise had to end.

Chapter Eleven

The court room felt as cold as her sub-zero, side by side refrigerator. Elizabeth sat shivering between her attorney and the studio executive assigned to her. Jeff sat next to his attorney, across from her, never able to make eye contact. The bailiff stood up and called, "Dr. Demfry to the stand."

The doctor sedately walked to the wooden chair next to the judge's oversized bench. He gave her a smile as he passed and the air in the room became a little warmer.

The bailiff swore Dr. Demfry in and opposing counsel started to question him. "State your name for the record."

"Dr. Weston Demfry."

"Tell us your connection with Miss Barrett."

"I'm her medical doctor."

"You testify the studio hired you to be Miss Barrett's doctor?"

The studio attorney stood up, "Objection, leading the witness."

A brief discussion took place. One Elizabeth did not understand, then Dr. Demfry answered the question.

"They hired me as the set doctor. The company films two shows, and my services were retained to treat anyone on either set if they have a medical situation."

"Did any situations arise?"

"Objection. This question is not relevant to the Cease and Desist order."

"Your Honor, we are here to establish the studio intentionally brought in a doctor for Miss Barrett's mental detcrioration."

"Objection." A flurry of angry comments flew from her attorney's mouth before the judge rapped his gavel. The two lawyers were called before the bench and then the questions continued.

"When did you meet Miss Barrett?"

"The day I started working for the studio. I don't have the exact date. It was last year in May. The assistant introduced me to every member of the staff."

"Were you introduced to Jeff Ledger?"

"Yes."

"What were you told about him?"

"I'm sorry. I don't understand your question." She recognized his confused look. She, too, felt confused. *What did this have to do with the allegations?*

"Who introduced you to the staff?"

Dr. Demfry's eyes looked upward and he paused before he answered. "The assistant to the director, Cherry Fields."

"What did Miss Fields tell you about Jeff?"

"I still don't understand your question."

"What's not to understand, doctor? Did she say his name? Give his title?"

"That's not what happened. The staff gathered around in a circle and I got introduced to the team as Dr. Demfry. Miss Fields told everyone they were to see me if they needed an aspirin, bandage or had a medical issue. Miss Barrett introduced herself and shook my hand. After she greeted me, each member of the cast said their name and shook my hand. Everyone but Mr. Ledger. I had to approach him."

"You approached him?" The attorney asked in such a way she wanted to yank his tongue from his mouth. He had used sarcasm. She looked at the judge to see his reaction. The thin man sat stoic. Dr. Demfry appeared calm. Mayhap both men had trained with the actors' guild.

"I approached Mr. Ledger. I wanted to say hello to everyone on the set. Didn't know until I extended my hand that he wasn't a member of the cast."

"Not a member of the cast? Did he say he wasn't a cast member?"

"Actually, he snubbed me. Refused my hand and said, 'I'm Miss Barrett's manager'. Deliberately turned and walked away. I asked Miss Fields about his role and she laughed. Said, and I quote her, "He's an ass. Has a contract with her, not the studio.""

"So she derided the man? Demeaned him?" The attorney said in an over-loud voice.

Dr. Demfry shook his head. "No. The man was rude, and she explained his behavior by stating he acts like an ass. I agreed with her assessment. He isn't part of the team I've been hired to treat so I dismissed him from my thoughts."

"So if he fell and bumped his head, you wouldn't have been called to treat him?"

"I'm a medical doctor. I'm required to treat everyone. The difference is, I would have sent him a bill."

Elizabeth chuckled. The attorney made some long-winded statement to the Judge she couldn't follow. She gazed at Dr. Demfry and relived their initial encounter in the space inside her mind holding Liz' memories.

Liz hadn't experienced a spark when they met. She had been polite, extended a warm welcome. She shook his hand deliberately, so the others would embrace him. Remembered the handshake. No thrill. No excitement. No tension. Nothing more, nothing less than a handshake. How odd!

Her reaction the day she fell in time had created butterflies and tingles. Elizabeth and Liz shared a similar body, yet they had different ways of doing, being, seeing, and sensing.

The Judge made some pronouncement and the attorney started to ask questions again. "You live with Miss Barrett, don't you?"

"Objection. The doctor's living arrangement has nothing to do with the Cease and Desist order. Your Honor, this debacle has gone on all morning. Reasons for granting this injunction don't exist. Mr. Ledger is delusional. He did not create this TV show. We already proved the writers of the production company created the show. Miss Barrett signed a contract with Mr. Ledger after she started her job with the studio. You have a copy of the signed contract." He waved the document in the air. "I don't understand why we have to continue this charade."

The Judge frowned, his jowls drooped, his mouth curved into a grimace. "I have your evidence. I also have a slew of cameras in the lobby. I want to figure out who used my court for publicity—Miss Barrett or Mr. Ledger. I don't take kindly to anyone who wastes my time."

The man glared at Elizabeth and she smiled serenely at him. She didn't need to worry. Dr. Demfry told her the American judicial system was fair, even to women. The Judge tried to frown as he looked at her, but she noticed his lips tipped upward before he shook his head. Then he glared at Mr. Ledger who quickly glanced downward.

Jeff's attorney stood up. "My client denies this is a publicity stunt. He has been wrongfully terminated."

The Judge interrupted him. "I'm not here to listen to a wrongful termination case. You filed for an injunction. What does Dr. Demfry have to do with the injunction?"

The attorney pointed to her. "The studio hired Dr. Demfry specifically to cut Mr. Ledger out of his fair share of the profits. The studio systematically used a number of individuals to run my client out of Princeton Pictures."

She couldn't contain herself. For the second time she burst into peals of laughter. Belly clenching, echoing, louder than life laughter.

The Judge smashed his gavel and told her she would be evicted from the courtroom if she could not contain herself.

She stopped immediately, frightened by his harsh demeanor. "I am sorry Your Honor, but Mr. Ledger's face is worth a king's ransom. I know not what he thinks with this yarn he weaves. He doesn't write the scripts. In fact, he's never made a worthwhile suggestion. Then he stood in the way of the writer's getting a raise."

She thought for a moment before she continued. "That didn't stop him from wanting more money for himself. He is a vainglorious man! One with no value. Why, I constantly chastised him by saying no, stop, and

241

don't to each and every one of his preposterous suggestions. I'm puzzled why we are in court. If I were older, I would be called a cougar because I have pursued the man. He didn't get me my position. I got him his."

The Judge scowled. "If he was such an albatross around your neck, why did you hire him?"

She blushed when she said. "He is a man. I…I allowed him to charm me."

The Judge crooked his finger at the two attorneys' and said, "In my chambers. Now."

The bailiff led Dr. Demfry from the stand and out of the closed court room. The silence stretched taut and chilly, like the temperature in the room. She decided to take the opportunity and talk with Jeff Ledger. She stood up and the studio executive grabbed her arm. "What do you think you're doing?"

"I plan to reason with him. He must have some honor. Does he not realize how badly this looks for him? He has filed a useless suit and the Judge is angry. I would like to know what he tries to prove."

The man loosened his grip. "He wants publicity. The tabloids pay him money to keep the public entertained. The bigger the farce, the more money he makes. He's been on every sleazy talk show. This is about money, greed, and wounded pride. We told you he would cause trouble when you fired him."

"I am sorry I did not listen to your goodly advice." She moved around her lawyer, started to walk toward Mr. Ledger. Her brother, Brian, who had been allowed in the court room, blocked her way.

"Don't do this sis. The studio's attorney will take care of the matter. Reporters are outside those doors and a mob of fans is on the courthouse steps. You make one wrong move, and this could cause infinite problems."

"I shall ask Dr. Demfry.".

That's how she found herself in front of a group of camera's calling Dr. Demfry's name. The man rushed to her side and bustled her back into the courtroom. Camera's followed. The Judge reappeared and so did his temper. The room cleared within minutes.

***

They sat around the pool as the heat of the day started to lift and the stars in the sky began to twinkle. The group congratulated themselves on a job well done. The Cease and Desist motion had been denied, along with a slew of other legal claims. The court appearance made the news, the paper, and Entertainment Today. The media portrayed Jeff as a grasping interloper.

Tina walked over to a chair next to her and dropped onto the cushions. "Don't get too comfortable, missy. Jeff means to make more trouble. Lots of trouble. Why would a successful woman such as yourself date him?"

She pulled up some memories belonging to Liz before she answered. "He charmed me. Pulled out my chair, buttered my bread, made sure taxis were available if we had too much to drink. Made me believe I was special. My father preached at me. Brian continually defended me. No one in my life ever went out of their way to make me feel special. Not until Jeff came along." She sighed, looked up, and noticed Dr. Demfry. He stared at her strangely.

"I know the man took advantage of me. He should be an actor because he played the part well." She nodded toward Tina. "You wouldn't butter my bread, but you did show me how to make toast. And you," she cocked her head toward her brother, "wouldn't dream of calling for a ride. You'd throw me over your shoulder, bring me home and dump me in the pool. Then you'd lecture me on the evils of over indulging."

"Yeah. That's me. Neanderthal man." He didn't sound pleased.

She rushed on. "Dr. Demfry opens doors for me. But, then, he opens doors for everyone." She gave a wave of her hand.

"I don't think I like this conversation." Tina started to get up from her chair, but Elizabeth placed her hand on the other woman's arm to stop her.

"I have not made my point, so you understand."

"What is the point, missy?"

"Each one of you has my best interest at heart. You wanted me to learn how to take care of myself instead of, what is the popular word I search for? Enabling. That's the word. You don't enable me. You help me. Brian, you want to protect me, so you make sure I behave virtuously."

Her brother grinned so she continued. "But you do act prehistoric with Tina." He frowned, and his mouth turned down in a pout. "And you, Dr. Demfry. You make me feel special without artifice. You don't sugarcoat the truth." She paused and said softly, "but you are gentle when you tell me." Her voice softened to a heartfelt whisper. "I love each and every one of you."

"And me?" Dr. Stoneherst quipped. "How come you left me out of this little *tête à tête.*"

"I left you out, doctor, because I do not believe you have my best interests at heart. You are bought and paid for by the studio. You are here at their request, not mine." The water in the pool lapped gently. Silence filled the night as a lone cricket chirped nearby.

Dr. Stoneherst stood. "I guess I'll say goodnight."

Dr. Demfry also stood. "I think we've celebrated a victory, but we still need to talk strategy. You're the company person. Let's talk about the future. You mentioned Miss Barrett would have a televised special. Tell us about this special."

The angry shrink downed the contents of her margarita glass and rushed toward the pitcher on the bar. After she poured another drink, she looked at the doctor. "You have been relegated to a nice man and I agree. You are a nice man."

Tina held out her glass. "Please pour me another one before you drink it all. I swear you can drink like a fish. And," she paused for a long moment, "I agree with your assessment. Dr. Demfry *is* a nice man. Thank goodness missy over here likes nice men."

She blushed. "Of course, I like nice men." Hoped her crush, Tina's word for what she sensed when the doctor stood near, did not believe her overly bold. Once again, the pool noises seemed loud, along with the clink of the pitcher on Tina's glass. Patio furniture creaked as everyone tried to get comfortable.

Dr. Stoneherst broke the silence. "What would you think about a special show with Cupid's Brooch? This wouldn't be a *Times Past* production."

She gulped. "I don't know. What type of special?"

"The studio thought you might be interested in telling the world how you traveled through time and ended up in Liz Barrett's body. You could give small details about eighteen hundred and twelve and then demonstrate the power of the brooch by trading places with Liz. The museum will fund the entire project."

"I bet they would." Dr. Demfry looked like a helicopter, as he propelled himself out of his chair and hovered over Dr. Stoneherst. Her eyes went wide as he put one hand on the right arm of her chair and his other hand on the left arm of her chair, blocked her in. "You're not Dr. Oz even though you want to command large audiences. A little bird told me you had an interview today. You angle for your own show and I am not about to let you use Elizabeth to get one!"

"Miss Barrett correctly stated I get paid by the studio. So do you Dr. Demfry. Don't forget who pays you. Now I'll ask you kindly to move your arms off my chair and get out of my space. I think Miss Barrett can make up her own mind about this project." The woman batted Dr. Demfry's arms away.

He stood in front of her chair. "And you plan to be the person who advises her? What happens when the brooch doesn't move her back in time? What then? Will Miss Barrett be required to lie? Act out a scene?"

Brian approached Dr. Demfry and tapped him on the shoulder. The man backed up and ran a hand through his hair. Brian didn't give him an opportunity to speak. "I agree with Weston. Lizzy will look insane."

Weston shook his head and groaned. "The studio counts on the drama. Great publicity for the show. The Judge questioned who got the word out about the Cease and Desist order and both sides lied and denied the leak came from them." He walked over to the fire pit. "Don't forget what happened to the actor who insisted he was a wizard. Great publicity until the media frenzy died. He got thrown out on his ass."

Tina wiggled in her chair. "Everyone remembers the crazy, tiger blood guy. They showed his rants for a while. In a space of two and a half weeks, he became old news. He's an old guy with a drinking problem and anger issues." Tina deliberately set her drink on the coffee table. Stood up, pointed her finger and demanded, "How do you intend to portray Elizabeth, Dr. Stoneherst?"

"If eyes were daggers, you would score a hit," came the snarky quip. She placed two hands to her chest in a contrived manner and said in a false voice, "I would never harm Miss Barrett."

Elizabeth didn't want the argument to continue. "Will this be scripted or do I ad lib?"

Dr. Stoneherst's reply was instantaneous, "Does it make a difference?"

"Of course. I don't want a script if I do this. I want to direct. This could be my golden opportunity." She hadn't been aware she thought about directing before the words poured from her mouth. *Golden opportunity? A great word choice.* She realized she had started to become Liz, their actions and reactions melded, like a great pot of soup. The flavors simmered together until the stock became a delicious mix. If she figured out how to take the best qualities of each personality, she would be a better person. Why, she hadn't bit her fake nails in days!

"I want control of who gets to be part of this special. Dr. Demfry must be by my side. He'll ensure I'm not injured, and the show stays ethical. Tina has been my support since I arrived in two thousand and twelve. I want the audience to know she is faithful. I need Brian to walk me on stage, like the considerate brother he has been. And I want the museum delivery guy to tell his story. He can explain what happened between Jeff and me. No one asked him for his version. He can tell the audience what he witnessed. This will stop some of Mr. Ledger's lawsuits. No one knows if he pushed Liz. Not even me."

Dr. Stoneherst looked amused. "I suppose all these people will need to be paid?"

"Naturally. If the brooch works, great. If our plan doesn't work out, I want them to have ten minutes of fame. Ten minutes will net everyone a fortune."

She became excited, driven. Pointed toward Tina. "You will be able to open your own hair salon. Dr. Demfry," she paused, "you'll be able to pay off your student loans and practice medicine. Practice with real patients, not the hypochondriacs you told me about from the studio. I know you have plans for your clinic, and I think Brian could be your accountant. He keeps my financial records straight."

She held out her hand to her brother. He walked over to where she sat and patted her shoulder. "You will have enough money to help father. Maybe we could find a way to get him a spot on the program."

"How much time do you need to create this production?" Dr. Stoneherst's interruption stopped her mental thought process.

Dr. Demfry and Tina looked slacked jawed and horrified.

She considered her friends before she replied. "I would like the museum man and Tina on the first night. They can talk about what they overheard. I want the conversation with Jeff explained. This can be a thirty-minute segment. A teaser of sorts. Definitely a special."

She realized she had figured this out without any serious contemplation.

"Brian can spend thirty minutes and tell the fans about my life as a child. We will air this the following night. Mayhap we can include Father. Next, we can have Dr. Demfry and you talk about my medical condition. Set up a way for people to call in and text their questions. Like the singing show I binged. On the forth night, I will wield the brooch."

"Whoa, whoa, whoa. Slow down and think this through. What will you accomplish?" Dr. Demfry didn't sound happy. His jaw had a tick and his hands opened and shut, as if he wanted to strangle someone.

"I intend to leave you with a way to remember me." The thought saddened her, but she rushed on. "Liz will reappear. She's a no-nonsense person so your lives will go back to business as usual."

Tina started to cry. Short sniffs quickly turned into loud sobs. She got up and ran toward the sliding glass door. "I don't want you to go. I like you the way you are, not the way you were."

Brian looked at her and said, "You don't have to prove your worth." He tweaked her curl, followed after Tina.

Dr. Demfry growled, "You should be disbarred. I don't want Elizabeth harmed!" The wrought iron gate clanged as he slammed out of the pool area and down the path to the guest house.

Dr. Stoneherst smiled and a chill ran down Elizabeth's spine. "I'll tell the studio you're ready to talk." The woman stood, nodded in her direction, sauntered over to the sliding door, gently shut the glass behind her.

Fear paralyzed her. *What have I done? What will happen if Liz doesn't reappear? I'll be written off as insane.*

She didn't want to dwell on what she set in motion. Got up and walked around, picked up glasses and put them on one of Maria's handy trays. The housekeeper had decided to make her special drink for their celebration. Even made a dip called *queso* which tasted hot on her palate yet fun to eat. The celebration and all Maria's hard work turned sour. Like Dr. Stoneherst. The most offensive woman alive. She picked at scabs and made people squirm.

She blew out the torches and candles. Gazed into the fire and watched the flames dance. Tina taught her how to roast marshmallows in this pit. Showed her how to eat gooey s'mores. In her time, they didn't even make marshmallows. She wondered when they were invented. Would she ever taste them again? She started to cry.

She smelled Dr. Demfry's cologne before he wrapped comforting arms around her. *Why had the man returned?* She didn't care, because the need inside grew.

She turned into him as his lips pressed against hers. *My first kiss.*

All thoughts stopped. Delicious sensations returned. The world became sensual and turbulent. She discovered the comfort of his arms. For tonight, she planned to taste the forbidden.

Chapter Twelve

Brian waited by the gate. Banged the door against the metal closure for the fifth time in two minutes. "What in the hell were you doing with my sister," he hissed when Dr. Demfry finally got his clothes adjusted and walked toward him.

"I kissed her."

"How dare you?" Brian's tone held cold fury. He stormed from the pool enclosure, glanced over his shoulder to make sure Dr. Demfry walked behind him. The two men headed to the guesthouse they shared.

Weston turned and nodded to Elizabeth. Her eyes had a dreaminess about them, her hair mussed, her mouth reddened. Her pink tongue darted out to lick her parted, swollen lips and he groaned. He wanted to race back and take her into his arms once again. Thankfully Brian had pulled them apart. If he hadn't, they would have been on the ground making babies.

The thought sobered him. Babies. He never dreamed about a family. His dream had been medical school and a healthy practice. A baby with Elizabeth didn't seem abhorrent. In fact, it…. well, he didn't need to think about a family. The love of his life would direct a show and get tarred and feathered and run out of Hollywood.

A new thought struck him. What if the brooch returned her to eighteen twelve? He had studied her speech pattern. She spoke with a mixture of old English and modern slang. It endeared. He did a mental head slap.

They had looked her up on the internet. Witnessed a picture on some educational web site of the Earl of Whittington. Lady Whittington stood next to him, only, she had the look of a minx and went by the name Liz. The article stated she had been adventurous, assisted the woman's movement and bolstered her husband's career. The Earl reformed child labor laws. When he read about the couple, he began to believe the unbelievable. What if Cupid's Brooch opened a time travel portal? Would Elizabeth be lost to him forever?

He accidentally ran into Brian's back. The young man shoved him away. "You're in love, aren't you?" Brian had a glare on his face and propped his two large, meaty fits on his hips. Waited for a response.

"I…I…," he ran his hands through his hair. "I don't want her to leave. I need to show you what I found on the web."

"The internet? I don't give a flying fig about the internet. I want to know what your intentions are toward my sister so don't try to change the subject."

"Your sister is from eighteen twelve and I want to marry her only I can't. She plans to travel back in time. Liz will return. Remember your sister. The queen bee. The one who called all the shots, liked to be in charge, and found pleasure when she managed her own money. She is not the young woman who I'm in love with. And really, Brian. Flying fig? You sound like Tina."

"Dr. Stoneherst has an agenda. I didn't know you had one to."

"Good God, Brian. I don't have an agenda, I'm in

love with Elizabeth." He wanted to make his point, so he decided to bring up the elephant that stood in the room each time they gathered on the back patio. "You know what I mean since you are in love with Tina."

"Don't bring Tina into this." The big man hunched his shoulders and deflated like a balloon. "Tina and I are different."

"You are the balance Tina needs."

"We're more like a teeter totter. Up one minute, down the next." He stubbed his toe in the grass, straightened his shoulders and demanded once again, "What are your intentions toward my sister?"

"I want to marry Elizabeth. Have babies with her." He realized he meant what he said. A little Elizabeth. Okay, that might be a bit much. He dampened his own enthusiasm.

"I can't have her because she's going back in time. The personality of your sister will return and then what? She's an ambitious woman. Elizabeth said she would like to follow me to Africa annually and help at the free clinic. I can't see Liz with chipped nails and bed pans." He inhaled so he could stop the panic swelling in his chest.

"Your sister Liz would be off on a safari." He had located a picture from the British Museum showing Lord Whittington and his wife on a big game hunt. Elizabeth wouldn't want to participate in blood sports.

Brian looked angry. "You want Elizabeth to help you in Africa? You realize your dream is a continent away with a large ocean between the two countries."

He wondered if Liz was the only person in the Barrett family to be born with a sense of adventure. Could be the reason why she whizzed through time. "I categorically believe your sister is Elizabeth. She's still your sister, only she has another personality in her body. I love Elizabeth. I respect Liz."

"I love my sister and I don't care if she acts like Liz or Elizabeth."

"You are lying to yourself. Liz relegated me to peon status when she lived in the body. She wrote off you and her father. Don't you understand? If Elizabeth leaves, Liz will return."

"I can deal with both of them."

"Well your face says different. You look like you sucked a lemon." He needed Brian on his side. Tried a different angle. "What you witnessed tonight…a mistake. I returned to the pool area because I wanted to make sure your sister didn't get hurt when we deserted her. I walked over to where she stood by the fire, her shoulders hunched, and I needed to comfort her. The embrace turned into…" he couldn't explain because he had never been out of control in his entire life.

Brian looked away, his face pink. "Doctor. You can't play with my sister. She already looks at you like you hung the moon. Elizabeth has had a mental break. She's not a time traveler and she will be more confused when this brooch doesn't transport her back in time. I don't want you to encourage her. What if she ends up on medication? Do you want a wife who needs medication?"

"I don't want to put on an act with you or your sister, Brian. I want you to know I will take Elizabeth even if she needs medication. I cherish her spirit and someday I would like to marry her. Only…" He understood this could be a big mistake. One of epic proportions. "I'm in love with Elizabeth. Not Liz.

Elizabeth. I'm worried Liz could come back from the past and ruin my future. I need to show you the web sites and the picture I found. Then you'll understand why I'm concerned."

They entered the guesthouse silently. Dr. Demfry booted up his computer. He went to the bookmarked pages and showed Brian what he had found. He gave him a copy of the picture the museum sent. As he stared into the eyes of Lady Whittington, Brian swore like a sailor.

Because the man didn't cuss, he realized he understood. "I'm concerned. That looks like Liz to me."

Brian continued to stare at the picture. "They look the same except," Brian shook his head. "Lizzy always had a tilt to her chin. Look," he pointed. "Elizabeth only turns her head a little to the left when she's being stubborn. Liz has walked around with that titled chin her entire life—like she can snub the world. I'll show you her third-grade picture. She had the same demeanor. Her innate way to say, 'get the hell out of my way or I'll run you over' look."

He stared at the picture. "Elizabeth isn't Liz! I suspect she's a time traveler. You've known her all your life. What do you believe?"

Brian shook his head as if that would clear his thoughts. "I...I...I don't know. I can't be certain."

He understood the man didn't want to admit the truth. "I'm furious with Dr. Stoneherst. She met with the studio. Told them she would talk Elizabeth into their special. I came home early, decided to do some research. The mind-doctor is a quack who wants stardom. The problem is she's correct about time travel and doesn't understand she diagnosed the situation appropriately…"

Brian groaned. Walked the room while he glared at the printed picture of his sister in his hand.

"I researched Cupid's Brooch. I don't know why Jeff borrowed the piece from the museum. Did he want to time travel or fall in love?" He clicked open a page from the museum's website.

Brian read the information and let out a long whistle. "Can people who transport from one century to another ever go back to their original time?"

"The pin is said to be a love brooch." He walked over to the small bar and got out the bourbon.

Brian smiled, shook his head no when asked if he wanted a drink. Then he went and set the Dr.'s glass to one side. "Weston. Look at this picture of Liz. She's obviously in love. Are you convinced she wants to return to our century? See all the organizations her husband belongs to. Do you think a man would be this involved in society unless he had a wife who inspired him? Liz looks like she's…like she's actually happy. If she is, she won't want to come back here."

"Yeah, but Elizabeth isn't in love."

"She will be if you keep kissing her."

He held up both hands because Brian had a strange look on his face. "I promise I won't kiss her again. I made a mistake. I won't make another error until I'm certain Elizabeth stays with us."

"The network will take a week to put together the special. Use your time to wine and dine my sister. You can kiss her but promise me you'll keep your tongue out of her mouth."

"Brian, why would I wine and dine her?" Anger rose from the pit of his stomach into his throat. He wanted to date Elizabeth only she made more money than he did. He would never live off her income. What a blow to his ego. And, hadn't she gone on and on about Liz giving Jeff money?

"Weston, she needs to stay put. Look at what my sister accomplished with father. The man has mellowed before my eyes. He didn't want to go back to his congregation. Elizabeth asked him to stay in Hollywood. Permanently. Tina drove him to a soup kitchen yesterday. He called after his interview and sounded serene. My father has never sounded serene. They hired him and gave him a room to live in. Plan to pay him. My old man hasn't had a steady income in years. Let's talk about Tina. She has a purpose in life. Her purpose is to help Elizabeth."

When Brian paused for breath, Weston interrupted. "Tina didn't have a purpose before Elizabeth?" He asked because he wanted to understand Brian's frame of mind. When the two of them stood next to each other, the air between them became taunt with emotion. Did everyone notice the same tightly drawn tension between him and Liz?

"Earth to Dr. Demfry."

He looked at Brian and realized his mind played tricks. "I'm back in reality. What's your deal with Tina?"

Brian had the temerity to laugh. "She's got a purpose. Elizabeth is right. If you marry her, Tina can open her own hair salon."

"Whoa. Whoa. Whoa. Who said we would marry?"

Brian gave him an evil grin. "You can't stick your tongue down my sister's throat and then not marry her," he said. "You need to step up your game and court her."

"I don't know how to court. I've never had time for a girlfriend."

Brian's enthusiasm stopped for a split second before he said, "Tina would know what to do." He picked up his cell and punched in a number. She must have answered on the first ring. He didn't actually listen to their conversation.

"Tina's on her way over. I need to show her this website and then we need to come up with a plan. If Elizabeth is in love with you, Doctor, then she can't leave. Cupid is the angel of love. She needs to be in love to stay."

Tina arrived a few minutes later. She looked as if she'd run across the massive lawn. Her chest heaved, her hair was windblown. Her unicorn PJs were plastered to her skin. A sure sign she ran through the sprinklers. The automatic system turned on every night like clockwork. Brian went into his room and retrieved a dry T-shirt. Handed the top to her and pointed toward the bathroom.

Tina pulled the shirt over her head, found a way to remove the wet one at the same time. "Blasted sprinklers. I never noticed them before. Of course, I don't ever leave the house this late." She handed Brian the soggy garment and demanded "sweat pants." Brian gasped so Weston told her he had a pair of biker shorts she could use. He told Brian to put the shirt in the dryer when he opened his mouth to protest.

Once Tina had on dry clothes, they asked her to sit at the table. The laptop sat in front of her.

"Here's the web site I told you about." Brian pointed, and Tina looked at the pictures. Clicked through to the other sight. Studied the photographs.

Held the copy of the photo sent to the doctor. Listened to their plan. She started to instruct the men in the art of courtship. The trio talked until dawn.

He decided to take a quick shower, then picked flowers from the garden. Tina told him, "Trivial gestures count."

"Trivial gestures?" Brian had a far-away look. "I thought women liked grand gestures."

"Grand gestures are for grand dames. Elizabeth is from another time and place. Can you write a poem?" she asked.

He didn't want to consider her idea. "I can't write poetry. I can't even write a complete sentence. I'm a doctor. We study science, not language. A poem?"

She shrugged. "We can find one on the internet and you can recite the composition to her."

He groaned loudly. "Next you'll want me to learn the lute."

Brian and Tina looked at each other, then Tina chirped. "Not a bad idea."

"I refuse to write a poem or play a lute. I can't carry a tune. I can bring her chocolates and flowers. I already open her car door. Can you believe Liz seemed impressed with Jeff for such a simple gesture?"

"Focus. This is Elizabeth. She stands regally by and waits until someone opens her door. Generally, you're Johnny on the spot. She expects the door to be opened. You have to give her the unexpected."

He didn't like feeling trapped. "All I know is medicine. I don't know how to date."

"Then talk to her about your dreams," Tina said, looked at Brian in a weird way before she continued. "The director mentioned Africa. Said you donate your time for necessary operations. Tell her about what you do when you operate. Details about how you save patients will fascinate her."

He highly doubted Elizabeth would be fascinated by the mechanics of his operations. She would lend a hand. That he knew. But..."Would you want to know about African women and their diseases?"

"No, but I'm not Elizabeth. I'm telling you Doctor. I understand her. She wants you to engage her mind. Tell her how modern planes use aerodynamics to fly. She loves history and big words. You should take her to the airport. You do realize she hasn't seen one up close and personal. On the day you two picked up her dad, she asked a million questions. Ones I didn't or couldn't answer."

He realized he needed a special way to connect with Elizabeth. "I have a patient who flies helicopters. I should take her up in one."

"Now that's a grand gesture." Brian gave him a high five.

"Liz would love a ride. Elizabeth," Tina shook her head, "not so much. She might want to know how they worked but going up in one? You guys are on the wrong track."

Brian and Dr. Demfry didn't listen. They were already on the phone.

***

The flowers at breakfast were a hit.

The helicopter ride turned into a disaster. Elizabeth puked on his pant leg, started to cry and couldn't stop. She apologized for 'lurching her lunch' and ran to Tina who whisked her away before he could utter "I'm sorry."

So much for grand gestures! Now how would he repair the situation?

Chapter Thirteen

"The harder he tries, the more he fails." Tina sounded disgusted, yet she had a lop-sided grin on her face.

"Who are you talking about?" Elizabeth wondered if she meant her brother, Brian. He had purchased an electric guitar and strummed a tune last night by the pool. Tina put on the annoyed act before she said, "The coyotes in the canyon sound better than you." The entire scenario made her laugh at his efforts. Her brother hadn't liked the rebuff, so he fled.

Then Brian gave Tina a chocolate candy bar with chili in it. What might have been declared 'cool' by consumer standards, didn't mean a lady had to like the taste. And how could a scorched tongue be cool. Terminology in this day and age had her connect her old self with the new-improved version she embodied. More and more of Liz's memories surfaced.

She thought about Dr. Demfry, blushed. He could court a lady properly. The man gave her flowers which made her insides flutter and cards with silly words. She especially liked the witty ones comparing men to chocolate. Those made her laugh.

Then she remembered the helicopter ride and the eatery at the top of an extremely tall high-rise. She sailed on a ship from America to England in the year eighteen eleven and never realized she feared heights.

How would she have known? The highest building in London hadn't compared to the ginormous skyscraper.

She considered the museum disaster. Dr. Demfry thought she became homesick viewing carriages. Not so! The coach brought back memories of her father's heart condition. They had ridden through a fashionable street, gawking like the Colonials they were when he grabbed his chest. If they had been in this era, her father would be alive. Hence, the reason for her tears.

The dear, sweet, doctor tried to comfort her. The more he spoke, the more she wept. She realized their days together were limited which only made her cry harder. Her heart wrenched as she realized she would never eat breakfast with him again or sit around the pool. She would never be able to chatter like a magpie in her century. Never feel his arm at her back when they walked into a crowd.

She dreaded her return to eighteen twelve. The thought made her hands tremble. Here, she had a life. Enjoyed friends. Had fallen in love with the great Dr. Demfry. No. She told herself to stop the thoughts swirling in her head. He would become a figment of her imagination when she went back in time. Would she even remember him? She hoped the answer would be a resounding no. She didn't want to remember what she could not have and would surely miss.

"Elizabeth." Tina waved her hand in front of her face. "You're wearing a serious look. I'll give you a penny for your last thoughts."

Her kooky friend went into her purse, retrieved a bright shinny penny and handed the coin to Tina who looked confused. Elizabeth pushed her sadness away and smiled. "I don't know why I have to pay you for my thoughts. You should be paying me. After all," she chuckled, "I am the director."

"Yeah. Well, start directing Dr. Demfry to step up his game."

"Is he playing a game? Where?" She looked around, tried to locate him.

"Never mind. Dr. Stoneherst wants to show you the brooch. We've been live all week. This is the final episode. The show will start in fifteen minutes. I know you had time to say goodbye to your father earlier today. We said our goodbyes last night. Have you said goodbye to Dr. Demfry?"

She couldn't speak so she nodded her head. Nods were acceptable in this day and age. Would she go back in time and no longer fit in? She realized Tina continued to talk and caught the tail end of her words. "Told me to tell you he doesn't want you to touch that pin until you start the show. I think he's afraid you'll disappear in a puff of smoke."

"I daresay I didn't come in a puff of smoke. More like I slid in on a rainbow of colors. Yes. That's how I can describe what happened."

Dr. Stoneherst overheard them and said, "What a great line to start the show. You can walk the audience through how you got here. I'll ask you questions, and you'll answer. Keep your replies short and to the point. Let's take our places now. Tina, make sure I don't have too much color, dear. I want to look my best."

Tina grimace. "I'm not your hair and makeup artist. Dr. Do-What-I-Say."

The therapist snapped her fingers in Tina's face. "Do your job."

Tina put her hand up like a stop sign. "Nobody tells

me what to do."

The doctor's face turned red and huffed. Looked over to where the director stood. "Make sure my color isn't too yellow." She smiled because everyone on the set heard her.

"Yellow matches your reality, you cowardly fraud."

Elizabeth decided to intervene before they started pulling hair. "Lady Stoneherst's older than us so we should show a modicum of respect. Brush the yellow streak away."

The older woman turned her back on them and marched to the two chairs in the middle of the studio. She hugged her friend close before she followed. The curtain had not been lifted. The black material didn't drown out the sounds from the audience. People laughed and talked, equipment wheels squeaked as they moved chairs in place. Brian waved at her from the sidelines. He had the opportunity to take charge of this final segment of the program. Soon enough, Liz would be back. She would commandeer attention and ignore her family.

Elizabeth disliked how she thought so badly of the woman whose body she possessed. The woman's single mindedness for her career overrode every decision. She thought her career would make her feel whole, when in fact, the people in one's life were what made one whole. She blinked the tears from her eyes and forced herself to refocus. Looked around and noticed the oversight. "Where is Dr. Demfry's chair?"

"I decided you and I will have a chat first. We can bring Dr. Demfry on stage if he's needed." Dr. Stoneherst turned her back and told one of the technicians to move one of the lights closer.

"No. I need Dr. Demfry next to me while we televise."

"Be seated. We don't have time to bring a third chair."

"Then I guess you will stand." Elizabeth walked to the sidelines, grabbed Dr. Demfry's hand, a desperate, forward gesture, and tugged him toward the two chairs. She needed him next to her. Wanted to look into his eyes right before she disappeared forever. Determination filled her. He had to be the last person she looked at before she vanished.

Dr. Stoneherst somehow managed to get a third chair on stage before the curtain lifted. She hissed as the camera began its countdown, "You can let go of her hand, doctor."

"No, I can't."

Her chest filled with warmth.

"Good evening," Dr. Stoneherst said to the audience and waved. Elizabeth waved with her left hand because Dr. Demfry had secured her other hand in his.

"The good doctor doesn't want to let go of his patient. I believe he is smitten."

She didn't care for the doctor's remark. The woman acted a guttersnipe. She held up their entwined hands. "This man is my life line. He grounds me to twenty twelve. I want to thank every one of you in the audience for your attendance tonight. I also want to thank those of you at home who have stopped your busy lives to view this special. You see, I came here from the year eighteen twelve. I'm here tonight to tell you a story. One I want to share with each of you."

She let their hands drop but together, so she could keep in contact with the man she loved as she went into her prepared spiel. Had practiced her speech with Tina last night. Intended to cut Dr. Stoneherst out of the picture as much as possible and this soliloquy would do the trick.

When she paused to take a breath, Dr. Demfry picked up her story, unrehearsed. "I walked into the room to find Elizabeth on the floor. Miss Davis held her hand, much as I am doing right now. She talked to Miss Barrett in a calming tone." He turned and gazed into her eyes. The same thrill raced through her body. They were meant to be together.

"You were pale and motionless. So surreal. When I touched you, the energy shot up my arm, straight to my heart. I fell in love with you the moment you swatted my hand away and called me a scamp." A sad, sappy smile appeared on his face.

They gazed at each other, the audience roared approval, and Dr. Stoneherst made an inane comment nobody listened to.

"You love me?"

"I do. I love you Elizabeth Barrett. I don't want you to go back in time."

"I love you, too." Her words came out in a strangled whisper. "What should I do? What if Miss Barrett wants to return? There are all manner of ills in eighteen twelve. A person can die of the common cold."

"Please explain yourself." Dr. Stoneherst interrupted.

She didn't need any encouragement. Talked about the common cold, typhoid, the plague, her father's heart failure, and a slew of other ailments treatable today.

"Women die all the time birthing babes. What if my counterpart gets in the family way or catches a cold? She might die young."

Dr. Demfry smiled warmly. "She doesn't die young. I looked her up on the internet. Liz lived as Lady Whittington for a long, long time."

"She did? How come you never told me?" She dropped his hand and glared.

Dr. Stoneherst motioned for the men to have the brooch wheeled toward them. Two crew members pushed the Plexiglas pedestal onto the stage.

Elizabeth glanced at the jewel and couldn't help but comment. "This piece is as ugly as I remember."

"What else do you remember?" The shrink sounded harsh, demanding.

She stood, picked up the brooch and shook her head. "This betrothal gift came from the Duke of Silverman. The present did not encourage me to marry him."

"You didn't marry Silverman. You married a Lord Whittington. He had the title of an Earl." Dr. Demfry's voice soothed her.

She took her eyes off the brooch. "I did. Lord Whittington? My guardian. Why would I marry him?"

"Liz married him." Dr. Demfry pulled the picture Brian printed from his jacket pocket and thrust the paper at her. "Here is a picture of the Earl and his wife in India."

"Oh my! I see a dead lion at their feet." She became faint. "I don't want to go back in time and kill large cats." She tried to hand the brooch to Dr. Stoneherst, but the woman ignored her, called for a commercial break. The minute the station cut to a commercial the shrink stood, grabbed Elizabeth's arm and shook her.

Hissed through clenched teeth. "You made a promise to the studio and you will keep your promise. I also made a promise. Said I would deliver Liz Barrett and you will comply with my wishes. Now pull yourself together or I'll have you committed to a mental hospital. I have the power and I'll do what I have to if you don't cooperate."

Dr. Demfry pried the doctor's hand from Elizabeth's arm and stood between the two women. He had his back to his beloved. Stood and faced the misguided doctor. "She will move the brooch as promised. You won't place Elizabeth in a mental institution no matter what the outcome." The microphones had not been turned off. A roar of approval sounded from the audience.

He turned his back on Dr. Stoneherst and held Elizabeth in a warm embrace. The curtains opened and the audience went wild—clapping, chanting, and a few brave people stood on their seats. Tina walked on stage and sang, "Two little love birds sitting in a tree. K I S S I N G. First came love, then came marriage, then came babies for the baby carriage."

She let go of her fear, decided to step off the cliff into the unknown. "I shall wield Cupid's Brooch as promised." She didn't care if the monitors were off. She had the brooch in her hand as she walked toward the front of the stage. Unbeknownst to her, the green lights on the cameras remained on.

"This brooch upset me. Look at it. Old and ugly. The stone is dull. The gold looks tarnished. I said to myself, would a man who loved me give me this unbecoming pin? No! A man in love would give me a gift that reminded us of some moment together. A man in love would give flowers and notes, open carriage doors and help me into and out of my cloak. It's cold in London, you see, and one wears a cloak or a pelisse or some form of cape with fur to keep warm. We wore gloves at all times, even when we drank tea. They were so tedious, those gloves. Like the man who gave me this brooch. I thought him tedious."

She looked toward Dr. Demfry. "Today you get to choose the person you want to marry. In my century, our fathers or guardians made the choice for us. I have known many a young lady who met the man she would marry at the altar." The audience booed.

"I know. Barbaric in this modern age. Today I would pick Dr. Demfry but back then, I had no choice."

"You have a choice." Dr. Demfry's voice sounded strong. "Liz figured out how to marry Lord Whittington and you said you were betrothed to Lord Silverman."

"Where is the museum curator?" She called. "I want him to explain exactly how this brooch works. Then I shall wave the pin like I did in eighteen twelve. We shall discover a great truth. If the brooch works, I will stay here."

Commercials aired as Dr. Stoneherst got ushered off the stage by the director. They found the curator out in the audience and brought him up on stage. Dr. Demfry could not get close to Elizabeth who huddled with Tina, whispering like co-conspirators, in the middle of the stage. Their microphones had been turned off.

Brian started the countdown for the program to

begin again and Dr. Demfry found himself seated next to the curator as the green light came on. Elizabeth stood behind him with the brooch in her hands. Two men wheeled the Plexiglas contraption offstage.

The scholarly man looked like he should be at home with a book. Under the camera lights, he wore an expression of terror. He cleared his voice three times and they had to adjust his speaker so he could finally be heard. "The metal was forged before Christ. Iron isn't pretty." He blinked rapidly.

"Please continue." She bent forward, smiled and patted the curator's shoulder from behind.

He focused on her, turned in his chair, his back to the audience. "We believe this a functional piece used to clasp material together. An old-fashioned cloak pin. At different periods, this brooch has appeared in museums and private collections. We can't trace the birth place, but we did find a scroll with the brooch's picture and know the piece has made an appearance in every century all the way back to ancient Egypt. It's called Cupid's Brooch. Donated to our museum in nineteen fifty-eight by a man who claims he lived in Egypt during Cleopatra's time. What else can I say?"

"You've given the audience enough general information about the piece to form their own conclusions."

"Can I go?" The man squirmed in the chair.

"By all means. Thank you for your help."

The man tripped over his feet as he rushed from the stage. Dr. Demfry turned in his chair so he could look over the back of the seat and see his beloved.

Music started, and she began to speak. "I stood in the parlor. We don't have those anymore. We now have living rooms and dens. Parlors have fringe and tassels, many tables crammed with bric-a-brac, hard chairs and a sideboard where the men keep their libations—or liquor, as you call it. I stood in the parlor alone. Hunger knocked at my ribs because the maids took all day to dye my unpopular red hair. For some reason I could not comprehend, I became miffed."

Her voice faltered. "Some man spied me from across a ballroom floor. The one and only ball I had the opportunity to attend. My whole reason for sailing from Boston to London had been to have a season. During a season, one attends numerous balls. I went to one and I get betrothed. The man had the title of a Duke. Imagine my embarrassment. When someone of the highest rank wants you, you don't say no!"

Comments and messages from the audience poured in. Brian stood behind a camera and gave her a thumbs up signal. The gesture saddened her. She would leave soon and miss these people who had included her. She shook off her unease like a cat shakes off water and continued with her saga.

"My chaperone, Lady Coldwell, told me how grateful I should be because I had been chosen. I didn't want to be chosen." She sounded petulant and spoiled but she didn't care. "I wanted to be loved. I don't remember the exact words, but I do believe they were heartfelt." She started to move the brooch.

Her heart lurched and instinctively she chanted. "I want to be loved for who I am." The brooch lifted upward, and her hands followed. She completed a figure eight motion and chanted again, "I want to be loved for who I am." The third time she made the motion her voice echoed from far away. Her mind and body became a rainbow slide as the colors churned, pushed, pulled.

She dropped through the rainbow of colors.

Sounds roared, weakened.

Lights blinked, twinkled, blacked out.

She collapsed, came back to herself in time to realize she had somersaulted over the back of the chair, and somehow, fell into her beloved's lap. She could not get a grip on what happened. A tingling sensation ran the length of her body. Dr. Demfry talked to her but she couldn't hear because of the loud harp music twanging from above.

Long minutes passed before her spirit settled inside her body. A gentle touch of her finger to Dr. Demfry's lips shushed him. Soothed the skin on his face. She lifted his mouth into a smile with her fingers. He gathered her close, stood up, and rushed her off the stage. Their eyes stayed glued to one another until he found an unoccupied storage room. He deliberately locked the door behind them.

"Elizabeth?"

"Dr. Demfry."

His husky voice sounded like a declaration. Made both of them crazy with pent up emotions. Their lips met.

She heard angels sing. When you know something, it is instantaneous and doesn't require figuring out. She realized she would never return to eighteen twelve.

Chapter Fourteen

They were at the pool, celebrating. The replay of her feet leaving the ground as she sailed over the chair to land in Dr. Demfry's lap went viral. Her father, who had to work the soup kitchen, called after the broadcast and told her, "I'm proud of you." Said he would be over to join the celebration after he closed the place for the night.

She had a family who loved her even though everyone knew her to be an imposter.

Brian had been the one to rescue the brooch from the floor and return the pin to the curator before anyone else could find themselves transported to other places and spaces. He had held the item by two fingers, one eye closed.

"The papers say you managed a publicity stunt as good as, if not better than Houdini." Tina read from her cell phone as she lounged in her chaise.

"Who is Houdini?" Elizabeth tried to find a picture in her brain and could not come up with a memory.

Dr. Demfry explained. "The Great Houdini. A stunt man whose repertoire included breaking free from chains while he swung from skyscrapers. He could get out of straitjackets under water, and once he let the public seal him in a milk can until he could break free. His biggest feat occurred when they buried him alive. He somehow clawed his way out of the coffin. He came from your time. Born in the eighteen hundreds and no one, to this day, knows how he managed his feats. Doesn't make sense what he could do. You've become like him. Everyone wonders how you faked your mid-air somersault."

Tina shrugged her shoulders. "Some mysteries are unsolvable."

"I am not a fake," she said and hoped her tone sounded indignant. "I am Elizabeth Barrett and I am from the year eighteen twelve."

"People believe what they want to believe." He tweaked her nose, rubbed a warm hand down her arm. Gently lifted her fingers, turned her hand over and kissed the skin of her palm. The most intimate part of her body got wet.

Her face flushed. Would he marry her? She decided, if he didn't, she would be one of those women. The kind who let a man have his way, no matter the consequences!

Brian interrupted them. "I need to talk to Tina for a few minutes. Can you come with me into the garden?"

"Your voice sounds funny. Are you all right?" Elizabeth asked. He didn't sound sure of himself. Did he plan to discuss what happened with Tina?

The studio had been furious when she deserted the stage with Dr. Demfry. Somehow Brian and Tina saved the show. They answered questions for her and the doctor. She would interview with the press tomorrow.

"Whatever you have to say, Brian, say in front of Elizabeth and Weston. We've all been through enough. I don't want secrets. Missy over here needs to be a participant since she's staying. We have to share all the news, good or bad." Tina shifted in her lounger, tried to get comfortable.

"What I want to ask you should be between us." Brian's voice sounded deliberate. His hands twisted together as he walked back and forth in front of Tina's chaise.

"Get on with your project Big Boy. I don't care to stand. I've been on my feet since five a.m. and I'm tired."

Brian pulled a jewelry box from his pocket. He knelt beside Tina's chair and she groaned. Brian's back turned away from Elizabeth and the doctor. They couldn't see the gift, but they could hear his voice. "I got you a nontraditional ring. One to wear in your nose."

Tina gasped, flung herself onto Brian with a loud, happy shriek. Grabbed the box out of his hand and showed the diamond to the two curious on-lookers. "A ring for my nose."

Brian held her close, talked into her neck. "I had the jewel made. Got the biggest diamond I could afford. I wanted you to have a non-traditional, unique type of wedding ring."

"You're asking me to marry you, aren't you?" Tina squeaked.

"I want you to be my wife. I can help with the business side while you run your salon. I get paid to manage my sister's accounts, Dr. Demfry's clinic, and I'll have time for you. I don't make a lot of money. This televised special netted us both enough cash to get your shop started. Maybe we can pool our resources and go look at property tomorrow."

"Oh Brian," Tina kissed him.

Brian kissed her back.

Elizabeth looked on in amazement. *When had this happened?*

Dr. Demfry interrupted them when he said, "You two need to get a room."

Brian came up for breath. "We're can't share a room until we're married."

Tina huffed. "Then we need to get married soon."

"We can get the license tomorrow when we apply for your corporation. Do you have a name picked out for the salon?"

"I don't have a name because I've been busy with Elizabeth's show. By the way, do I have to change my name from Davis to Barrett?" Her facial expression soured.

"You can keep your name, but I insist you wear the wedding ring in your nose. I'll buy you a new one every anniversary. You'll have a large collection."

"Oh Brian." Tina started to kiss him again. "I'd love to be a member of the Barrett clan."

It was embarrassing to see the two of them. Elizabeth cleared her throat and asked, "Can we go with you to look at property?"

"Of course. You'll be my maid of honor. And," she paused to take her old nose piece out and put the new one in. "I'll need you two to be our witnesses."

"You mean to get married tomorrow?" Her tone sounded incredulous.

"Of course," Brian laughed. "After your interview."

"You better believe we want to get married immediately." Tina replied. Both of them wore grins only love-sick fools could conjure.

"Oh my. Maybe we should eat that delicious dinner

Maria prepared first, then go into my bedroom and find an outfit for you to wear." She had a multitude of designer clothes in her closet.

Brian coughed again. "I know you're not traditional, so I found a Middle Eastern gown on line and bought the outfit. You don't have to wear this if you don't like the way it looks."

Tina hands made a grabbing motion. "Let me see, let me see."

Brian stepped behind the bar and pulled out a box. The package hadn't been opened. "I hope this will work. If not, we can send the outfit back and purchase what you like."

"Whatever did you pick?" Tina tugged the box opened. She laughed and clapped her hands in glee. Finally, the happy young lady pulled bright, flowing pants from the over large envelope. Held up a brilliant blue fitted bra top so all could see. Coins dangled along the seams, creating a merry jingle. A fitted hip belt richly decorated with beads and embroidery completed the ensemble. "This is exactly what I would have picked. Oh, Brian. How did you guess?"

He looked ashamed. "I tried to find the most outrageous outfit I could think of to be married in and figured you'd like what I found."

Dr. Demfry's curiosity got the better of him. "What do you plan to wear?"

"An Armani suit and tie. Come on Doc. You know I'm the traditional type. One other detail." His voice trailed off, his eyes looked at the furniture but not at the three people on the patio.

Tina giggled. "So far you've batted home runs. What's this one detail?"

"I know we can get married by a judge we've never met tomorrow but..." he paused. Looked terrified to say what he had to say. "I want dad to marry us in a religious ceremony. I might have to convert him to the idea. Will you do this for me?"

"Absolutely. Makes marriage more real than a run-through at the court house. I've always said Vegas weddings never last. Can we use your rose arbor?" Tina asked Elizabeth.

"You want to be married outside?"

"You bet," said Tina.

At the same time Brian replied, "Of course."

With the details settled, the group decided to eat before the food got cold. "Your meal is better than any chef I've tasted," she told Maria when the caretaker appeared on the patio.

"I'm here of see if you need refills." She picked up the empty plates as she bussed the dishes into a plastic bin she carried.

"I'm so glad I'm still here to enjoy your preparations."

"Me too, Chica. I answered the phone earlier and your father will be here in a few minutes. I told him I saved a plate of green enchiladas since those are his favorite. Do you want me to feed him first or send him here to the patio?"

"Let him eat, first. We plan to have a wedding in the garden. I would love some of those famous Mexican Wedding cookies you talk about."

The women beamed at her. "So, you and the good doctor plan to marry?"

"No silly. Brian and Tina are getting married."

Maria stood up, hands filled with plates, and

looked at Brian with a frowny face that made her laugh. She told Maria, "They want father to preside."

Tina interrupted. "Don't tell Mr. Barrett yet. Brian wants to be the one to let him know."

"Your secret is safe with me. I assumed you two would kill each other. Now I hear you plan to marry. Loco." She gathered the rest of the dishes sitting on the bar and muttered under her breath. "Estas loco." Brian opened the sliding glass door for her to enter when she hefted the bin. Told him, "You should be glad I like to work with crazy people."

The group decided to walk to the back and inspect the rose arbor. Brian and Tina went first, hugged as if they were afraid the other person would disappear.

She strolled along at a slow pace, and the doctor stayed by her side.

He put his hand on her arm to stop her. Faced her. "I noticed you laughed when Maria asked you if we were the ones to marry." Weston titled her chin upward with his finger.

"How else could I cover my embarrassment?"

He took his finger off her chin and stepped back. "Do I embarrass you?"

"Never," she clapped her hand to her mouth. "I am never embarrassed by you. Quite the opposite. I am the one who is an embarrassment. You are such a great doctor so you can't be stuck with a crazy wife. An actress is allowed to be crazy. Different. But a doctor's wife must be impeccable."

He stepped closer and she could feel his breath on her face. "You're a time traveler, not a crazy person."

His simple sentence made her shiver with delight.

"I am so glad you believe in me," she whispered.

Dr. Demfry cleared his throat. She noticed his jaw muscle tighten. "I do believe in you. I believe in us, only I don't make the money you're used to, Elizabeth. I am in the process of building a medical practice, which takes time. When I do have money, I'll spend my salary on medical equipment instead of gardeners." He waved his hand in the direction of the newly pruned rose bushes. "The equipment I purchase will be shipped to Africa. I plan to volunteer a month of my time each year to perform operations in Central African Republic." She stood patiently, nodded, and waited. Her gesture encouraged him.

"I don't always have the best disposition. I am not a morning person and my hands shake when I don't eat regularly. I will bitch at you. Brian says I'm worse than a woman. Only this morning, I complained on the way to the studio because he left his towel on the floor in the bathroom. We will have arguments over silly issues like towels and socks and muddy shoes. I'm not one for grand gestures, I don't play an instrument, and I'll never sing out loud except on your birthday. I can sing Happy Birthday."

He paused and looked at her face. Her expression made him feel as if he had hung the moon. "I can't make a lot of promises but the ones I make are forever. I will never leave you. In fact, I will expect you to go to Africa with me for one month out of the year. You don't have to wash bed pans, but I want you by my side. I will give up a portion of my year to dedicate to your career. I know you have a contract and I'd never stand in the way of your success."

He put his hand under her chin. "I will look up the answer to all your questions, since you ask so many of them. I will never, knowingly give you false information. I hate to admit when I don't know the answer, but you have a lot of questions I will never know how to explain. I want a traditional wedding, in a church, with you in a long, white dress, not some skimpy bohemian outfit like Tina."

He got on one knee, pleased the grass didn't feel wet. "I don't have a lot to offer you except my intention to love you more each and every day. Will you marry me?"

She dropped to her knees, across from him and said. "I am stubborn and willful. I am red headed and bad tempered when I don't get my own way. I have found I do like large audiences. How extremely vain of me. I plan to go with you to Africa and I intend to make myself useful. Mayhap, roll bandages. I am not sure I have the nose for cleaning bedpans. I will not ride an elephant and I do not see a need to parasail. I would like to try a motor boat, but I can't guarantee I won't lurch on your pant leg. If you can put up with me and my foibles, I shall marry you."

They leaned toward each other as her father barreled around the shrub and bumped into them. The three of them were on their backs, laughing when Brian and Tina returned.

She pulled her friend, Tina, onto the grass beside her, "Let us star gaze."

"Do you know what you're looking at?"

"No," she replied, "but I believe in the magic of the heavens. I did see stars as I flashed through time."

Everyone replied at the same time. Each one with a different comment yet, they agreed magic was in the air.

Chapter Fifteen

"I'm glad we found more information about Liz and Lord Whittington." Elizabeth clutched a large, cracked journal to her chest. "The introduction we read said this fairy tale holds the family legacy. I guess the Barrett's decided to hand the brooch to the first-born son for the last few generations. Imagine, calling their story a fairy tale. I guess they didn't want to get tarred and feathered and run out of London."

"We've only read the first few pages. I like the sketch of the brooch. Looks accurate." Tina folded Mr. Barrett's pants and stacked them neatly into a donation bag.

"I wonder if father read this. He had the journal in his junk drawer. A drawer he dumped into a box when he relocated. I never realized the junk drawer contained mother's possessions." Brian pulled a lace handkerchief with their mother's initials from the drawer. You could still smell a hint of scent. "I'm surprised dad kept mom's stuff. He hated her."

"I always wondered why he accepted the fact I came from the past. Father never condemned me for my beliefs. We didn't understand him. I'm sorry he's dead." She sniffed back a tear. She had created a relationship with the man his own daughter couldn't. They sat together without talking, content to listen to classical music and church hymns.

Brian unfolded a piece of paper. He whistled, and Tina instantly flew to his side. "You found your mother's death certificate. Didn't you tell me she died the year you changed residences. I remember a story you told about leaving Santa Fe dragging a U-Haul behind a dilapidated station wagon."

"Look at the cause of death. Head trauma sustained in car accident."

She stuffed her hand in her mouth to stifle a sob. "I always wondered why she didn't look me up when I became famous."

Weston sat on the bed next to her in the small, crowded room. He leaned close and gently pulled her pony tail. "Is that why you went into show biz? So, your mother could find you?"

They reminisced about Liz's mother. Looked up from the journal to find Brian staring. "Yes. I wanted contact with my mother. Father moved us from New Mexico when she ran off. What do you remember, Brian?"

"I can tell you because father's dead. They fought over money. Mom wanted to buy you a new dress for Easter and father said no. He kept harping about over indulgence. Mom slammed out the door of the rectory. She didn't come home. Neither did the assistant pastor. Did mom run away with him or did she run off to the store and got killed on the way?"

She gasped. "Father never said she ran away with someone. The church secretary told us. You remember her. She slapped me once. Mother told her she would be kicked out of the congregation if she dared touch me again." The hidden memory surfaced clearly. The slap. The confrontation.

Then another set of memories surfaced. A police officer at the door who whispered with her father. He had left her and Brian with the secretary to go downtown. "I don't think father told us mother ran off with another man. I think the mean-spirited secretary made up the entire story to humiliate us. She's one of those mealy-mouth types who cloak themselves with biblical quotes."

Brian nodded his head. "You're right. Father said, 'Your mother's gone, and she won't be back.' A week after his pronouncement, we piled into the car and drove to the border. I hated our year in Mexico. This obituary is dated a week before we left. I remember because we were on the road the day after his Easter sermon. Maybe father's assistant gave mom a ride to the store. I do remember she defied father from time to time."

"I'll open my laptop and see what I can find. Do either of you remember the man's name?"

She loved how her husband continually looked up information on the internet when she asked a question. And she asked a fountain of questions. "Father Brandon. I remember because I wondered if Brandon was a first name or a last name."

"Keep on with the clean-up and I'll see what I can find. Give me the obituary date. The easiest way to find out more is to look in the newspaper archives. I hope they have those old papers on-line."

Brian gave him the date.

Hot tears streamed like rivers down her cheeks. She wondered how she could access memories and feel someone else's pain. Liz thought she had been abandoned. She hoped she had found the right person to love.

Weston pulled her close. "You've had a slew of new experiences since you landed here last year. You found out you were an actress and then won an Emmy award. You married a knucklehead and had to help set up a charitable foundation. I still can't believe we are building a hospital on another continent. You gained a father who learned to love you like a daughter. I'm so sorry he died in his sleep. I'm also glad you got to know him. You've had to process a lot in a short period of time. Not to mention everyday events still seem foreign to you since you didn't grow up in this century."

Tina chimed in. "I got to know your father since he helped out at the salon when I needed someone to shampoo. He had a gentle touch and the ladies adored him. Who would have thought? Maybe he grieved for your mother and both of you misunderstood. He never once said I would go to hell after our initial meeting."

The room fell silent. A lot had happened since they met. They had argued, become friends, and married.

"This new information fascinates me. Like the stolen brooch. This will be our highlight of the year." Tina grunted.

"What about me?" Brian stopped rummaging through the dresser drawer, a pout formed on his face.

"Our marriage took place last year. The highlight of two thousand twelve. This is two thousand thirteen. We have a successful business and now we get to solve mysteries."

Brian frowned. "What mysteries?"

"Your mother and the stolen brooch."

"The mystery of your mother is solved." Weston

286

broke in. "Here's the article the newspaper ran and a picture of the crashed vehicle. A big rig hit the car when he lost his air brakes and both parties in the vehicle were killed instantly."

Tina peered over Weston's shoulder. "I wonder how the driver got on after the tragedy. Did you find his name?"

"Yes."

"Don't give Tina his name!" Brian stood up, his hands on his hip.

"Why not?" Weston had been around the couple long enough to see their pattern. They planned to have a loud argument. Thankfully his wife did not argue for the sake of argument.

"She'll want to go visit the guy. Find out if her mom had a dress in the car. Tina, you're not a sleuth. I already told you to stop bugging those guards at the museum." Brian stood with hands on hips in front of his wife.

"I want the man's name. We have to go see him and let him know he has been forgiven. I'm sure he's carried terrible guilt over the accident. Imagine the scenario, Brian. Your father may have been so grief stricken he left town without a trace. The man never even had the chance to apologize."

"Tina, you need to keep your nose ring out of this." Brian ushered her from the room.

Elizabeth looked at her husband and said, "Come here knucklehead." She rubbed the side of his head with her knuckles, kissed his hair, neck and finally his cheek. "You are the best person I have ever met."

"Do you want to keep Tina from snooping into your mother's death?"

"No. Let her find the guy and absolve him. She likes to make situations right. I want to finish up here, go home and read the journal. Then I plan to question Tina about the museum guard."

Weston groaned. "You plan to find the brooch?"

"I want to find out if another person is here from a different century. The person would be confused and frightened. Might not have found such kind people. I could help."

"How can you be sure the brooch hasn't used up all its magic powers. Maybe the pin only works for Barrett's."

"Remember when we were in Las Vegas last weekend? Tina and I had our first interview with the wife of the Egyptian guy who donated Cupid's Brooch to the museum. He died from a case of the measles. No one dies of the measles unless they had never been exposed to them."

"Your first interview?" He held her chin gently and looked into her eyes.

"I didn't want to tell you until we had more information. Tina and I are penning a book together."

"Hum."

"That's all you have to say? Hum?" She could not keep the puzzled look from her face.

His tone sounded resolute when he said. "I want to be present when you have your next interview. And, I want you to explain why this had to be a secret. Why wasn't I invited?"

"You were at the hospital, inspecting the donated equipment and Tina pulled me aside. She said you would salivate for another hour over those old x-ray machines. Asked me if I wanted to go with her and scout out a fancy new salon. I figured we would give you and Brian time to figure out how to ship your equipment overseas. I didn't know where we were going until we arrived."

She realized her husband waited for the rest of the story. He tapped his foot on the floor. Such an endearing gesture, full of restless patience. "I meant to tell you the night we got the call from Maria about father. I'm sorry. With so much happening," her hand went up in the air. "The police, the stolen brooch, the press, my father's death. I forgot to explain where we went, and you didn't ask."

Weston stared at his wife, pulled her close, kissed the end of her nose. "I could have gone with you."

"I know. I'm glad Tina didn't tell me until we were in the Taxi."

"You didn't want me with you?"

"I know how much this hospital means to you. You get all sentimental when equipment is donated. I couldn't ruin the moment. But I do want you with us next time. You ask better questions than Tina. Funny, she started out as my chaperon, but I seem to be the one who watches out for her."

"She plans to find the stolen brooch."

"Yes."

"Okay. Let's read the journal tonight and tomorrow we will start a formal investigation. We may not get far. The police haven't discovered who stole the brooch from the museum."

"Brian will be mad."

Her husband kissed her. "Brian will join us. He hates to miss out on the action."

"You are a man who understands people."

"I am a man who loves my wife. I will indulge you in every way until I sense danger. Then you must promise me you will stop the investigation."

She snuggled against the man she loved. "I am the luckiest woman alive. I hope the next person who transports with Cupid's Brooch will find everlasting love."

A word about the author...

Donna Ann Brown loves her life. She blogs for clients; a holistic clinic, a veterinary clinic, and on her own writing website, donnabrownwriting.com. She sends monthly newsletters to her hypnosis clients and has created over 250 memes for her Yelp profile.

In her spare time, she writes romance, creates inspirational card decks, plays make-believe with her grandsons, and watches stories with subtitles on Netflix. Her first book, *Lady Cathrine Brandon's Leap Day Adventure*, is a Regency Romance. Her second book is a self-published allegory called *Dare to Love Yourself*. Her motto: All you can do is all you can do and all you can do is enough.

Thank you for purchasing
this publication of The Wild Rose Press, Inc.

For questions or more information
contact us at
info@thewildrosepress.com.

The Wild Rose Press, Inc.
www.thewildrosepress.com